香港華人名人史略

黃慕松題

獻 此 於 吾 族 兄 吳 鐵 城 主 席

TO

MR. WU TEH SHING

CHAIRMAN OF THE GOVERNMENT OF KWONGTUNG PROVINCE

FROM WHOM I HAVE RECEIVED KINDNESS.

照 小 者 編

PROF. WOO SING LIM, THE AUTHOR.

吳醒濂・字肇醒・粵中山縣人・現年四十五歲・民國三年・畢業交通部上海工業專門學校（即今交通大學）・旋留學美國・民國九年・在滬創設南洋商科高級中學・歷任該校校長達十五年之久・民國十三年・赴滇出席第九屆全國教育會聯合大會・雲南督軍兼省長唐公繼堯・聘充省長公署顧問・後再度漫遊歐美・民國二十三年・受美國加省士丹佛大學之聘・充任漢文文學教授・曾著「芝加高世界博覽大會之批評」一文・分登美國各報・並著有「美國檀山菲島華僑合誌」一書・其在滬所手創之南洋商科高級中學・因一二八之役・受日軍轟燬・損失甚鉅・難以為繼・現已讓上海市總商會接辦・改稱為上海市總商會商業中學矣・民國二十五年來港・微編是書・

Born in Canton, 1893. Graduated from the Government Institute of Technology (now Choa Tung University) Shanghai 1914. Special student of Columbia University N. Y., U. S. A. 1916. Principal of The Nanyang Commercial Academy Shanghai 1920 - 1935. Adviser of the Governor of Yunnan Province 1924. Professor of Chinese literature of Stanford University California U. S. A. 1934. Author of "Criticisms of the A Century of Progress International Exposition Chicago" 1934. Author of "The Chinese in America, Hawaii, and Philippine Islands" 1936. Author of "the Prominent Chinese in Hongkong" 1937.

序

襄史官世其家‧崇其位‧厚其祿‧史之重可知也‧周末，孔子修春秋‧正名份‧嚴一字之褒貶‧使君君臣臣‧以喜以懼‧史事遂屬學者‧喀萊爾(Carlyle)謂世之史‧大人先生傳記耳‧華夏自司馬作列傳‧始易左傳紀一事物‧而傳大人先生也‧傳，傳也‧其道可稽‧昔儒以德，言，功‧苟有一可式世者‧胥足傳‧傳固非易也‧史，執正而持中‧司馬遷寧逆漢武以獲罪‧不易‧『今上本紀』‧持史筆者不畏禍‧毋刧於勢‧不喜功‧毋誘於利‧然後其義生‧史之信亦難矣哉‧宗兄醒濂，幼嘗同學鳳山書院‧長嘗共事修來學校‧既棄筆海上‧曾遍遊歐美各大埠‧以稽華人海外掌故‧曾成『美國檀山及菲島華僑合誌』諸書‧世頗有嘉其勾稽得間‧使遠民之德‧弗潛於世者‧吾兄今復以修『香港華人名人史畧』告，梅鶴曰，史為德音‧音出宜響孚其聲‧英人哥德斯密(Godsmith)謂『史應孕道德，生產，智力』‧德人陸宰(Lotge)張為慎察智力，產業，美術，宗教，政治五者‧而史之響‧乃應乎其聲‧夫聖賢尤以博選為本‧以正世為用‧人益顯其誠能‧其道乃弗可去‧兄之述‧其有志於斯乎‧則豈局於一地一世‧直百世之器矣‧

民國廿五年十二月中山梅鶴吳瑺昌謹叙

自序

嘗游考察教育。觀光文化。幾度漫遊歐美。目覩各大都邑紀載名人事績之刊物。至為普遍。即我國出版界。近亦有中華當代名人傳等書面世。其適應潮流。獨標一格。所以滿青年之讀慾。資後學之楷梯。當為大雅所許。寧以史官自居耶。香港開闢。將達百年。現蔚為遠東第二大商埠。吾華人才薈萃。名流迭出。其間能造成社會幸福。推進中英邦交者。不鮮其人。偉績豐功。尚無專書。分別紀述。久易湮沒。殊為可惜。此是書之所由徵編也。況輓近風俗日偷。人心不古。而文人無行。貶節趨時。修談神怪。艷說風流。導青年於陷阱者。更有以公妻共產之學說。小學生文庫之傳記類等籍刊行。其體裁分紀中外聖賢豪傑，忠臣烈士之史實。思矯其弊。遂有少年叢書，岳飛，文天祥，耶穌，華盛頓，林肯等。惠美矣。然以古代異方之人物示範。徒供仰止。以近世當地之人物表率。切實於香江人士之前。亦冀世道人心。於親近。易於仿模。抑有進者。尚友錄一書。我國之標準名人錄也。歷朝人物。均應基於道德。否則功業失其價值。濂對於書中人選。敢不兢兢於此點乎。自古真名之所歸。太上在立德。其次在立功。又其次在立言。蓋人之立身建業。均應列其中。才兼文武之曹操。屏而不錄。取舍之嚴可知。曹操而不錄。不嘗驅天下後世之人相率而為大奸惡也。名譽文武之曹操。抑自創基業。而能獻身社會。香港之華人。多出於商賈一途。因機會所限。欲建三不朽之業。殊非人人可得。使有專門學問。或特別技能。或自創基業。而能獻身社會。致力公益者。傳之也。其誰曰不宜。至香港華人名人。範圍之大小既清。則詭異與譏嘲之來。可以止矣。濂既以香港華人名人為範圍。人史署八字名其書。顧名思義。可知其中所載。晉香港之名人。而非全中國或全世界之名人。然則謂香港華人名人值得錄於是書者。將盡於此區區八十餘人耶。是又不然。此次主撰是編。搜羅資料。窮八月之光陰。工作人員。聘五人為助理。終因囿於見聞。不免掛一漏萬。且港中縉紳名流。及商業鉅子。或因公忙。或因謙遜。微求未必即應。滄海遺多遺珠。事與願違。實深抱歉。而同時對於寄表同情慨然加入者。愈覺感激。其次對於盧伯禎，郭子超，楊應聰三先生。及姚秀容。黃志忠兩女士。或佐編中英文稿。或代訪今古史實。亦應致謝。微諸名流之應徵。此書不能蕆事。微數子之襄助。亦未易成功也。

中華建國二十六年吳醒濂序於香江客次

PREFACE

Included in this book, are the photographs and biographies of about eighty prominent Chinese in Hongkong. Political, commercial, financial, industrial, educational and professional circles are represented herein. As the existence of this book, distributed throughout Hongkong and China, will act as an encouragement, to some one, as well as a deterrent, to many; the author has endeavoured to make careful selections.

The biographies of this book are principally written in Chinese. For the sake of convenience of those who learn English language, an addition of English translation to each biography is necessary. However, as the English translations are only the outlines of the ideas of the Chinese texts, they are not to be translated words by words and sentences by sentences.

It is very difficult to determine in just what order to place the biographies. Certainly I cannot please all in this matter; but I wish to state that the order in which they are placed does not indicate the order of importance in the affairs of Hongkong. It is merely what I believe to be the most satisfactory manner of arranging them, and was done with no intention of being partial to anyone.

I wish to acknowledge the co-operation given to me by every one whose biography included in this book. I also wish to thank Messrs. Chi Chew Kwok, Ying Chung Yang, Park Ching Loo and Misses Yao Shou Yung and Wong Chi Wai, without whose assistance in compiling and collecting the materials, my work would not have been a success.

Hongkong, April, 1937.   WOO SING LIM.

名留海宇

孫科題

滄海之廣不愛

愛源萬籟之底

不忘愛東

于右任

嶺海俊彥

王寵惠題

海外球圖

邸永

香江人瑞

曹養甫題

寔至名歸

饒宗頤

編　例

（一）此書之編．中文為主．西文為輔．兼以編排關係．英文祇可舉領提綱．愧未能全篇對照繙譯也．

（二）是書紀載之次序．係以覆函應徵之先後而定．究與其本人在港中地位無關．編者對於袞袞諸公．一致景仰．更不欲有所軒輊．稍存成見．

（三）書中人物．年齡有老壯之分．功業有多寡之別．撰述或簡或繁．實非輕彼重此．

（四）此書延攬之今古名流．必以其人一生事業．多在香港．或現居香港者為限．不敢勉強牽附．如孫總理中山．幼讀於皇仁書院．並曾留港業醫．如伍博士廷芳．卒業聖保羅書院．後曾署九龍巡理府．又充定例局議員．為華人代表第一人．終因其大部份勳績．屬於全國．未敢加入．餘可類推．

（五）其他名流史畧．未經調查而脫畧者．諒尚有其人．將來擬再努力徵集．在再版時補充．以彰賢才．

何東爵士

SIR ROBERT HO TUNG

何東爵士○字曉生○現年七十六歲○朱籍廣海○僑寓香江○父早見背○遺孤七人○母氏綜賢○幸採不精覽假○爵士少歧嶷○以家清俊○徙就學私塾○母日與銅錢三○作午餐用○彼擄有存積○合數旬將四十餐錢○一日途遇老乞丐○狀甚貧苦○憫之○竟以平數相贈○其尚俠與好義○於幼時已見其端倪矣○迨七齡○其母忍治生計○挺令較學○改習英文○欲究其材○詢免所費○仍俟留請於塾中者數載○故爵士於漢學頗具淵源○十二歲轉入中央學校○（即今皇仁書院）六年畢業○博覽西史○海通群籍○為謀菽水之歡○曾留校充助教○越年○政進粵垣海關○襄理稅務○兩年後○因應友召○辭謝近港○英商怡和洋行總司理人風聞其名○亜謀借重○延任該行副買辦○爵士固辭不獲○乃就職任事○延任裹助理○咸慶得人○又越二年○香港火險，廣東水險，兩公司分行○遂以組理要席○聘請兼領○而辦理諳精詳○興利剔弊○規畫精詳○爵士總任數職○復關重要○務繁雜○中肯綮○業務蒸蒸○爵士總任數職○復關重要○年頭日上○未幾怡和洋行復振其為正買辦○爵士展鴻才○且至公元一九零零年○始以積勞告退○該行重遠其懲○勉從所辭○然銘鐫紀封○賻畀叙功○其盛德之感人○勞苦功高○有如此者○詢後爵士自營商業○李然奇計○范蠡宏猷○利涉風帆○如操左券○義取之貨○茂干存○仍俟留請於塾中者數載○所費○仍俟留請於塾中者數載○故爵士於漢學

書院）六年畢業○博覽西史○海通群籍○為謀菽水之歡○曾留校充助教○越年○政進粵垣海關○襄理稅務○兩年後○因應友召○辭謝近港○英商怡和洋行總司理人風聞其名○亜謀借重○延任該行副買辦○爵士固辭不獲○乃就職任事○延任裹助理○咸慶得人○又越二年○香港火險，廣東水險，兩公司分行○遂以組理要席○聘請兼領○而辦理諳精詳○興利剔弊○規畫精詳○爵士總任數職○復關重要○務繁雜○復關重要○爵士總任數職○復關重要○精詳○興利剔弊○規畫○中肯綮○業務蒸蒸○捐巨款之獎勵金○於香港大學堂初立○更大解義橐○竭力助贊○前後輸捐○迨二十六萬○其他獎掖後進○孜孜不倦○於港大書院曾慨顧，獎品，及基金三桂○爵士史念學校稅多○港中精其成績之學校○多蒙其伙助○所捐分學但賢爵于弟○殊少遊校機會○送出巨金○遊設義務夜學於九龍地域○以謀教育之普及○又以啟重於九龍抱境○九龍兩地○以謀教育之普及○乃剏設學校○伴西方學序○統籌其成○一九三一年○爵士畢生忠士林○誠無相涉○一九三一年○爵士畢為忠士林○在新界建築兒童幸福會一所○以平數身充本港資女教育貴○一九三四年○又捐款十萬○在香港仔建設一兒童工藝學院○復撥款建一盲生收養所○以賻本港之柴虛言生會○香港自開剛後行金將典禮時○復慨然捐貲二十萬圓○以平數

之○非其德尤不足以致之也○爵士曾任保靈銀行買辦○蓋行舊有規定○華人供職其中者○須殉臣資保證○案門下戶○抱有長才○每有尚隔於公益事業○熱心輸助○更無或吝○塔桂人才於皇仁大書院○曾慨獎掖後進○孜孜不倦○爵士他免偷之○人皆感戴盛德○生平對游器重○兩年後○因應友召○幸辭近港○英商怡和洋行○爵士固辭不獲○乃就職任事○延任該行副買辦○爵士固辭不獲○乃就職任事○賢

原設東華醫院○房室狹小○病者恆以簾滿見遺○華人商其中者日多○五方雜處○疾疫時有○以賻本港之柴虛言生會○香港自開剛後○藝所○以賻本港之柴虛言生會○香港自開剛後景慕○紫榛黃榜○貫行倉陳○非其才不足以濟朋具淵源○十二歲轉入中央學校○（即今皇仁

○兩辭剮空史復闢知○遇有求治之人○苦留醫
之無所○時抱缺憾○又以港側遇有疫症發生○
勸運入西人分隔所○於華俗起居飲食○每感不
便○爵士時在任束華總理○慨焉憂之○引爲己
到於今受其賜○十餘年前○本港米荒○幾釀亂
事○乃首捐助束院○創設疫局○旋設疫局○民
方奔走○卒賴蓋籌○以挹紛紜○人
心大定○地方秩序○賴以維持○暨夫粵束洪澇
爲虐○華北旱魃爲虐○
濟○存活至眾○則仁人之利溥矣○一九一五年
○歐洲風雲○暴德恣狡狂權○征服世界○英興
協約國○以維持人道故○起而鷹戰○爵士義形
於色○捐飛機二架○及救傷汽車數輛○不惜鉅
貲○以捐公道○同時港府因籌助軍需○特頒
新例○增設差餉○租值凡百抽七○令由住戶繳
納○爵士爲香港最大之業主○本其好義之心○
為摩地之舉○將名下租出房屋○所有加
抽之款○概歸其繳納○共數凡二萬五千金○港
人稱頌弗置○一九二二年○香港海員以加薪要
挾○群情憤激○卒中英兩政府派員協助調停○

副全民一致之要求○就一九三六年後之我國奧
正統一○實基於此○客歲我國人籍祝半奉長蔣
公壽辰○獻機以實國防○爵士斥金十萬○慨獻
一機○其對於祖國之熱忱○尤足於式○爵士為
人○不任中英推重○亦將各國尊崇○一九一五
年○將英國爵士榮銜○一九二二年○付我國一
等○將葡萄牙一等勳
章○一九三二年○將法國大勳章○及德國一等
勳章○及比利時爵位勳章○一九三六年○將愛
全國紅十字大勳章○一九三三年○將愛爾蘭爵位
勳章○及我國光遠大○智

三十八歲後○蔚為港中星案保險船務及出入口
各行商案之領袖○其營案托國○且遠至華北及
南洋瓜哇列濱等地○現港中最大商行○舉之
任董事或主席者○凡十有八○足微其為最有名
人也○爵士於一八八零年受室○其
夫人殊有賢德○樂善好施○曾發英京聖約翰救
傷隊榮譽獎章○

SIR ROBERT HO TUNG, Kt. J. P.

Sir Robert Ho Tung (widely known as the "Grand Old Man" of Hongkong) was born in a humble home in Hongkong in 1862. As the eldest child of a family of seven, he early acquired and developed those qualities of organization and leadership which paved the way for his brilliant career later on. Being poor, he learned from his childhood days the lesson of frugality and wise employment of limited resources.

Young Robert showed signs of promise from the very first. At the age of seven he was such an adept pupil in Chinese that when his mother had to withdraw him from school on account of poverty, the teacher offered to continue teaching the child without fees. This teacher became so attached to his pupil that when the little boy had to commence his English studies at the Central School (now Queen's College) there was a reluctant parting. As an English student at the age of twelve Sir Robert quickly showed his ability, for after only six years of study he was chosen as a pupil teacher of the School. Then after a year of teaching (that is in 1878) he sat for a competitive examination for a post in the Chinese Maritime Customs at Canton under Sir Robert Hart's regime. Though he was the youngest candidate at that examination Sir Robert easily secured the post. After two years at the Customs young Ho Tung resigned. He then commenced his association with Messrs. Jardine, Matheson & Co., Ltd., which has now lasted over 50 years. His business abilities and his energising will soon became apparent and in two years he was promoted from a junior position to become the Manager of the Chinese department of the leading business firm in the Far East as Compradore of Jardine's. Sir Robert soon multiplied the business returns and connexions of the firm.

A Millionaire before he was 30 years of age, the once poor struggling youth soon became associated with practically every important business enterprise in the Colony. When he resigned his compradoreship in 1900 (at the early age of 38) Sir Robert Ho Tung was already known as the leading expert and merchant in Hongkong in property, insurance, shipping, and import and export business, with agencies in Java and the Philippines. From 1900 and onwards one company after another invited him to serve on its Board of Directors, until to-day he is a Director of 18 of the leading companies in Hongkong & Shanghai as well as being Chairman and largest shareholder of a number of them. A genius in all matters touching finance Sir Robert Ho Tung's opinion has been constantly sought after not only by the Government of Hongkong but also by the Chinese Republic whose High Adviser he is. In Hongkong he has served on many of the leading Committees and Commissions dealing with the economic life on the Colony. In particular he, as Chairman, was mainly responsible for producing the report of a Sub-Committee on the economic resources of Hong Kong and its Dependences in 1920. In 1922 he contributed much towards the settlement of the Seamen's Strike.

Sir Robert Ho Tung also takes a keen interest in the welfare of the Colony. Education in all its forms receives unstinted support from him. He has given $260,000. to the Hongkong University and defrayed the cost of building the old Kowloon British School. Many free evening schools on the island and the mainland are being maintained by him, while almost every school of importance in the Colony for both boys and girls has received something from him either in the form of scholarships or prizes or donations.

The poor and needy also have always had his sympathetic support. Sir Robert was the Chairman of the Tung Wah Hospital as far back as 1898, and during his term of office he was responsible for extending the hospital structurally, by raising funds for a new building as an Extension and Plague Hospital. In 1931 Sir Robert celebrated his Golden Wedding, and announced a donation of $200,000 to mark that occasion. Half this sum was applied to the building of a Children's Welfare Centre in the New Territories and the other half was devoted to the free education of poor girls in Hongkong. In 1934 he defrayed the entire cost of erecting a home for abandoned dumb animals and presenting it to the S.P.C.A. Thus from dumb animals to needy human beings, Sir Robert has held out the helping hand. In the same year he gave $100,000 towards the cost of an erection of an Industrial School for boys at aberdeen so that the poor children of Hongkong may learn a craft as well as the three Rs.

During the Great War he presented two aeroplanes and a number of motor ambulances to the British Government. Among some of the best known of Sir Robert's many public and social activities mention must be made of his efforts to end Civil Warfare in China by setting up a Round Table Conference between the various warlords. Though his efforts were not immediately successful they stimulated a demand for national unification which became an established fact in 1936. He also personally interviewed famine and flood Sufferers in China on various occasions. Another prominent part played by Sir Robert Ho Tung was at the British Empire Exhibition at Wembley in 1924 and 1925, which he attended as the Honorary Associate Commissioner of the Hongkong Section.

Sir Robert was a member of the Committee which organized the Reception to Duke of Connaught, and the then Prince of Wales as well as the celebrations in honour of Queen Victoria's Diamond Jubilee and the King George V Silver Jubilee.

In 1936 Sir Robert presented the Chinese Government an aeroplane costing $100,000 to mark the Fiftieth Birthday of the Generalissimo Chiang Kai Shek. Honours have been heaped upon Sir Robert from many countries. In 1915 he was knighted by His Majesty the King. He has been a Justice of the Peace since 1889, being the senior one on the list, and received several honours from the Chinese Government. To-day his imposing list of honours includes the following:—Knight of Grace of St. John of Jerusalem (1925), Knight Grand of Officer of the Order of Christ of Portugal (promoted Grand Officer in 1930), First Class Order of the Excellent Crop with Sash of China 1922, Knight Commander of the Legion of Honour 1932, First Class National Red Cross of Germany 1932, Knight Commander of the Crown of Italy 1933, Knight Commander of the Crown of Leopold of Belgium 1933, Knight Commander of the Imperial Dragon of Annam 1936. He is also Senior Honorary LL.D. of the University of Hongkong as well as the Colony's Senior Justice of the Peace. Sir Robert has travelled extensively throughout the world and his visits to Europe, U.S.A. and North China have been frequent in recent years. Many local societies claim him either as their Patron or President or Hon. Vice President.

In 1880 Sir Robert married Lady Ho Tung who is a Lady of Grace of the order of St. John of Jerusalem and assisted Sir Robert at the Wembley Exhibition in 1924 and 1925.

周壽臣爵士

SIR SHOU SON CHOW

周壽臣爵士○名長齡○以字行○廣東省寶安縣人也○現年七十七歲○乃香港耆、德、望，三者兼備之人也○清同治十三年（一八七四）○由南洋大臣曾國藩○北洋大臣李鴻章○退充官費學生○赴美留學○修業於紐約哥林比亞學校○光緒七年（一八八一）○回國○由北洋大臣李鴻章○奏派往朝鮮辦理海關稅務○光緒二十年（一八九四）○著理朝鮮仁川領事○光緒二十九年（一九○三）○由北洋大臣袁世凱委充天津招商局總辦○光緒三十三年（一九○七）○委京奉鐵路總辦○賞戴花翎○因辦理日俄交戰中立事宜○由日本帝國英對四等旭日勤章○光緒三十四年（一九○八）○欽加二品頂戴○因辦理進加按察使街○宣統元年（一九○九）○蒙山海關監督○來政充錦新營口分巡兵備道○

因籌餉出力○議敘加一級○又因防疫出力○傳旨加獎○凡在任四年○悉準所屬各府各州縣○辦理民事，刑事，外交，稅務○勤政愛民○去任之日○萬民脫隔○口碑載道○各商民餽送萬民傘○

道○旋組織外務部奏調以外務部參議上行走○民國元年（一九一二）○大總統袁世凱○給予三等嘉禾章○民國七年（一九一八）○晉給二等嘉禾章○民國八年（一九一九）○大總統徐世昌○頒給紀念章○醫校二等大綬寶光嘉禾章○由民國六年起（一九一七）○充香港太平紳士○民國八年（一九一九）○

委充香港大學堂董事○民國十一年（一九二二）委充香港潔淨局局紳○旋奉英政府十年（一九二一）充香港大學堂董事○委充香港定例局議員○民國十五年（一九二六）○委充英廷賞賜壽臣爵士榮銜○民國十六年（一九二七）○委充香港議政局員○民國二十二年（一九三三）○委充香港議政局員○英皇賞賜銀牌紀念章○民國二十四年（一九三五）○香港大學堂給予博士學位○

在港凡廿餘年○由香港政府委派者○和圖防局○研究財政分任值理○研究兒童工藝院值理○東華醫院永遠顧問○公立醫局顧問○定例局值理○工務分任值理○財政分任值理○保護兒童會等名譽會長○中華全國體育協進會名譽會長○南華體育會○華體育會會長○其屬於社團者○兒童幸福會○華董育嬰等名譽會長○其屬於商業者○則南洋兄弟煙草公司，香港電燈公司，香港電話公司，香港置地信託公司，香港電車公司，屈臣氏藥房等董事，中華百貨公司，中華糖房，及東亞銀行等董事局主席○華探樂五金公司，香港電車公司等董事局主席○勤業麗納○福和漆廠○香港華人中○平與其四○元配葉氏○兄孫甚眾○

SIR SHOU-SON CHOW, Kt. J. P.

One of the most distinguished personages in Hongkong is Sir Shou-son Chow. He is a native of the Po On District, Kwongtung Province, but he was born in Hongkong and is now seventy-seven years of age. Having attained a good knowledge in Chinese literature he was then selected as a free scholar by the Chinese Government to study in the Columbia University, N.Y., U.S.A., in 1874. He returned to China in 1881, and held an important post in the Chinese Customs in Korea. Three years later, he was transferred to be consul-general in an important city in that country. In 1903, he was appointed president of the Chinese Merchants Steamship Navigation Co., Tientsin, and in 1907, president of the Peking Mukden Railway. During the Ruso Japanese War, he was presented by the Japanese Emperor with the Medal of Brilliancy, and since then, he was in the position of various Mandarins in Northern China and his excellent reputation was spread far and abroad.

After the Republic of China was founded, he was honoured by the late President Yuan Shih-kai with conferring of the Order of the Chia Ho (Excellent Crop) Third Class. The Second Class of the same Order was given him in 1918, while the Second Class Medal of Brilliancy was bestowed on him by president Hsu Shih-chang in the following year.

Since 1917, he became Justice of the Peace of Hongkong and besides this, he has the chair in the Directorate of many important firms and Public Utility concerns such as the Bank of East Asia; the China Entertainment and Land Investment Co., The China Emporium., The Hongkong Telephone Co., The Hongkong Electric Co., The Hongkong Tramway, The International Assurance, A. S. Watson, The Hongkong China Realty and Trust Co., The Nanyang Brothers Tobacco Co., Ltd., and many others.

Sir Shou-son Chow was a member of the Sanitary Board since 1922 and in the same year, became member of the Legislative Council. The Honour of Knighthood was conferred upon him by His Late Majesty King George V in 1926. In the following year, he became member of the Hongkong Executive Council, and in 1933, he was conferred by the Hongkong University with the Degree of LL.D. Another Honour bestowed upon him by His late Majesty King George V is the Order of the Silver Jubilee in 1935.

Sir Shou-son has been noted to be publicly and privately connected with various branches of philantrophic activities and is the president of the Hongkong Society for the Protection of Children and Patron of the Chinese Mission to Lepers as well as being in the Committee of various charitable associations. He is a member of the District Watchmen Committee, Permanent Adviser of the Tung Wah Hospital, Public Dispensaries and the Po Leung Kuk. Though he advances in age, his spirit is vigorous and kind; for he takes as great delight in sports as in business. He is adviser to the Chinese General Chamber of Commerce and Hon. President of the South China Athletic Assiciation and the Chinese Recreation Club.

Sir Shou-son was married in his youth and has many sons and plenty of grand and great-grand sons.

羅旭龢博士

羅旭龢博士○現任香港行政局華人代表議員○生於香港○先世集商○現年五十有七○髫齡肄業於香港皇仁○拔萃兩書院○復從游宦儒○研求國學○其他日進語○玫詩英文○復從此○致詩儒可貴○且天資聰穎○過目不忘○履公不特學貫中西○實宇坫宏○撫諭令○各繳文○兼愛政術○養通牲密○年僅十六○已擢龍效用中○居恒覽群籍○初呂四等文員供職於香港警察○兼主慈善○教育○公益○至關於政事言○公益○則殿任香港定例局前華人代表議員○國防局○縣○賓呂長才為上游實誌○於一九一三年○破

DR. R. H. KOTEWALL

紳董○工務局工程委員會委員○員會委員○公立醫局委員○研究莊宇事宜委員會委員○中紐代理行政局議員七次○而在定例局委員亦歷三屆之多○聞時凡十二年○在公益言○尤為夸重○恆時港前例必○打破前例○不因難絀而困失○尤為夸重○博士之力植新利害○不因難絀而困失○然風潮恆時○居港維持社會治安○交遊盪復○然風潮恆時○居港維持社會治安○交遊盪復○則殿任香港社名譽副總裁○在教育顧問○鐘聲慈善社名譽主席○保良局顧問○禁止虐畜會商會總顧問○兼主席○兒童遊樂場管理委員○養通牲密○年僅十六○保良兒童會會長○兼主○慈善○教育○公益○至關於政事言○則曾任香港大學漢文考試委員○香港大學學務監考官○西商會商語學務監考官○一九二六年香港大學特時先生呂為「三千萬國代付的演批」又舉其呂為「歌吉」也○一九二六年香港大學特時先生呂法學博士名譽學位○一九二七年英廷復校長先生呂C.○此「聖雲吉耳及堅佐治勳位」此勳位○譯義為「聖雲吉耳及堅佐治勳位」又舉其呂為「歌吉」也○一九二六年香港大學特時先生呂法學博士

論榮之○此一九一六年專地○後七年○即被選為香港定例局華人代表議員○在任各所建樹○凡於胞福利有關○恆應力呂赴○一九二五年香港大罷工風潮發生○則向內地交涉斷紀○恆心○博士不投腕力○不因難絀而困失○尤為夸重○博士之力植新利害○不因難絀而困失○然風潮恆時○居港維持社會治安○交遊盪復○然風潮恆時○居港維持社會治安○交遊盪復○博士為南華體育會○政為每屆墊請○政成南華體育會副主席○博士為南華體育會○政為每屆墊請○政成南華體育會副主席○博士公餘恆事著作○已出版者有英文合璧之『政治與國計之關係』等書○有『羅旭龢演祝詞彙編』一書○一九二一年曾編撰金叔Uncle Kim」一劇○造經排演籌助款之唯一樂善之濟○一九二二年○英廷君『即今之常義將之滿○『羅旭龢演祝詞彙編』『跳之劇演為○博士卽將我國某某劇政編為『蝶娘娘』『粉劇之排演為博士卽將道趣劇政編○居代有提演戲劇者○以博士卽將我國文化藝術之介紹○自中華文化藝術之介紹○本身神商挾善持家政者十餘人○不幸於一九三六年底仙遊○其而為善善持家政者十餘人○不幸於一九三夫人郭氏○其而為善○本身神商挾善持家政者十餘人○不幸於一九三六年底仙遊○其而為善持家政者十餘人○生有子女九人○備受庭訓○現張於香港旭龢道○

格據為裁判司署前席文案○太平紳士○一九一六年○旋游抵香港○後呂立志向商業發展○後解本職○當于狀旭龢洋行○及股任香港和聲唱片公司總理○華人及業香地小輪有限公司○電話有限公司○司○香港油蘇地小輪有限公司○中華汽車公司等○九龍汽車公司有限公司○凡此礦務○均股兼任○至關於贊助社會義務○政公益○工商等六項○在政事言○則殿任香港定例局前席華人代表議員○國防局○則殿任香港定例局前席華人代表議員○國防局○

長一切委務○未就○徐不勝枚舉英○德履士初呂童年服務警界○同像彈基其優俊○半已破提目之○及觀其治事○金呂為能○造足欲敬○則裁判司署前文案特○破務繁劇○時人進呂著理裁判司署前文案特○破務繁劇○時人進呂著理尤殷殷○而上業亦易聯州有資○時人進呂時人非富於法學者○博士則羽羽有資○時人進呂奇才則○而上業亦易聯州有徐呂此○未魏報升布政司署前文案○凡此種種○尤見精密○破務常年預算○逾其例超○尤見精密○破務常年預算○逾其例超○院大臣所稱計○解緻之外○尤見精密○破務常年於贊助社會義務○政政事○公益○逐趨英廷理藩於贊助社會義務○政政事○公益○逐趨英廷理藩相恭頌○港府當身面謝其勤勞○褒崇備至○時相恭頌○港府當身面謝其勤勞○褒崇備至○時

Dr. R. H. KOTEWALL, C.M.G., LL.D.

Dr. R. H. Kotewall is a member of the Hongkong Executive and Legislative Councils. He was born in Hongkong in 1880. He obtained his early education at the Diocesan Boy's School and the Queen's College. He takes pride in the fact that he has risen to the present position without a college diploma. What was deprived of him in the University halls he made up with books. What he missed in the college rooms he learned in the school of hard knocks. At home he has his own library where he spends two or three hours every day to read books, newspapers and magazines. He is a typical Chinese leader, modern and modest.

Dr. Kotewall was appointed as a 4th clerk in the Police Headquarters at the age of sixteen. Young in age but old in experience, he was promoted as the first clerk in the Magistrates' Court, Victoria, in 1913. In 1916 he was appointed as chief clerk in the Colonial Secretrate and at the same year he was made a Justice of the Peace, an appointment never before, nor since, given to a Chinese civil servant of Hongkong. Dr. Kotewall resigned the civil service in 1916, to start business. He was officially thanked by the government for his efficient and trustworthy services.

He has been nominated as a Chinese member of the Legislative Council in 1924, and of the Executive Council in 1936. The Hon. degree of LL.D. was conferred on him by the University of Hongkong in 1926. His late Majesty King George V decorated him with the insignia of C.M.G. in 1927.

Besides being an extremely capable Government official, Dr. Kotewall is connected with various social and commercial organizations either in the capacity of a president or a director. He is the principal of the R. H. Kotewall & Co., Ltd.; director of Hongkong Telephone Co., Ltd., director of Wo Shing Co., Ltd.; Hon. Vice-president of Hongkong University Union; Vice-president of Hongkong branch of the English Association; Vice-patron of St. John Ambulance Association; school committee of Diocesan Boys' School; Hon. Member of the Hongkong University Law & Commerce Society; Hon. president of South China Athletic Association; Hon. President of Chung Shing Benevolent Association.

Dr. Kotewall spends a lot of his time for Public Welfares. He has even not forgotten the Street Urchins. There is now a club for Boot-blacks and Newspaper Sellers Street Urchins sho would have otherwise no means of recreation or free tuition for a better future. Dr. R. H. Kotewall is one of the sponsors of the Club which has as its patron-His Excellency the Governor.

Though he is always busy yet he likes art and literature very much. His writings include "Forestry", and "Government in its relation to national welfare", which were written both in Chinese and English. In 1921 he wrote and personally produced a play entitled "Uncle Kim" in aid of charity, which was a great success. He also adapted a play named "The Maid of the Hills" from an old Chinese play, which he produced in honour of H.R.H. the then prince of Wales during the latter visit to Hongkong in 1922.

香港華人名人史略（一九三七）

曹善允博士

曹博士善允○粵之中山縣人○於遜清同治七年，(公元一八六八)誕於澳門○現年七十歲○先德消糺公○濱江服役○今閱久彰○以能致力地方公益○為華僑晉校蔔廈勘學之第一人○用是

DR. TS'O SEEN WAN

見如于清廷○獲欽賜二品榮銜○頂戴花翎之賞○博士生富裕家○無騎奢習○幼已馳譽好學○頭角崢嶸○招華十四○使子馬貝笈玫讀國學於香華文人萃萃之濱瀉○四年面壁○可謂功深○兩成之春○避學英國○以益新知○及秋玫遜畢○爾歐成大書院讀律○四歲學成○即與該地名法家鄒成尼君訂約為輟肄生○期滿○史在英京藏恥卷之律卸撰習○追光緒二二年，(一八九六)

初，作古閩人何啟爵士等○欲與博士叛辦一程度較高之學府○廣育港地英才○使卑業俊○可遞進英大學○免浪擲寶貴光陰○與有用金錢○戀至善也○惜浪遷成○未幾金○納牧師，附偹尼士他副主教○熱心興學○尤許幫忙○遭獻鎮由公等領街○傖肥基捐六萬圓○必能促其實現○如其言○卒○中西南洋各地華僑○即富時○名卷秘書由博士住之○另組一純粹華人之籌募委員會○主席由何啟住之○於一九○九年○再由熹制米名流○成立籌募委員會○主席由何啟住之○由港主其事恭○時值英儲君(即今遜邑)來遊在列提相道○翌年，因地點不適中○至一九二六年○遷在

應英國律師檢定試○以成績優異○獲領執業文憑○將出席英京高等法庭○翌年近歸○開業香江○獨力經營○凡三十載○至民一九○○始與英人學洵君合辦○逐以兩人之名○顏其律師樓曰英○博士雖生長於馬交○但親友顧多在香島○其赴英也○寶家卑辦寶珊之照拂○故學成近港後○○素徐料理社會各種事業○恆惟卑志趣高尚○且故生平志趣高尚

瞻○從而與華僑領袖何啟爵士通力合作○而享光榮之終○博士曾提議問時興辦一○為人類進步及快慰之兩大要素○故數十年來○無日不以提倡興家為己任○○今光就教育言○

(一)聖士提反男校一○博士秋舉為其中之一○大學之緣起○○○請其主其事恭○時值英儲君(即今遜邑)來遊在列提相道○翌年，因地點不適中○至一九二六年○遷在

聖士提反女校也○成立時期○為一九○三年○至一九○七年冬○兩該校前屆學業○領獎之兒○寄割峯提攜○本港應有一大學○英翁富紳毛地和之○寶胎胞於此校○今該校學移日形發達○故香港大學○○避赤社者○均投規此宏偉之學府為○寶家卑辦寶珊南中○以為叛辦人才之一○追今常董其事○○○學成近此校○乃開辦於卑廈士道○故一九○四年○乃開辦於卑廈士道○翌年○因地點不適中○斯時狼跟因陋○少艾赤聯翻慶止○而代表致校致謝詞者○為已納副主教與提攜翻慶止○而代表致校致謝詞者○為已納提攜

(二)聖士提反女校　當爾料堂士提反男校之小綠校舍移起○而建校者○均投規此宏偉之寶財○未償學以倡○

(三)香港大學　香港大學之基○萬○博士秋舉為其中之一○(三)香港大學　香港於一九○九年○再由熹制米名流○成立籌募委員會○顧捐捐校舍以倡○討論其事○預籌基金百萬○乃在接受毛君貢獻之前○應先預籌基金百

兩廣總督○赤曹予以助力馬○治一九一一年，

家鄒成尼君訂約為輟肄生○期滿○即與該地名法得此數○以作華辦經費○是即令日鼎鼎大名

兩廣總督○赤曹予以助力馬○治一九一一年，

誃大學為宛裕基金。舉行賣物會。名譽秘書一席。亦為之博士。同年誃大學規例選准港府通過。以博士曾與起草之列。被聘兼為委員。博士因辭不獲。至一九一四年而始就。同時兼充校內之聖約翰。整座理之管理委員。一九二九年。史醫住誃大學立例。及董事。兩禮科堂之管理委員。

○一九二八年。誃校據增建術舍。博士亦被為委員。教育部。本港教育部成立於一九二○年。博士被選為秘書。○（四）至保原男爵書院董事。兩度勸捐。

羅男書院董事。始於一九一四年。同年誃大學因擴充原址。遂組委員會籌款。博士任內助力爭走。勤勞義舉。又伍延芳夫人捐建之何妙玲博士者之。迨一九三○年。院章重理者也。○雅利氏及那打素醫院。在本港具有悠久歷史。且為歲完美之慈善機關。勤勞義舉。亦附庸誃院。又有獎學金。博士廉不錫力爭走。博士也。○（一）雅利氏分布醫教育者也。○一九○三年博士被選為誃院財政管院。緣就慈善言。

民生書院。○泉舉博士任董事長。○此其貢獻矣。

本港教育會。○（六）民生書院。一九二六年。報科牛痘者見三十六萬人。於是倡行普編之微求。亦善其言。進旗應即舉行普編之微求。以遂於今。計拖行僅四個月。○華民政務司特召集博士等。與衛生局共同討論。防止傳染病之妙。博士房中贊助其賛甚益。○乃行表決。計拖行僅四個月之力也。○（五）潔淨局（即今之市政衛生局）一九一八年。博士被委為潔淨局局紳之一。服務凡十一載。○（六）東華醫院。一九二五年。被聘為東華醫一九二○年功竟。蓮科啟德汽車公司。以利九龍

○（二）公立醫局。一九一○年。博士被選為華人九二○年功竟。蓮科啟德汽車公司。以利九龍

公立醫局董事。○翌年。被推為西環公立醫局董事會會長。○（三）贊育醫院。西環為貧民住宅區。婦孺醫院。尤宜設立。一九二二年以前。未有注意及之者。誠屬莢急。乃自博士主持立醫局於斯。委料及接生科教授宛誃醫院之婦科及接生科。教授宛誃醫院泉堂。○臨時組織特別醫隊。○博士則舉命組織華人警察後備隊。及巡街命史練。未幾。港府成立華人警察後備隊。博士遂以華人身份任名譽總裁為○（丙）為華人求永遠墳場之力也。一九一一年。向港府爭得安樂墳地一。以及掃桿埔水遠墳場之地。博士均為其管理○一九○五年。本港工潮發生。政府特治華人墳地一。○委料工業潮持會。為辦持治安。博士則舉命組織華人警察及新墳地之交通。迨一九二七年。第二期完成方進行第三期之際。官方卒蘭收四所絵地綾。用建啟德飛行場。與全部計劃。其能實現。○因而為可托也。○（乙）鎮壓飛工潮及新墳地之交通。迨一九二七年。第二期完成

香港華人名人史略（一九三七）

23

Dr. TS'O SEEN WAN, C.B.E., LL.D., J.P.

The Honourable Mr. Ts'o Seen Wan, C.B.E., LL.D. J.P., was born in Macao on the 10th November, 1868. He is the son of the late Mr. Ts'o Yau alias Ts'o Wai Chuen, a well-known merchant of Macao who was the first Chinese in Macao decorated by the King of Portugal with the Insignia of "Commenda De Nossa Senhora Da Conceicao" (Palmeira De Reino) and had the Honorary title of the 2nd Degree with the Red Button and Peacock's Feather conferred on him by the Emperor of China Kwang Hsu in the year 1880.

Dr. Ts'o went to Shanghai for his Chinese education in 1881 and returned to Macao in 1885 when arrangements were made for him to go to England for his English education. He left Hongkong for England at the end of February of 1885 and entered Cheltenham College in September of the same year. After passing his Law Entrance Examination he left College after the Mid-Summer term in 1890. He was articled to Mr. W. G. Gurney of Messrs. Winterbotham and Gurney, a well-known firm of Solicitors in Cheltenham and served the last year of his articles at the office of Messrs. Waterhouse, Winterbotham and Harrison in London. He passed his final law examination in April 1896 and was enrolled as a solicitor of the Supreme Court of Judicature of England. He came to Hongkong and set up in practice on his own account as a solicitor in 1897; was subsequently joined by Mr. P. M. Hodgson in 1927 and thereafter has practiced with him under the firm name of Messrs. Ts'o and Hodgson.

Although Dr. Ts'o's ancestral home was in Macao, his family had many friends, business connections and interests in Hongkong. On his return to the Colony he at once associated himself with the late Sir Kai Ho Kai and the late Sir Boshan Wei Yuk, two leading members of the Chinese community, and assisted them, unostentatiously, in various matters of public interest; Sir Boshan Wei Yuk being the gentleman who was responsible for his going to England, and looked after his welfare during the whole period of his sojourn there. His chief interest seemed to have been directed towards education and medical work among the Chinese; holding, no doubt, the principle that sound knowledge and good health are essentials to human beings for progress and happiness. He possesses a quiet disposition and unobtrusive manners and much dislikes coming forward into the limelight. And yet, by the weight of his public services, he was forced to the front and recognized as a leading member of the Chinese community in Hong Kong. His services to the Chinese community have been many and varied and it may be said that they cover the whole expanse of a human life from birth to death as the following list of institutions with which he was and is still connected will show.

EDUCATIONAL

St. Stephen's Boys' College.

This College was opened in 1903. Dr. Ts'o was one of its founders and has taken interest in its affairs since its opening. The object of founding this College was to give Chinese students a higher standard of education so that any one of them who may desire to go to England for a University course of education may enter a University without much further preparation for entrance and thereby save himself from longer residence there and the expense attendant thereto. An attempt to establish such a College for the Chinese was made by the late Sir Kai Ho Kai, Dr. Ts'o and other leading members of the Chinese community a few years previously. But for certain reasons, the scheme was not proceeded with, until the Rev. Mr. (afterwards Archdeacon) E.J. Barnett came to Hongkong in 1902 when he and Archdeacon (Afterwards Bishop) Bannister approached Sir Kai on the subject and undertook to start such a school if the Chinese would promise to support. This promise was readily given by Sir Kai Ho Kai and his associate. One of the two houses known as "Ball's Court" situated between Bonham Road and Western Street was then taken as a start for the school. Under the Wardenship of Mr. Barnett the school flourished. The other house at Ball's Court was also taken the next year. In 1905 it was found that further accomodation was required for the school and a 21 years' lease of Ball's Court with its extensive ground was taken with the object of adding a new wing to the existing buildings; the Chinese supporters of the school provided a sum of $60,000 for the purpose. It was not until January 2, 1910, that a Board of Advice was founded of which Dr. Ts'o was an original member. This Board was changed to a College Council of which Dr. Ts'o was also an original member. The College has now its own school building at Stanley situated on a beautiful site with every facility and ample ground for games and sport. It was at a Prize-giving Day at St. Stephen's College (December 1907) that Sir Frederick (now Lord) Lugard the then Governor of Hongkong suggested that Hongkong itself should possess a University. His suggestion was taken up at once by the late Sir (then Mr.) H. N. Mody, who offered to erect entirely at his own expense the necessary buildings for a Hong Kong University. The idea of founding a Hongkong University, it may be said, originated from St. Stephen's College.

St. Stephen's Girls' College.

When discussing the establishment of the Boys' College, Dr. Ts'o suggested that a kindergarten school for Chinese boys and girls should also be opened as a nucleus for a girls' college. A kindergarten and girls' school was started in 1904 in a building at Breezy Point but only a few very young girls attended. It was subsequently found that the parents of grown-up girls objected to the locality as being too far from the centre of the town and it was, therefore, removed to No. 59 Caine Road the next year 1905. Many grown-up girls then came and the school prospered. It may be said that St. Stephen's Girls' College was founded in that year.

Dr. Ts'o took great interest in the College from its start and it was not until 1922 that the present College building at Lyttleton Road was erected, the foundation stone of which was laid by His Royal Highness, the Prince of Wales in that year; Archdeacon Barnett and Dr. Ts'o as representatives of the College, had the honour of presenting to His Royal Highness, and address of welcome and thanks. The College Council was not instituted until 1926 and Dr. Ts'o has been a member of the Council since that year.

Hongkong University.

When Mr. Mody offered to erect the necessary buildings for the Hongkong University, a committee was appointed by His Excellency, Sir Frederick Lugard, to consider the matter and it was decided that, before accepting the offer, an Endowment Fund of at least $1,000,000 should be raised. The leading Chinese in Hongkong were asked to form a Sub-Committee to assist in raising the Endowment and at a meeting held at Government House in 1909 on the invitation of His Excellency Sir Frederick Lugard, a Chinese Sub-Committee was formed; the late Sir Kai Ho Kai was elected Chairman, and Dr. Ts'o the Honorary Secretary thereof. Appeals were made not only to Chinese in Hongkong, but also in China and abroad. The Viceroy of Canton was approached who took special interest in the scheme and gave substantial help to the Endowment Fund. A University Bazaar of which Dr. Ts'o was the Honorary Secretary was held in 1911 to raise more funds. This Committee continued to function for a few years after the opening of the University collecting further funds for various objects of the University such as for the playground, the union, etc.; and particularly in obtaining funds for starting an Arts Faculty. When the University Ordinance was passed in 1911, Dr. Ts'o was appointed a member of the Court; but he resigned his seat in favour of another gentleman, and was not until 1914, appointed a member thereof. Since 1929, Dr. Ts'o has been (ex officio) a member of the Court as well as the University Council. He was also a member both of the University Sharp and the University Gollan Commissions.

University Hostels.

Dr. Ts'o has been a member of the Board of Control of St. John's Hall since April 1914; and also a member of the Board of Control of Morrison Hall since 1914.

St. Paul's College.

When St. Paul's College was re-established, an extension to the old College building was required. A Committee was appointed in 1914 to raise the necessary funds for the extension. Dr. Ts'o was appointed Secretary to the Committee. He was also a member of the Committee for raising funds to build a hostel in 1918 and a member of the College Council since 1914.

Board of Education.

Dr. Ts'o has been a member of the Board since it was instituted in April 1920.

Munsang College.

The establishment of this College was part of a scheme for the development of the Kai Tack Reclamation. The late Mr. Au Chak Mun left by his will a sum of 10,000 for the purpose and Mr. Mok Kon Sang, a shareholder of the Kai Tack Co., also contributed another sum of $10,000 for the same purpose. When the first section of the reclamation was completed and houses were built thereon, the need for educational facilities seemed apparent and in 1926 the College was first started Dr. Ts'o was elected Chairman of the College Council.

MEDICAL

Alice Memorial and Affiliated Hospitals.

Dr. Ts'o became a member of the Finance Committee of the Alice Memorial and the Nethersole Hospitals in 1903. He took part in raising funds for the building of the Maternity Hospital and the Institute for the Training of Nurses. When Madam Wu Ting Fang presented the funds for the building of the Ho Miu Ling Hospital, Dr. Ts'o was Treasurer of that fund. The last mentioned institutions were affiliated to the Alice Memorial and Nethersole Hospitals all of which were under the management and control of the London Missionary Society. In 1923, a new Constitution (for the draft of which Dr. Ts'o was responsible) was adopted. The Finance Committee was then changed into a General Committee. Dr. Ts'o was appointed Chairman of the Committee in 1930 and (ex officio) he was also Chairman of the Executive Committee. The Nethersole Hospital Building after forty years of useful work was pulled down in May 1935. Dr. Ts'o is making every effort to raise funds for its rebuilding.

Chinese Public Dispensaries.

He was a Member of the Chinese Public Dispensaries Committee in 1910 and became a Chairman of the Western Public Dispensary in 1911.

Tsan Yuk Hospital.

This is a Maternity Hospital in the Western district built in 1922. As Chairman of the Western Public Dispensary, the Tsan Yuk Hospital was under his management and control. As the district was a poor one, the need of a clinic for women's diseases and one for babies became urgent. The Professor of Gynaecology and Obstetrics of the Hongkong University was invited to take charge of these clinics. This Hospital was, for financial reasons handed over to the Government in January 1934 for management.

Vaccination Campaign (1916—1917)

When an epidemic of small-pox broke out in the Western District of Hongkong towards the end of 1916, Dr. Ts'o was requested by the Secretary for Chinese Affairs and the Medical Officer of Health to consider the best means of preventing the spreading of the disease. Dr. Ts'o suggested universal vaccination. He guaranteed that the Chinese would not go against vaccination if certain concessions be given to them when a case occurred in their house. The concession was agreed to by the Medical Officer of Health, Dr. Woodman, subject to the approval of His Excellency, the Governor. His Excellency gave full power to Dr. Woodman to adopt, at his discretion, any suggestion Dr. Ts'o might make during the campaign. The campaign was successful from the very beginning. It commenced in November 1916 and ended in March 1917. No less than 360,000 children and grown-ups were vaccinated during that period. A second campaign took place three years afterwards in which Dr. Ts'o also assisted.

Sanitary Board (now Urban Council)

Dr. Ts'o appointed a Chinese member of the Board in the year 1918. He served on the Board from that year until he resigned his seat in 1929.

Tung Wah Hospital.

Dr. Ts'o has been a member of the Advisory Board since September 1925. Apart from the great interest he takes in the educational and medical works, Dr. Ts'o has also taken great interest in the general question of over-crowding in Hongkong. Many Chinese came to Hongkong to reside when the revolution took place in China. The late Sir Kai Ho Kai, Dr. Ts'o and Messrs. Au Tack and Cheung Sum Woo formulated a scheme for the reclamation of Kowloon Bay foreshore. Sir Kai Ho Kai was requested to negotiate with the Hongkong Government for a concession to reclaim Kowloon Bay. After long negotiations, the concession was ultimately granted by the Hongkong Government in April. Unfortunately, Sir Kai died in May of the same year and Dr. Ts'o was left to carry out the scheme. A private company was formed to take up the concession and the name of "Kai Tack" was taken in honour of Sir Kai and Mr. Au Tack. War broke out in August 1914 which caused many obstacles in the progress of the reclamation work. However, the first section of the scheme was completed in 1920 and buildings were erected on that section. The Kai Tack Bus Company was specially instituted to give facilities to residents of Kowloon City and the reclamation, and formed part of the scheme for the development of the reclamation. However, after the second section had been fully completed, the Government required the whole reclamation, except the first section, for air service. The remaining area was surrendered to the Government in 1927 and it is now known as the Kai Tack Aerodrome.

During the emergency in 1925 on account of labour trouble, Dr. Ts'o was appointed Chinese Labour Controller by the Government. While engaged in this task, he organized a Chinese company of special constables and also a number of street guards to meet the threat of incendiarism. After the experience of 1925, it was thought by the Hon. Inspector General of Police that a police reserve force should be formed. Dr. Ts'o was requested to organized a Chinese Company and was made Hon. Commissioner of the Police Reserve Force.

In 1925, he was appointed a member of the District Watch Committee and a visiting Justice of the Po Leung Kuk and has been a member of the Permanent Board of Direction of the Po Leung Kuk since 1929.

He has been connected both with the Hongkong Society for the Protection of Children's Playground Association since their foundations in the capacity of a Vice-president.

He was one of the original members of the Committee to apply for a Permanent Cemetery for the Chinese in 1911, and a member of the Board of Management of the Permanent Cemetery when the Board was formed in 1913. He became the Honorary Secretary of the Permanent Cemetery in 1919.

He is also associated in various ways with many other organizations in public life including the movements of St. John's Brigade, Boy Scouts & etc.

The Rotary Club of Hongkong appointed him their President for the year 1933.

He was nominated as a Chinese member of the Legislative Council on 17th January 1929 and is serving his second term which will expire on the 17th January 1937.

He was made a Justice of the Peace in 1918. The Hon. Degree of LL.D. was conferred on him by the University of Hongkong in 1924.

He was created an Officer of the Order of the British Empire by His late Majesty King George VI in 1928 and Commander of the same Order in 1935.

He is being invited by the Hongkong Government to represent the Chinese in Hongkong at the Coronation of his Majesty King George VI on the 12th May 1937 to which invitation he has accepted and will proceed to England next April.

香港華人名人史略（一九三七）

周埈年大律師

周埈年大律師

法家埈年先生。原籍廣東東莞縣。而生長於香港。乃前本港華人代表周少岐之公子。而現任之香港華人代表也。幼秀楚。十七歲已畢業於香港聖士提反書院。越年。赴英留學。習律於牛津大學。及西曆一九一四年。學成歸國。得大律師及文學士榮銜。在港中社會服務多年。曾任東華醫院總理。保良局紳。西曆一九二三年任太平局紳。華商總會會名譽董事。一九二九年。任潯海局紳。物業維持會主席。內河輪船商會主席。保險兄童會司理。整理港口會委員。東莞商會主席。華人核數試官。南華體育會正會長。中華體育會名譽會董。華人體育協進會名譽會童。受子軍港分會長。華人體育協進會名譽會童。聖約翰救傷隊名譽會童，兼財政委員。華商會所主席。防範海盜會委員。電話會委員。英容會司理。內河輪船會委員。

庫業司理。一九三一年英政府以先生服務精忠。委充定例局議員。先生史勢勵盡職。對港政府法例方面。貢獻良多。而對於華人利益。尤能策劃及保障。一九三五年。第一任期滿。政府不計辭卷董事。一九二九年。故現連任職職。先生現年四十四歲。退休。前程無限量。

救濟水委員。荒會委員。又任慈幼會司理。大司庫。庫。港大學女等斜。宿舍司。

Hon. Mr. CHAU TSUN NIN, J.P.
BARRISTER - AT - LAW.

Mr. Chau is one of the most influential social magnates of Hongkong. He is a native of the Tungkoon District, Kwongtung Province, but was born in Hongkong is 1893. When he was but seventeen years old, he was graduated from the St. Stephen's College and in the following year, he set sail to England to continue his studies and to attain a thorough education. He was graduated with the B.A. degree and the title of Barrister - at - law from Oxford University England in 1914 and ever since, he practices his profession in the Colony. Bright and smart as Mr. Chau is, he has rendered himself to the commercial world. He is general manager and director of the Yuen On Steamship Co., Ltd.; The China Emporium, Ltd.; the Chun On Fire Insurance Co.; manager of the Hongkong & Kowloon Land & Loan Co., Ltd.; director of the Wo Shing Co., Ltd.; committee of the Fire Insurance Association of Hong Kong, Marine Insurance Association of Hongkong & Canton. Besides these, Mr. Chau is partner or stockholder of many firms in Hongkong.

Though he is always busy with his own work, Mr. Chau is, very attentive in social affairs. He is a member of the Legislative Council, which he began consumation since 1931; and member of the Sanitary Board. He was appointed Justice of the Peace of Hongkong since 1923 and has been holding important positions in different public - welfare organizations. The most note - worthy ones are finance committee of the St. John Ambulance Association; Hon. president of the Chung Sing Benevolent Society; college council of the St. Stephen's College; Hon. Vice - president of the Hong Kong University Union; Hon. President of the South China Athletic Association; Vice - president of the Boy Scouts Association; Hon. Director of the Chinese General Chamber of Commerce; Ex - president of the Tung Wah Hospital; Justice of the Po Leung Kuk; ex - president of the Inland Steamship Association; and director of the Hongkong Society for the Protection of Children.

Speaking generally, Mr. Chau has done, a great deal to the Hongkong Government as well as to the Chinese population living in the Colony.

香港・澳門雙城成長經典

羅文錦大律師

師律大錦文羅

文錦律師羅先生者。紳士長蓁翁之長公子也。生於西曆一八九三年港寓。賦姓溫和。容貌英偉。自少精敏。學貫中英。踔厲風發。薪然嶄頭角。泉謂羅氏有子矣。及長。賦笈英倫。銳

清海衛生局等議員。去歲復委為定例局議員。兼香港大學校董及參事。孔子所謂學而優則仕者。先生以之。其服務於社會也。則尤華商總會。東華醫院顧問，體育俱樂部。兒童保護會等主席。香港扶幼會。歐美留學生聯合會等會長。其致

力於商業也。則任香港中華電力公司。香港大酒店。省港澳輪船公司。司等董事。此不過先生半生服務之大旨情形耳，其餘猶或殊委於官廳。或見重於社團。聘書及函。史償數數。然最顯著而為僑肥頸于鋸慶者。則英提議撤銷華報檢查苛。蓋言論自由。為文明國之公例。而民之喉舌。莫容久遠摧擊。先生激於大義。提議撤銷。殊不幸竟遭否決。而正義所在。中外咸欽。淘不愧為華人之代表。偽肥愛戴。讓日不宜。今先生方年富力強。正大有為之候。其造福于人羣者。寧有艾耶。羅代表。羅先生。吾將馨香以祝之也。先生淑配何氏。乃何東爵紳之女公子。賢夫良婦。相得益彰。現有子女五人云。

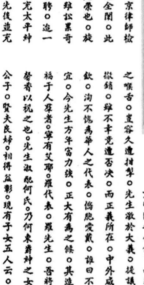

志法律。一九一五年學所業。迷願英京律師檢定。名譽等試。初已及第。蝶則名冠全閒。此固羅君之美譽。抑亦我國留學生之光榮也。按即束裝歸港。行其所學。業救律師。辯訟黑奇。鞫。片言立折。故使譽大振。訟者爭聘。追一九二一年。英政府以其廉明精幹。委充太平紳士。一九三二年。又委為國防局紳。先後迭充

Hon. Mr. LO MAN-KAM, J.P.
Solicitor

Mr. Lo was born in Hong Kong in 1893. He was bestowed with such talents that he was usually highly commended even when he was a youth. Having graduated from Hong Kong, he went to England for higher education. He passed the Solicitors' Final and the Solicitors' Honour Examinations in 1915 and came first in the First Class in the latter case which was considered to be one of the glories among the Chinese students who studied there.

He returned to Hong Kong in the same year and since then he practises his profession in the colony gaining most recommendation and praise of his line.

Mr. Lo is an influential factor in social affairs. He was appointed Justice of Peace in 1921, Member of District Watchmen Committee since 1932, Member of the Legislative Council in 1935 and Member of the Sanitary Board and afterwards Urban Council from 1932 to 1936. Besides these, Mr. Lo has usually been appointed important positions in various social and commercial organizations. The most note worthy ones are Director of the Hong Kong and Shanghai Hotel Ltd., Hong Kong Canton and Macao Steamboat Co., Ltd., China Light & Power Co., Ltd., Member of the Hong Kong University Law & Commerce Society, Committee of the Law Society, Hon. Vice-president of the Hong Kong University Union, Vice-president of the Hong Kong Branch of the English Association, Ex-officio and former president of the Rotary Club of Hong Kong, Vice-president of the Hong Kong Football Association, Vice-president of the Hong Kong Lawn Tennis Association, Hon. President of the South China Athletic Association, Committee of the Hong Kong Chinese Recreation Club and Legal Adviser of the New Territories Agricultural Association of Hong Kong. He is also Member of the Advisory Board of the Tung Wah Hospital, Permanent Member of the Committee of the Po Leung Kuk, and Hon. Legal Adviser to the Chinese Chamber of Commerce.

Mr. Lo married in 1918 to Ho Kam Chi. They have five children.

Speaking in general, Mr. Lo is one of the most prominent Chinese in Hong Kong and has wrought wonderfully for the good of Chinese Community. One example for which the fame and name of Mr. Lo shall never be faded is the protest against the censorship of Chinese news papers.

李樹芬醫博士

李樹芬博士。原籍廣東台山人。而生長於香港。現年五十三歲。久著名香港之華人西醫生。新就職之華人代表也。少時。肄業於港中拔萃書院。精長。隨父兄到美國之波士頓埠。肄業九二四及一九二五兩年。

DR. LI SHU FAN

母一九一一年。即民國元年也。當時我國共和政府始初成立。首都暫設廣州。未幾我國首都遷於南京。政府廣東省衛生部長。未幾我國首都遷於南京。之唯一療養院。遂從事將該院改組。以訓練看護人材。增設附醫部。及設看護學校。以訓練看護人。

博士仍被委充廣東省衛生司長。一九一三年。博士辭職返港。遂在港中自行開設醫務所。一村。擴築五層樓院。添置最新式醫科用具。

從此結束。至今港人猶稱道之。於罷工風潮時。急後。博士以跑馬地養和醫院。乃華人所設立之唯一療養院。遂從事將該院改組。以訓練看護人。燦然一新。因對於該院勞苦甚大。故歷被舉為該醫院董事長凡十年之久。除此之外。博士在港中各機關團體所任職務至多。計歷任東華醫院副會長。中華醫學會香港分會會長。中華醫學會總會副會長。香港大學醫學會副會長。

○參加廣東公醫學校。改組大學事宜。及廣東公醫科大學成立。後。即被聘為該大學校長兼外科大教授。當時國父孫中山正在廣州組織軍政府。被舉為大元帥。聘博士為大元帥府醫官。聘博士為

院顧問。醫務局局員。非官議太平局紳。潔淨局議員。市政衛生局議員。香港孔聖會名譽會長。歐美同學會會長。廣東銀行董事。我國國民經濟建設運動委員會廣東省分會委員。今年史被委為本港定例局議員(華人代表)。博士生平最喜行

於美國中學。既弱冠。攷進香港西醫學堂。攻醫科。西曆一九零八年畢業。領有該校執照。攷得清廷資選到英國愛丁堡大學免攻外科學院攻讀。卒膺故學院外科博士衔。一曆一九二二年。博士再赴英國。追完丁堡密士聖約翰救傷會醫官。整水遊會會員。保護兒童會幹事。東華

士之銜頭。攷內外全科。一九一零年畢業。授得故風潮最烈之頃。港幣金元泰弄bonds。以博士曾為九二五年。博士由英返港時。正為香港大罷工外科學院攻請。卒膺故學院外科博士衔。一莊宇審查會會員。香港孔聖會名譽會長。一九三五年香港

官醫生。攷內外全科。一九一零年畢業。授得故中國政府官吏。托任說人。博士遂弁走省港間。大學內外科醫學士學位。越年。又榮膺故大學後。公牘報帶一槍一物。很於對邦之外。三十

熱帶病學兼衛生學碩士。選由英返港。時為西以進行制作工作。卒不辱使命。使罷工風潮。年如一日。故授術甚精。而皖皖亦甚壯。

Dr. LI SHU FAN,

J.P., M.B., Ch. B., D.T.M. & H., F.R.C.S. (Edinburgh)

Dr. Li was born in Hongkong in 1885. He received his early education at the Diocesan School and later in Boston, U.S.A. In 1908 he graduated from the Hongkong College of Medicine with the degree of L.M. & S. Thereafter, he proceeded to Europe under a Chinese Government Scholarship and enrolled himself at the University of Edinburgh, where in 1910 he obtained the degree of Bachelor of Medicine and Surgery and in the following year a special Diploma in Tropical Medicine and Hygiene. After several years of medical practice in Hongkong he returned to Edinburgh in 1922 where after a course of post-graduate work, he was elected a Fellow of the Royal College of Surgeons.

Upon his return to China in 1911, the year of the foundation of the Chinese Republic, when Canton was the Capital of China, he was appointed Minister of Health and Later when the seat of the Government was removed to Nanking, he continued to serve in Canton as Commissioner of Health for the province of Kwangtung. Being the first Minister and Commissioner of Health in the history of the country, he had undertaken studpendous pioneering legislative and organization work.

Returning to the Colony in 1913, he commenced the practice of his profession up to the present time. From 1924 to 1925, however, he had served a two years' contract in Canton, being engaged in the reorganization of the Kung Yee Medical College, with the object of bringing it up to the University Status. On the completion of that work, he was appointed President of the Kung Yee University Medical School as well as Professor of Surgery. This school is now incorporated with the Sun Yat Sen University.

During his stay in Canton, a signal honour was bestowed upon him by the Chinese Government in appointing him Medical Officer to the Generalissimo and President of the Republic, Dr. Sun Yat Sen.

During the big strike of 1925 he again returned to the Colony, and in this connection he acted as one of the intermediaries between the Hongkong and Canton Governments, at the special request of the then Governor of Hongkong, Sir Cecil Clementi. His work had helped in no measure towards the settlement of that strike.

Having been back in the Colony, he was primarily responsible for the reorganization of the Yeung Wo Hospital at Happy Valley, now known as the Hongkong Sanatorium and Hospital. This, he completely reorganized, adding thereto a charity department and a training school for nurses and midwives, and in 1932 the present magnificent new hospital building of five stories was completed, designed on up-to-date lines, and equipped with modern appliances. He has now served the Hospital continuously as Chairman of Directors for ten years.

He had been elected as Vice-president of the Far Eastern Association of Tropical Medicine, Vice-president of the National Chinese Medical Association, President of the Hongkong Chinese Medical Association, and Vice-president of the Hongkong University Medical Society. He is also member of the Court of the University of Hongkong.

He is an Honorary Director of the Chinese Chamber of Commerce, a member of the Tung Wah Hospital Advisory Board, member of the Medical Board, as well as a member of the Sanitary Board. In 1935 he was re-elected to serve a second term as member of the Sanitary Board, which is now the Urban Council. He is a non-official Justice of the Peace. He has been nominated as a Chinese member of the Legislative Council 1937.

In addition, he is a member of the Executive Committee of Society for the Protection of Children, for twenty years he was as active member as well as life member and Corps Surgeon to the St. John Ambulance Brigade and Association. He served as member of the Sanitary Legislation Committee, in connection with the Scheme for the Reorganization of the Medical and Sanitary Services of the Colony. At present he is a member of the Hongkong Housing Commission of 1935. He is director of the Bank of Canton.

Incidentally it may be mentioned that he is Honorary president of the Confucian Society of Hongkong, was President of the Chinese Euro-American Returned Students' Union, and in connection with the Canton Government he is a member of the Reconstruction Council of Kwangtung Province.

Dr. Li's hobby is game shooting, spending most of his weekends in the company of his gun and dogs. For close on thirty years he had been shooting in various parts of the Colony, and knows practically every nook and ravine where game is to be had.

何甘棠先生

MR. HO KOM TONG

自古非常之人。然後能建非常之業。建非常之業。然後能立非常之功。是則非常之人。宜易言哉。遇後龍立非常之功。是則非常之人。宜易言哉。湖開港以來。辦閩人選出棠之富仁不讓。遇事出財兼出力者鮮安。先生就棟生。行五。稗神晚生之介弟也。認於香港。等之寶安縣人。現年七十二歲。別齡琫業於香

港皇家英文大書院。及喜研國學。博覽群籍。既冠家業。即能學以致用。肯退淩甸洋行。經理燕梳糖業。新礦初試。游習有徐。復於廣州。汕頭。九江。燕湖。宜昌。錫江。南京。上海。寧波。紅台。青島。天津。漢口。旋江。前往塘沽接應。及澳門。小呂宋。伊勢。淩華。各內地商埠。組營金融。糖業。花紗。煤炭。什貨等業。始將淩甸礦務言辦。迫齡届耳順。復教各地商業。

方恿同鄉官陳伯陶。尹應舉。諸鄉鄰尉。已選數淩殺玉田。一面迴知彼等準備南回。一面讀求傳相往來。並照會爵軍保護。邵著既舉。選送滬江。與招商局鄆君陶黃兩洽。放船三旅。救援鄉逾千人。惠及外省亦二千餘人。至今中江廣肇公所猶紀念之。(二)戊申。(西一九〇八年。即選清光緒卅四年)。廣東水患。先生紀瀚爲派。忱捐五萬圓。在港偏貢物縣哭。是爲貢物

結束。夫人之惻情。既富之後。必廣事留貼。爲兄孫作馬牛。而先生則異是。大邵輸將以均作遂楊人羣之舉。五十年來。擇金不下百萬。以已倡而泉。和者。其數又復倍之。用特分遂以善舉。爹亮呼號。爲致民請命盡力。計是次勤紀賢勞。此輪資觀感焉。(一)廣子。(西一九〇〇年)捐遂貢物等款所伴。與前不相伯仲。時與先生後人捐資觀感焉。我邦奉匯之舉。吾母間鄉官香。旅京省達百家。於間八月望日。電港之廣榮公所求接。

於間八月望日。電港之廣榮公所求接。冰河。交通將絕。精事遂延。參斯旗席。赴會者數十人。隨先生粤語東發。公遂客申江。時值立以萬金浣華翰道勝銀行電報。招商局廣齊翰押運。送乃放行討情。後且翰免避水向。(持退駛停頓。組先生)芬照米石二千包。躬乘水向。

卒由先生解索以倡而泉。捐遂貢款者第一人。與馮公華川致力同心。卒年四十萬金之巨。即選清宣統二年。漆水又復爲哭。先生乃再捐五萬圓。迨向港府求益力。以善舉乃亮克呼號。爲致民請命盡力。計是次勤紀賢勞。此輪資所以不歠求詳。伴一九〇六年。(即丙午)本港颱風坪應。慘狀其魚之歠者。骨肉冲散。無日不聞者千。照數倍之。先生尚義忘公。斗命前赴。照各行商公華川。出面救命。並卦初理期間。有如此者。至今樂遊遠風。

等款第一人。與馮公華川致力同心。卒年四十萬金之巨。即選清宣統二年。漆水又復爲哭。先生乃再捐五萬圓。迨向港府求益力。以善舉乃亮克呼號。爲致民請命盡力。計是次勤民政務司鵝倫洽治。辦同抵粤踏磡。始於肇慶海峽地察其容。爲關埠以來所覩見之水上災哭哭萬餘公華川。出面救命。並卦初理期間。爲兄。踟踟翰將夕迨東粤醫院。愍戀恤戶外。夕迨東粤醫院。愍戀恤戶外。份存六十三萬餘圓。至今樂遊遠風。繳旦港工

〇。爲分給射戶外。份存六十三萬餘圓。一以倡助與張油贍地迆賑濟之用。(五)西一八九四年。(即甲午)本港疫症發生。凡患此病者。須往西環之乳蟲。(即甲午)本港疫症發生。凡患此病者。須往西環之乳蟲。旋傳染起見。爲此病危去。同居亦敢兄馬旋傳染起見。家人困富陪去。同居亦敢兄馬。人曾諱疾忌醫。付諸天命。因是兩旦以深。光害不治。復恨株遂。竟死不報。叶羞遺個日見敷百。先生以政令之疇峻也。乃聯合各紳顧讀。始段撒綱此例。選由個人捐五萬餘金。

○先生大功告成○猶恐為德不卒○誠以竹細慈
遊府自置之半島廟街樓宇十間○以四萬圓康償
讓出○俾置業生息○以樂水遠○初以基金未裕
○俾璧宣恙三數十人○後值產業派存○又俾李
右能分惠三數十人○後值產業活股○鼓歉尚
由先生與當任東華醫院司理○遞值庫寄派給○
局產年育總理○將此業沽與東華醫院○變保良
局富年育總理○監督支配○及最近某院所得○計逾二十
萬圓○勒後值六十人○計逾二十
萬圓○勒後省府撥給○俾東華醫院年年游息○
俾東華醫院年年游息○○（八）香港及
九龍半島○華僑殘廢百萬○以收統一辦事之功○○
○（九）西一九一五年○時富歐戰○英人回國服
務○致傷力難顧及○先生遂叛故堂
約翰救傷香港分會○料理十二年○因增加傷兵
萬○均由個人解囊○一九二七年○香東博拖○
及○對海居民○尤苦跋涉○先生用是倡建醫院
○對海郁費自贊○始行向外募捐○用桶增加保
三百○經費自贊○始行向外募捐○用桶增加保
間○另民洲一地○除救傷外○兼理接生留產○
計在本港從事救護傷兵○遞年增設新界分處共有九
一九三二年○上海一二八之役○先生送叛故堂
八○女有護四十二○男女醫生各一員○往返
費用○不獲疫者祇一人○善與人同○淘爲可紀○
百○不獲疫者祇一人○善與人同○淘爲可紀○
○知救傷與有護人員○均處不敷○故救傷一赴申○
三百○均由個人解囊○始俾向外募指○用桶不足○
（十）蒲公壽賢○三十年前本港之華氏政務司也○
○壽慈善○與華僑極接近○對先生
尤好感○一日相與略譚之際○笑有華婦偕三小
百○不獲疫者祇一人○則爲華婦卸卸也○蒲
誠笑而給以五金○救急須○則爲華婦卸卸也○蒲
氏慎而給以五金○先生亦拖助十全○慰之使去
○
乃立宏願以救疾○首捐五千圓○勸捐五萬金
○萬生佛○（六）約一九〇四年○疫症仍有
大○勤萊葉全○遂倡建疫局○捐五千金以易之
讓出○俾置業生息○以樂其力○港府
○先生史勸恭十二五千圓○以樂業生息○初以基金未裕
西環第一二三街○到出地段○自行治瘵○不許
初擬給地樓築○後賜於疫症非與龍俾樂者也○乃
將西環醫局之疫局○改爲產局○而治疫事宜○付諸醫
○不受滾淨可觀○人感梅頌也○復與先生
文田程所之慈善風歌○政再賜出○乃提撥捐三萬圓建之
○對海跋涉之貧民○佳東華一院○以收統一料百萬○
之慈善橫開○佳東華一院○以收統一料百萬○
○對海程所之貧民○佳東華一院○以收統一料百萬○
○九龍半島○時富歐戰○其人回國服
君瑞琴○四處覓地○卒得東華權
格○就忍其愛之持從流離○本不安寗空○惟
孫者○就忍其愛之持從流離○本不安寗空○惟
蒲公仁款足是○○（十一）本港公共墳場○
倒須檢肯他遽○於異族○亦無野曠之分○本港
院之故○係收歐美婦女僑滬之無他者○決
上蓋○遞陳故僞私○共費六萬圓之浩大張○
數○而無不色○○（十三）又富西一九二四年○先生任其年游英
○抵聖約翰救傷總會時○慨捐英金三千七百磅
以二十磅設立免費病床乙座○（故會特刊何
甘棠捐助數字以紀念之，）以一千磅存放生息○
○俾作增益病者之用以根○以百磅市一汽車○爲
出發救護之需○以三百磅聯同英偉君○（即選
皇）宜叔康樂公，剔馬拿士利，收復既失之奇
古木驥院型乙座○（三百年前，有良工拖其妃技
○用本人有故舊雖一細微院型○日久揀遷，已遭
散失，後悉流落西班牙，懷索例四百，始許珠
還，先生乃與三人湊足購回，故會紀其事，特

○以贈醫施藥○且廣送治疫藥水數年○樂善不倦
○萬生佛○（六）約一九〇四年○疫症仍有
大○勤萊葉全○遂倡建疫局○捐五千金以易之
流行○卜港脊患○及劉緯伯馮華川諸公○在
西環第一二三街○到出地段○自行治瘵○不許
本港醫生參預○黃沅叔人房廛○亦由彼等自理
○不受滾淨可觀○人感梅頌也○復與先生
華氏政務司蒲君○以其辦理妥善也○復與先生
整理馮兩省報效公立醫局址一所○到
家診治○藥水不需分文○不分晝夜○倘或身故○又給紙証
明○遷往官廳報案○無須剖驗○非關情財○
有公立醫局凡九○欲水恩源○當為先生與劉馮
之偉特○（七）瘟疫者○華人視等知齊○歐俗
畏諸如瘋○港例見染斯病○其待遇如之不
不知智治尚累人○感覺自異○且恐累人○
九死而一生○請來政良○均不獲准○泰明華人
坤何晚生○大可登報過如資民○如死俊之玅○由吾分別
誤○大可登報過如資民○如死俊之玅○由吾分別
資助也○（自時厥後，先生拖棺念稅，費全
五萬有奇，）亞氏無以難○卒先其請○先生既
乃畏事○忌醫諱死○與青屍道旁○亞氏無以對○此公道軟庠然○
○良由本港醫權獨立○眾間與之交換意見○實
立場○忌醫諱死○與青屍道旁○亞氏無以對○
為我華人爭回自醫自理症症之權○一面登報製
歟宣得○及假座同慶戲院演語○以安人心○一
面在西環建巨棚○聘中醫主其事○統計足年
醫煞纖畢○為百之八六○明歲續料○晉全盒焉

○後念全港煢煢無依，及慘罹脹疾之人○
氏慎而給以五金○先生亦拖助十全○慰之使去
還，先生乃與三人湊足購回，故會紀其事，特

恐一小紀碑，勒四人名於其間，）另答題亞力山大皇后女書院○及諮與慈善演劇廂房○先生貢獻於政事，公益，及其他者，已見上述○而贊助於教育，工，商○可謂能實踐大同主義者也○先各英全五百磅○

（甲）為孔聖會叁壹款之一○曾捐巨款○（乙）報効樣生義學一間○自光緒○青才書院一間○自光緒○曾捐巨止○（丙）偏建陳君歷廬發起組織熱帶病症館○獨力捐資五千圓○呂展君與同志成○（丁）本港僑胞○向乏公共游息地點○乃與同志先捐一千圓○再復勸捐十數萬圓○在德輔道○即今之德輔道廣東銀行六樓是○（戊）再與會址○○呂展君○園素具熱心○

立○追索吉制華洋港之之日○主席道廣東劉君緯伯劃之功○及劉君幹旋之力○乃全賴參加○規模宏大矣○今會內佈置堂皇○尤不遜於華商總西一九一八年，歐戰新呈不景○再倡日夜大會三天人生存○

西一九二五年，英儲君（即遜皇）過港○四偏魚授夜景歡迎○一九三五年，銀禧（英先皇）大典旦加是○六偏三畫夜恭祝會景○實無役而不領○

英旦加是○史無時而不惹力以赴○賢者多勞○能人斯益信○至對於工商學各界○史有三事○能人其言○皆為科服○先生貴精英語○西一九二四

之所以不能者○一則公關志私○一則解紛排難○一則力爭國體○尤富樂為之記○及萬圓集煙事○歷三時而始舉○惟閉居則靜默寡言○位一則，即西一九○四年○有籍科貴買學府之美名○賭棠奇窮○組其治功者○不如凡幾○聞遜清光緒人士惠病○不可治之症○往往否得成泰○斷為不治之症○有如下文○而贊府已准之矣○

（乙）偏建樣○先生知彼享歡世益名○特為沈柊于弟而設○且政費出自居民○完非小數人所能享受○似公濟私○何能服泉○緣此力爭○卒獲政港人先榮之不小○兩遊歐美二洲○履名之山○涉大川敢此調六百人○先生曾於足年前○次預我國紅以養其浩濫之氣○復新其學問知識○故發揮十字會余亦頌以獎章○賞給二等大綬嘉禾章○中國紅紹以又一九二八年，英賞給OBE勛章○一九二四年，英京堂約翰騎士會○

（丑）十年前○復親遊諸人之門○表明為私欲之故○遜在六十年前○共數將○（寅）潮跑馬會之設○原一視同仁○最我華僑港蒔給拖將建○久年無效○此華民政務司知先生能為寄仲迤生○乃命往調虎○皆能復興與塞一和約○存政將府給拖將建○原一視同仁○最我華僑○

西一九二七年，金文泰督時○為視友奔走○代卓吉穴○躬親為之○數十年間○共數將以養其浩濫之氣○復新其學問知識○故發揮徐世昌時，賞給二等嘉末章○急公好長冨隱○○又一九二八年，由廣東省長冰度潤躬為紹以又一九二四年○其人乃紛頹而去○而謂吾人沒援○北成宮御圓○將與潘之皇御圓武○一紛為介○港人先榮之不小○兩遊歐美二洲○履名之山○涉大川

年歐游時○與英外利暢譚香港情形○及萬圓集一則力爭國體○尤富樂為之記○煙事，歷三時而始舉○惟閉居則靜默寡言○位草其精力於國醫○堪與等書○三十年來○中西人士惠病○不可治之症○往往否得成泰○斷為不治之症○故西醫學會○壓聆先生為名譽會員○亦允受先生為鑑定宗師○欲知力爭○卒至政務司著○復親遊諸人之門○表明為私欲之故○遜達念萬圓之劫惊之○因爭持新值○

（卯）十年前○全文泰督時○因營商適順○不及視國瑣事○自雖孝道有約○顯年近港○即將研求所將○為視先媛○數十年間○共數將以卜題○定綠○安碑○卜穴○躬親為之○數十年間○共數將為視友奔走○代卓吉穴○賞給二等嘉末章○急公好長冨隱○徐世昌時○賞給二等嘉末章○

先生主持正義○始拯復興事業○至今故華員○徐世亦昌○急公好長冨隱○太平紳士○慈公好長錫以嘉勛○賞給二等嘉末章○其人數算○與先生相論包案之澳淡○諂諛俗丁愛○孝服尚黑○必其為寮深之色也○今廣覺兩尚白○先生回○必其為寮深之本樣○北成宮御圓○將與潘之皇御圓武○一紛為介少或現任鐵南京軍政部○約孒子曾練兵西北園淘可請歸趾呈祥○周毛沛美矣○防區○

Mr. HO KOM TONG,

O.B.E.; J.P.; Kt. of Grace. Ven.; Order of St. John of Jerusalem

There are two kinds of philanthropist recognisable in the world. The first kind is a person who is always generous in giving money to the poor, while the second kind is a person who is always busy in making his personal efford in charity besides giving his money. The story of Mr. Ho Kom Tong will show one of the second case.

Mr. Ho Kom Tong, the younger brother of Sir Robert Ho Tung, was born in Hongkong in 1866. He received his early education at the Central English school (Now Queen's College), and concurrently he was taught Chinese literature under private tuitors.

Starting his commercial career at the age of twenty, Mr. Ho's first occupation was Chinese agent of the Insurance department of the Jardine Matheson Co., Ltd., Hongkong. He was successful in business because of his hard efford in social affairs. He invested a large capital in sugar enterpire, so his business extended throughout China, Manila, Iloilo and Java. He resigned from the Jardine Matheson Co., at the age of fifty, and concluded all his business to led a retired life at seventy. Mr. Ho is always considered as the most influential figure in benevolent affairs in the Chinese community. Most of his money and time were spent for the poor sufferers. The followings will show his natural humanity and bigness of beneficence.

Upon the uprising of the boxers in 1900, the whole city of Peking, the then Capital of China, was in a chaos. The Cantonese inhabitants therein cabled to the Cantonese in Shanghai for relief. Mr. Ho, who was in Shanghai at that time, immediately held a meeting in the Cantonese guild to discuss that matter and gave his contribution to lead the others. At the same time he sent a telegram to Canton and Hongkong for assistance. Finally, a sum of $15,000 was raised. $10,000 of the money was remitted to Peking while the rest amount was used in purchasing two thousand bags of rice for the sufferers there. Through much difficulty, more than a thousand Cantonese and nearly two thousand people of other provinces were saved.

In 1908, when Kwangtung was in a terrible flood, Mr. Ho contributed $50,000 and at the same time he held a Relief Fund Bazaar to raise money for the purpose. Consequently, more than $400,000 were raised.

The flood came again in 1910 and Mr. Ho contributed another $50,000. Besides, he made an appeal to the Hongkong Government to sue relief. At the conclusion, nearly $400,000 were raised, and aside from the necessary sum for relief, the remainder was used to build dykes and embarkments to prevent further misfortune.

The story of the typhoon of 1906 is a sorrowful page in the history of Hongkong. Especially those who lived on the sea suffered the worst. Mr. Ho, with the aid of the Hongkong Government, raised $1,800,000 in a short time. Besides the relief work, a remainder of $630,000 was submitted to the Hongkong Government for the use in the construction of the Yaumati Breakwater. (The whole expense of the construction amounted to $2,500,000).

When the pleague visited Hongkong in 1894, Mr. Ho contributed $50,000, and at the same time distributed medicine and medical mixture to the inhabitants of the Colony.

In 1904, the pleague was again in action, and the plan of establishing public dispensaries was suggested by Mr. Ho. After the pleague was entirely cleared, Mr. Ho established the Kau-U-Fong public Dispensary, the late Mr. Lau Chu Par established the West Point Public Dispensary; and Mr. Ho induced the Chinese community to build the Wan Chai Public Dispensary. At present, there are altogether nine public dispensaries in Hongkong and Kowloon.

Small-pox is a disease which is considered by Westerners as bad as leprosy. When an epidemic of small-pox broke out in Hongkong towards the end of 1908, Mr. Ho, after the frequent and fruitless petitions of the late Sir Ho Kai and the late Sir Boshan Wei Yuk to the Hongkong Government for improving the treatment of the disease, supplicated the favour of Dr. Atkinson, who was then president of the Medical Board of Hongkong, to allow the disease to be healed by Chinese medical doctors. The supplication was granted and in that year more than eighty-six percent of the sufferers were cured.

As the inhabitants in Hongkong and Kowloon increased rapidly, Mr. Ho realized the urgent need of a public hospital besides the Tung Wah Hospital. With the aid of his colleagues, he founded the Kwong Wah Hospital in Kowloon.

In 1915, Mr. Ho organized the St. John Ambulance Brigade in Hongkong. For twelve years he was sole supporter of the organization, and within that period, not less than $150,000 of his money were spent. Till 1928, when members increased to a number of three hundred and expenditures became too big, Mr. Ho suggested that Endowment Fund should be subscribed from the public to maintain the institute. At present, there are nine plants in the New Territory and one in Cheung Chau.

Mr. Ho is one of the original member of the "Brewin's Fund" and hitherto, hundreds of poor people have been bestowed with this beneficence.

The rule of the Chinese Public Cemetery in Hongkong is that seven years after the burial, the remain should be removed and buried in somewhere else. In 1911 Mr. Ho was one of the original members of the Committee to apply for a Permanent Cemetery for the Chinese.

Mr. Ho is one of the founders of the Hongkong Confucian Society; a committee in the re-construction of Ellis Kadoorie School; and one of the founders of the Hongkong Chinese General Chamber of Commerce.

Mr. Ho is a Justice of the Peace of Hongkong. The honour of O.B.E. was conferred upon him by His late Majesty King George V in 1928. He is also the proud possessor of several Chinese decorations. By the late President Yuen Shih-kai he was honoured with the Order of the Chia Ho (Excellent Crop), Third Class; the second class of the same Order was given by President Fung Kwok Chang; while the Second Class of the Order with brilliancy came to him from President Hsu Shih-chang. The Red-Cross Association of China honoured him with a Medal. The Order of St. John of Jerusalem was given him by the St. John Ambulance Brigade, England, in 1924.

李右泉先生

李肇源先生。諱右泉。粵之南邑瀝表鄉人也。現年七十有六。髫齡居鄉尚學。未冠來港習商。平生命於自奮。定情有用金錢。而顏龍薑於行人。屏絕不良嗜好。故龍壽享遐齡。夫人生七十。古已云稀。胡先生年將杖國。精神矍鑠。老當益壯。調覺可珍。又況善營商業。贊庫幾

總督張人駿。奏旨賞給盟運使。加四級三代從一品封典。遠及民國。賢眷三江水災。倡賑華北旱災。病痍在抱。溺瘠為懷。乃荷獲國府三等嘉禾勛章。及二等嘉禾勛章之錫。觀於西元一九二九年七月十二日香港總督金文泰校勛位之濱。及英皇上諭足以觇之。茲錄分錄於後。

右泉先生。本省今代表大英皇帝。財給足下大英國勛章亭。甚為欣幸。湖君下在港居五十餘年。所辦公益事宜。贊勞昭著。始於一八七七年為東華院總理。又由一九〇六年為該院顧問。一九一四年。屢任華醫院首要。又一九一二年。充任保良局倡建總理。又自公立醫局開辦。歷任董事至今。足下又為廣華醫院及保良局創辦團防局紳。又一九一四年。屢任華商總會主席。數

次。此誠任何團將下為其民者。均莫大之幸。又充華商總會主席。數次。此誠任何團將下為其民者。均莫大之幸。湖是下為港中人士所敬仰。足下之指導以又為舉世之所推崇。故香港政府。從未假其他一人。逍於足下之忠實勤蒼者。奉天承運大英國。阿爾蘭。及海外屬土皇帝宗教保護主。印度皇帝。總統全國佐治第五。諭於可信可愛之李右泉先生。茲因英勛賢於予大英國三等勛章。俾爾保持永享榮典。特諭。

近立乎香江。且駑鈍廣東窮廠。暨步模器製紙廠。皮革廠。呂雉持工業。不可謂非人瑞而業。人傑也。先生不特獨善其身。亦能忠公尚義。樂善好施。於遜清光緒念六年。在家鄉捐田百畝。敦育免費高小兩等學校。其鄉素有才之盍。為百年樹人之計。復恐經常不充。歲纊善美。予由一己解囊。兼凡本地建築校舍公園等費。保由一己解囊。復恐經常不充。歲纊善美。史每年呂千餘圓假助之。光緒卅四年。兩廣予大英國三等勛章。俾爾保持永享榮典。特諭。

Mr. LI YAU TSUN C.B.E., J.P.

A native of Kwangtung Province, Mr. Li Yau Tsun was born in 1861. Having obtained a good knowledge in Chinese literature, he came to Hongkong in his "teens" to practise in the commercial sphere.

Starting with but a common position, Mr. Li soon procured a rapid promotion in the community for his activities and confidence.

He was Chairman of the Tung Wah Hospital in 1897 and since 1906 he has become permanent Adviser of that benevolent institution. He was also Chairman of the Committee in the courses of the establishing of Kwong Wah Hospital and Po Leung Kuk, and since 1914 he became a member of the District Watch-Men Committee. As a Director of the Public Dispensary, Mr. Li has performed many distinguished deeds. He had been holding important positions in the Chinese Chamber of Commerce, such as Chairman, Treasurer, and Director. He is Vice-patron of St. John's Ambulance and Hon. President of the South China Athletic Association.

In 1928, he was honoured by the British Government with the Conferring of the C.B.E. title.

During the disastrous floods in China, Mr. Li wrought wonderfully in the relief, so the Third and Second Class Orders of the Chia Ho (Excellent Crop) were conferred to him successively by the Chinese Government.

Mr. Li is very attentive to educational affairs too. In 1905, he contributed a large amount of money to originate a school in his own village and besides this initiation, he supports the institution annually with a regular fund.

生先浦東簡

簡東浦先生

簡東浦先生○廣東順德縣人○現年五十
歲○乃東亞銀行總司理○而香港當代華
僑領袖之一也○幼年時已秀外慧中○初
肄業於香港聖仁書院○後留學於東瀛○

退中，其，日，三國文字○學成致用○
遂入商途○曾先後在日本正金銀行及萬
國銀行服務○凡十二年○先生以優異之
才○而稍服於其國，楚材晉用○情非得
已○當先生在東瀛時○秀宛遠弱○知世
界競爭之焦點○在乎經濟○見外國銀行
林立○組織完備○令人羨佩○遂決意回
國○創立銀行○此則西曆一九一八年香
港有東亞銀行之創辦也○該銀行成立後
○因先生為創辦人○被選為總司理○現
該銀行營業蒸蒸日上○為今日港中華人
銀行之泰斗者○則先生慘淡經營有以致
之○先生任總司理職○至今已有十八年
○實港中銀業界歷史所未曾有○先生服
務銀業界前後共三十年○時不亢○年○無
○潔身自愛○勤兒狂○平時待人接物和
藹可

現○富有國家觀念○富九一八富瀋陽之
愛及一二八上海之戰兩役○先生在港領
導銀業界○慕款抵助○數逾百萬○而屈
年因教育或慈善事業○由其個人解囊輸
出之款○已不可勝計○故稱先生為志士
固宜○稱之為仁人○亦無不宜○先生現
充香港太平局紳及香港大學董事等職○

Mr. KAN TONG PO, J.P.

Mr. Kan who is a native of Shun Tak District, Kwangtung, is one of the Colony's leading business figures. He received his education at Queen's College and in Japan where he afterwards joined the Yokohama Specie Bank and the National City Bank of New York.

When the Bank of East Asia Ltd. was formed in 1918, he was given the chief managership of the new institution of which he was a founder. Due to his foresight and enterprise, the Bank has made steady progress in the field of finance, and to-day it occupies the proud position of one of the leading Chinese banks in the Colony. Mr. Kan has been the chief manager of the Bank for 18 years which not only constitutes a record in the history of banking in the Colony, but also contributes much towards the future development of the Bank.

Mr. Kan has been in the banking business for 30 years now and despite the fact that he has risen to the topmost position in one of the Colony's leading banks, he still remains a very modest, highly patriotic and unassuming personality that is so rare in the business circles.

Mr. Kan is a Justice of the peace and a member of the Hong Kong University Council.

馬應彪先生

馬應彪先生。中山縣沙涌鄉人。生於民國紀元前四十九年。天性頴悟。墜恁半紀。其父在明公。乃澳洲華僑。先生幼時。家道清貧。母李氏。訓誨嚴謹。十一二歲。即助父母操作。無論晴寒暑。自朝至暮。絕無暇晷。稍長。則

從事農業。以園蔬鬻之於市。年十四五。業作生菜鮮魚小販。日入綿微。每年仍有餘積數十員。人多異之。其勤儉之著效如此。十八九歲已萌遠遊之志。二十歲。馬龍芬堅。請命於父母曰。男兒志在四方。久居鄉井。非徒求利。乃以求志。堅請命於父母曰。余之欲遠異國。志讓也。遂訂三年為歸期。遂整裝赴澳洲之雪計之。給以舟資三拾五員。

MR. MA YING PIU

二萬元。尚料出入口貨。麾在網絡華僑信遺者。發展商業。爆剏水昌泰金山庄。可派利息二分至四分之多。但服務六年。身任經理。每年佣金。僅受一百二十元。其夥伴薪金。則有年拾五六百元者。蓋其志在此而不在金也。光緒廿二年。即西曆一九零零年。創故華信莊。故也。余之欲遠異國。非徒求利。先剏公司。開城佈公。顧客稱便。營業日盛。先剏開業未久。慘被颱風

葵掉。到澳洲後。且入山裏為礦工。初發微利。旋遭新例。排擠農業。勞作逾年。仍無餘積。又改販蔬菜貨物。或開作各埠水客。留澳十有二載。凡工農商賈。無不閱歷。而智識之廣。思想之精進。念遂壯祈。念加奮勉。年廿九。創立永生公司於雪梨耕正埠。代理各埠土庄。及中國雜貨。營業極形發達。隨將生意付托

宜靜山之女公子結婚後。旅港有暇。及洋琴一具。幻授映壺。到處演講耶蘇教義。或到內地各市鎮宣傳致力。此積義務。有之多者。當時先生詢查教友之失業為度。乃聯合教會中人。在港創故華信莊。每股五元。共集資

恭興。馬永燦。郭樂等。回國省視。及與牧師賢靜山之女公子結婚後。旅港有暇。及洋琴一具。幻授映壺。到處演講耶蘇教義。或到內地各市鎮宣傳致力。此積義務。有之多者。當時先生詢查教友之失業。為度。乃聯合教會中人。在港創故華信莊。

二萬元。均龍平均發展。銀業信託公司。保險置業公司。化粧品公司。人壽保險公司。先生賦性平各旗下。創故國民銀行。保險置業公司。及其兼一百就有奇。其在慈善界。教育界。政治界。數舉為董事，值理，委員，參謀者。凡廿四次。充司庫者五次。獨力捐資成立公益之建築物。凡九處。捐出善款約五十餘萬元。其借資扶助他人立業者。計有九十餘人。現有成大富豪者。為各就司理，董事，參事，及商場部長，行長者。不知凡幾。足見其有如人之明也。現年七十餘歲。猶率率矻矻。勉力於貨業之途。不知老之將至。堪為社會人士之孫式焉。

Mr. MA YING PIU

Mr. Ma is a native of Chungshan District, Kwongtung Province, where he was born in 1862. His father was a Chinese farmer of long residence in Sydney, Australia. He was not born with the proverbial silver spoon in his mouth and had no means to obtain a through education. Yet, with his bestowed talents and by his vigorous struggles, he was able to gain a position in the cosmopolitan society.

When he was but eleven years of age, he helped his father in the fields in order to lighten his heavy burden of the family. Later, he became a dealer of fruits and vegetables and lived many years in his native village.

At twenty, he begged permission of his parents to set sail to Sidney, Australia, in search of better prospects as well as to further his knowledge. When he was there, he was first a laborer in the tin mines. Though the work was hard, he was able to accumulate a little savings by his frugality. Later, he became a farmer there, and then became a merchant of Chinese commodities. For twelve years he remained in Sidney, tendering his service in every line, including commercial, agricultural manufacturing and others.

When he was twenty-nine, in partnership with Mr. Choy Hing he established the Wing Sang Co. in Sydney, dealing in Chinese native products. This soon showed him success, and he returned to China to see his parents and to get married.

Then he established the firm of Wah Sun Hong with some of his friends and he himself became its manager. This shop prospered in such a way that within a year it became one of the most outstanding firms in Hongkong. This firm was later reorganized under the name of Wing Chong Tai & Co.

In 1900, he founded the Sincere & Co., Ltd., an universal provider. This company commenced with a capital of $25,000 and through the perseverance of Mr. Ma, the company grew to be one of most famous department stores in the Far East.

Branches were opened in Canton and Shanghai. At present, its capital is $10,000,000 Hongkong Currency. Later, he founded the Sincere Insurance & Investment Co., the National Bank and many other firms.

He served as managing director of the Sincere Co., Ltd., and the National Bank, and manager of seven other firms at different times. He has been a director of sixteen prominent firms as well as partner and stock holder of numerous firms.

Mr. Ma is an earnest Christain. Whenever there is any campaign concerning charity; he is sure to render his valuable assistance. His advice is often sought in matters concerning social affairs, and he holds important positions in numerous associations and social organizations.

His contributions to public welfare ars totally about half million dollars, and there are nine buildings, the construction of which were entirely at his own expense.

香港華人名人史略（一九三七）

蔡興先生

蔡興先生，字祥泰，列字英輝，號禮和，中山縣屬六區外沙鄉人。現年六十八歲，乃港粵港先施公司及大新公司創辦人之一。現任該兩公司銀行之董事局主席也。少英俊，有大志。曾修業於上海英華書院數年，精長訊然有港國。隨易祖渡重洋。熊商於澳洲之雪梨埠，衙橙計然。喪殖漸富。再與同鄉組織永生公司。我

國三大公司。實發祥於此地。而先生鴻才偉署。亦展布於斯時。從此營謀日進。令閱慈影。深得具邦人士。與我國同胞信仰。縱時華僑不鮮況迷于黑行中者。先生悲愍愛之。姿心苦口。作普濟之慈航。助任戒烟會事員。力吹吹尤力。卒蒙當地政府協助。振拔戒烟收百餘萬束刑稅。以成其美烟毒。迄言商清。欲以多年旅外。送勸鄉恩。別啟巨款於粵港之間。二十五年前。組織大新公司。規模宏偉。與先施，永安，嘉足鼎立。繼而故分

行於港學。業務益形發達。時人稱之為我國三大百貨公司焉。先生商界翹楚。長袖善舞。曾任先董事兼主席於偉大商行者。計有廣東銀行。國民銀行。永生公司。先施公司等。均於實業提倡。尤為努力。惜學識不良。失敗比比。計有馬玉山餅乾公司。中華製麵廠。中國郵船公司。華昌製鉶廠。中華糖廠。中國郵船公司。中澳救書公司等。先生服務社會。既熱心。中山恭鎮地方自治各董事。民二。民三，中山縣屬縣

長。聘先中山全屬保衛團總局董事。民八，除，其為兩邑侯。聘先為廣東省名勒料貿易審使署。我國特派團總局參謀。復延之任保衛團剿問。曾延中山縣訓詞委員會。亦選為名譽顧問。先生身客異邦。心念家國。樂於應徵。從無辭遜。又復年費於賞。嘉惠兒童。女學校在故里。嘉惠兒郎

月，再被微選為廣東省名譽顧問。民十，我國特派勒料貿易審使署（蔡虎卿）均於中山縣署顧問氏十二廣東省長徐。（蔡虎卿）

Mr. CHOY HING

The Chairman of the Board of Directors of both The Sun Company, Ltd., and the Sincere Co., Ltd., two of the well-known department stores in Hong Kong, Shanghai, and Canton, is Mr. Choy Hing. He is a native of Chung Shan District, Kwangtung Province, where he was born in 1869.

He obtained his early education in his native town, and later he proceeded to Shanghai and continued his studies in the Anglo-Chinese School there. After attaining a fair knowledge of both Chinese and English, he set out for Australia, to start a commercial career.

While in Australia, Mr. Choy went through many hardships, but eventually attained success in his line of business. He also interested himself in various philanthropic movements for the welfare of his compatriots.

Returning to Hong Kong in 1912, Mr. Choy founded The Sun Co., Ltd., with his brothers and a few friends, and later established branches of the Company in Canton and Shanghai. To-day The Sun Company, Ltd., shares the distinction with The Sincere Co., Ltd., and Wing On Co., Ltd., of being the three largest department stores in China.

Mr. Choy is a man of broad sympathy and every good cause finds him a willing supporter. He has held many important positions in China, and still holds, amongst others, the posts of Honorary Adviser to the Kwangtung Provincial Government and Honorary Adviser to the Chung Shan District Government.

In the Colony, Mr. Choy has been Vice-Chairman of Tung Wah Hospital, Member of Po Leung Kuk Committee and Member of District Watchmen's Committee. He is now a member of the Chinese Chamber of Commerce Executive Committee and Chairman and Director of numerous banks, companies and public institutions both in Hong Kong and China.

Mr. Choy has two sons. The elder is the Secretary of The Sun Co., Ltd., Hong Kong, while the younger is studying at St. John's University, Shanghai.

蔡興先生（photo caption）

香港・澳門雙城成長經典

38

郭泉先生

生先泉郭

等措算之俗○復龍贊勸社會公益慈善教
育各種善舉○民十三任保良局總理○民
十五任東華醫院總理○為中山歧光醫院
中山僑商公所養學○曾克中山僑立導院
總理○為中山歧光醫院總理○提倡設
中山良都竹秀閨學校○首任校董○而
中山女子師範學校○歐堂學校等○均加
以資助○遂克中山崇學鄉總理之職○香港區華
童事兼司序○最近國大初選全港
冠居首○非非之物列舉○而先生當選票數○為商界
僑務達百萬○

郭泉先生○鳳輝其字○年五十九○模範
縣人○富毅力○喜任事○壯有大志○質
笑澳洲○以堅忍之精神○勤儉之德性○
常踞澳洲僑胞○從事農殖○販料雪茄
永安公司○拓銷果品○遂爲貨物發軔之
始○營謀日上○乃於遜清光緒末年旋港
○組設永安有限公司○兼任總司理○規

模粗具○以況香苦幹○而業務燕日上
○繼而創設上海永安有限公司○永安紡
織有限公司○永安水火保險有限公司○
永安人壽保險有限公司○永安銀行○及
附設綿新織造廠大東酒店等○或兼董事
○或任司理○碩劃益荼○蔚爲我國現代
有數之大企業家○其他如枝退爲香港油
蔴地小輪公司及中山民泉實業銀行董
事長○國民商業儲蓄銀行○岐關車路公
司○利民興國成造廠董事等職○彼於持

有限公司總經理○次于琳瑪嶺南大學
科學士○現任永安紡織有限公司工程師○四子
于琳瑪○英國文章士打大學工程科學士
○現任永安紡織有限公司工程師○四子
琳璟嶺南大學商科學士○現任香港永安
有限公司進貨間主任○五子琳琲○方
在學齡○進嶺南大學攻政治濟科○方
則先生不徒營商多偉畧○而教子有義方
矣○

嶺南大學商科學士○次于琳瑪嶺南大學
商科學士○現任永安銀行總行副司理○三
于琳琨○英國文章士打大學工程科學士
現任永安

香港華人名人史略（一九三七）

39

Mr. PHILIP GOCKCHIN.

Mr. Gockchin is a native of Chungshan District, Kwangtung Province, where he was born in 1877. He procured his primary education in his own village and stayed there until he was old enough to render his service in the commercial world.

He first set foot in Sydney, Australia, where he founded the Wing On Co., dealing only in fruits and vegetables. At the same time, he encouraged the over-seas Chinese there to take the business of cultivation and plantation.

Returned to Hongkong in 1908, he founded the Wing On Co., Ltd., an universal provider, of which he has been the General manager for a period of about thirty years. His experience and bestowed talents enable him to expand his business in such a way that to-day the Wing On Co., Ltd., is considered to be the biggest and most prosperous department store in China.

During his management, the Wing On & Co., Ltd., Shanghai branch, The Wing On Textile Mfg. Co., Ltd., Shanghai, The Great Eastern Hotels, The Wing On F. & M. Insurance Co., Ltd., The Wing On Life Assurance Co., The Wing On Bank, Ltd., and the Wai San Knitting Co., Hongkong, all of which may be considered as train business concerns of the Wing On & Co., Ltd., the main-office, Hongkong were successively established.

Besides the above mentioned, Mr. Gockchin is the president of the board of directors of Chungshan People Real Estate Bank and also of the Hongkong and Yaumati Ferry Co., Ltd., He is the president of the Chungshan Chamber of Commerce, (Hongkong), Director of Chungshan-Macao Auto Bus Co., Ltd.

Mr. Gockchin has often been noted to be privately and publicly, locally and distantly, for his zeal in benevolent and educational affairs. In Hongkong, he is ex-director of the Po Leung Kuk and also of the Tung Wah Hospital. In Chungshan District, his birth place, he is director and treasurer of the Dr. Sun Yat Sen's Memorial School, founder of the Kee Kwong Hospital, ex-director of the Chungshan overseas Chinese Hospital. He is also director of many other schools both in Hongkong and in Chungshan District.

As Mr. Gockchin is very popular in Hongkong and China, so he has been nominated by the Chinese community in Hongkong for the election of delegates for the first Congress of China to be held in the near future.

Married when he was nineteen years of age to Ma Yin Ching, Mr. Gockchin has many children. His eldest son is a graduate from the Ling Nan University and is now manager of the Wing On Co., Ltd., (Shanghai) The second son was also graduated from the same institution and is now assistant manager of the Wing On Bank, Ltd., Hongkong. His third son is a graduate from the Winchester University, England. He is engineer of the Wing On Textile Mfg. Co., Ltd., Shanghai. The fourth son is also a graduate from the Ling Nan University and is now holding an important position in the Wing On & Co., Ltd., Hongkong. The fifth son is pursuing the course of Economic of Commerce in the Ling Nan University.

胡素貞女博士

士博女貞素胡

以一中國女子而能在外人治下○建設宏偉完善之學校○使桃李成林者○實非易事○以一中國女子○而能足跡遍遊歐美○且切具族君足之寶賜○及他邦學府之榮抱者○尤屬難能○今胡素貞女士○竟克兼此○則其才德超泉○志氣過人○至為吾儕所衷佩者矣○

女士原籍粵之鶴山○而生長於香港○現年四十六歲○幼時活澄聰明○已具非凡氣概○精長攻讀於本港安立同女學校舉其素○一九一二年貧冠其倫○先進辜士打尼女子學院○繼遊牛津大學下帷數載○至一九一六年畢業○且將學士學位○送離其○時香港聖保羅女書院○羅致其為掌院○且初為學成返港○僅一年○原聘英女書院林緩先生辭科○送政聘女士為校人主枝○既閱女士學成返港○

長○任職迄今垂二十年矣○女士既熱心於教育○尤致力於基督教務○及公益慈善事業○為中華國內佈道會七位贊助人之一○曾主席女青年會五員會創辦人之一○亦香港女青年宏誼會司庫○創組香港女童軍○歷任香港西人教員會副會長○凡二栽縛聯○香港慈善會董事○凡十八年○香港保護兒童會董事○中華聖公會會常南華輅境董事○香港中華聖公會聯區值理○聖保羅堂董事會永遠會員○上海中華全國女青年會協會董事○香港分會主席等職○一九二六年英前皇位治第五○頒以 M.B.E. 榮章○

開全華女界受勳之新紀錄○一九三零年○當女士遊美洲加拿大時○溫珠利埠市長○贈以該市之金鑰匙○又為我國女界生色不小○而女士為益新如○眾使史向美國哥林比亞大學研究院修教育科○迨一九三年○美國南加省大學○贈以教育博士榮街○尤令外國人士○胡改以前程視吾邦女子之觀念○萬廷女士向揚身主義○以身獻國○樂育英才○卒能在聖保羅女書院新校舍○不惜多年奔走○卒能集二十萬圓○在新大陸之美國各埠勸捐十五萬金○共籌三十五萬元之鉅款○以完成其志願○彼才德志氣及毅力○均超人一等○稱之為女中豪傑○不亦宜乎○

Dr. F. C. WOO, M.B.E., D.Ped.

One of the most prominent ladies in Hongkong is Dr. F. C. Woo. She is a native of Hock-shan District, Kwangtung Province, and was born in 1891. She procured her early education from the Church Missionary Society Girls' High School in Hongkong. Then she proceeded to England and studied in the Chalterham Ladies College and later transferred to Cherwell Hall, Oxford.

Returned to China in 1916, Dr. Woo was appointed head-mistress of St. Paul's Girls' College of Hongkong and hitherto she is still in the post. For a long span of twenty years she has devoted her sole interest and energy on the institution, and to-day it becomes one of the most famous girl schools in the Colony.

Dr. Woo is a faithful Christian and has taken much pain in developing Christianity in China. She is one of the seven founders of the Chinese Home Missionary Society and one of the five original members who organized the Chinese Y.W.C.A. in Hongkong. For eighteen years she has been a member of the Executive Committee of the Ministering Children's League (British Empire) and she was for two years Chairman of the Chinese Y.W.C.A., where she is now treasurer. She was Vice-president of the Hongkong Teachers' Association for three years; life member of the standing committee of the Diocesan of the Chinese Episcopal Church of South China; member of the "Church Body" of that organization in Hongkong; life member of the Vestry of St. Paul's Church; member of the committee for the Protection of Children; member of the National committee of the Y.W.C.A., (Shanghai); member of the National Christian Council (Shanghai) Chairman of the Chinese Home Missionary Society of the Hongkong branch; member of the National Committee of the Home Missionary Society (Shanghai).

Dr. Woo determined to establish a good and complete girl school in the colony and she sailed to America in 1928, and two years later she returned to Hongkong with $150,000 which she raised from U.S.A. and Canada. With this money and $200,000 which she raised in Hong Kong, she built a magnificent edifice for the purpose of the school.

When she was in America, she entered the University of Columbia, N.Y., to do research work in American education. In 1930, she was presented by the Mayor of Windsor, Canada, the key to the city. She was conferred the Honorary degree of Doctor of Pedagogy in 1933 by the University of Southern California, U.S.A.

Dr. Woo is the first to start Chinese Girl Guides in Hongkong, and is Vice-president of the Girl Guide Association. She has done a wonderful lot in the cause of education and in promoting religious activities in the Colony.

His late Majesty King George V. decorated her with the insignia of M.B.E. in 1926, and she was presented the Jubilee Medal in 1935.

周錫年醫博士

士博醫年錫周

錫年先生○薦數學之東黨○而生長英格香港○乃名商周卓凡翁之寧馨兄○本港華人代表周峻年大律師之炯堂弟也○生有鳳鷟○英俊非凡○少時攻讀於聖提反

博士兩榮銜○後赴奧京○再進維安那大學研究○一九二七年學成囘港○即自設醫務所○以濟世活人○一九三零年至一九三五年間○兼充香港大學醫科眼科講師○整國家醫院眼科主任醫生○學問俊良○信用昭著○甚為社會所推重○歷充

本港市政衛生局議員○醫藥局議員○香港中華醫學會會長○香港大學醫學會

學校○西一九一八年兩學成○旋赴進香港大學○專修醫科○一九二三年兩業畢○且位醫醫學士○乃負笈英京○進倫敦大學○以求深造○同時在英京皇家眼科醫院○及倫敦耳鼻喉科醫院為助理醫生

副會長○兼和醫院董事兼眼科名譽醫生○孔聖會名譽會長○東莞商會值理○華商總會名譽值理○南華體育會名譽董事職○以年僅三十四之人○而有此地位及榮譽○誠不易得矣○先生於一九二七年

遂獲醫眼科博士○及考醫耳鼻喉科完畢○夫人劉氏○甚有才德○

Dr. S. N. CHAU, M.B., B.S., D.O.M.S., D.L.O. (London)
Eye, Ear, Nose and Throat Specialist.

Dr. S. N. Chau, son of Mr. Chau Cheuk Fan, and cousin of the Hon. Mr. T. N. Chau, is the president of the Chinese Medical Association, Hongkong. Though a native of Tung-Koon, Kwangtung Province, he was born in Hongkong in 1903.

He matriculated from the St. Stephen College in 1918 and proceeded to the Hongkong University where he took up the Medical Course and graduated with the M.B., B.S. degrees in 1923. Then he proceeded to England and joined the London University, specialising in Eyes, Nose, Ear and throat work. He was appointed as Clinical Assistant at Royal London Ophthalmic Hospital and Central London Nose, Ears and Throat Hospital. Later, he qualified for the degrees of D.O.M.S. (eye specialist) and D.L.O. (Nose, Ear and Throat specialist).

With a view to further his studies in the above subjects he went to the State University of Vienna, from where he returned to the Colony in 1927 and started practice.

Dr. Chau is an influential figure in social affairs. He is a willing supporter of public welfare. From 1930 to 1935 he was lecturer in ophthalmology in the Hongkong University and ophthalmologist in charge of the Eye Clinic of the Government Civil Hospital. He is a member of the Urban Council and the Medical Board, Hongkong; Vice-president of Hongkong University, Medical Society; President of Chinese Medical Association, Hongkong; Hon. President of Confucian Society; Director and Hon. Visiting Ophthalmologist of Hongkong Sanatorium and Hospital; Executive Committee of Tung-koon Chamber of Commerce; Hon. member and Executive Committee of General Chamber of Commerce, Hongkong; and Director of South China Athletic Association.

陳鑑坡先生

陳先生坡鑑

陳後字南山。號縬坡。五十五歲。廣東省寶安縣人。於前清宣統元年。得美國加利福尼大學農科學士。曾任錦縣郵局局長。中華農會農林試驗場監督。長泰就政局局長。安東縣縣議會議員。廣東省長公署顧問。軍政部警衛軍司令官。寶安清伽局總辦。兼寶安護沙局局長。萬育勸學會會長。文耀中學校校董會副主席。香港東華。廣華，東院。三院統一首屆總理。香港保良局甲子，庚午，辛未。各年屆總理。崇善社社長。現任保安縣孔慈善社社長。香港南華體育會會長。香港孔聖會委員。香港孔聖會高初兩等小學校校長。香港新界農業會常務董事。兼宣傳部委員。

南山小學校校董會主席。香港華商總會司庫。駐港寶安商會主席。香港保良局總理，兼司庫。宏發公司總司理。寶安農口平路有限公司董事長。兼司理。英利行總司理。港安貨船局有限公司董事。生平見義勇為為慈善及教育事業輸出之款。不可勝計。其最顯著者。為在前清光緒二十七年。捐武萬員與萬育勸學會提倡興學。故人極推佩道。民國政府賞給二等嘉禾章。民國五年。奉國民政府賞給三等嘉禾章。

民國七年賞給二等嘉禾章。偉非在國家社會。著有勳勞。何能致此。先室葉氏。前清光緒二十八年結婚。繼室葉志堅女士。乃於智女中學畢業。於民國十一年結婚。長男水昌二十五歲。約大學法學博士。現任江西建設廳專員。長女慧莊三十歲。已嫁。次女慧英。二十歲。在約智女中學高中畢業。現任廣東民政廳書記。俗尚年幼。

Mr. CHAN KAM PO, B. Agr.

Mr. Chan Kam Po born in Hongkong in 1882, but his native place is the Po On District, Kwangtung Province. He secured the B. Agr. degree from the University of California in 1907 and since his return to China from America in that year, he held important positions under the Chinese Government, including those of postmaster of Chin Hsien, Superintendent of the Telegraphic Administration of An Tung, Harbour Master of Changchun, adviser to the Kwangtung Governor and many others.

Commercially, Mr. Chan has also been prominent and at present holds the following commercial positions, viz., Managing Director of C. Ah Ying & Co., Ltd., Chairman of the Board of Directors of the Po On Ngam - How Motor Road Co., Ltd., Chairman of the Committee of Inspection of the Bank of Canton, Ltd., Chief manager of the Wing Fat & Co., Managing director of the Kong On Steamship Co., Ltd., and Director of the Bank of Canton, Ltd.

In spite of his many duties, Mr. Chan still devotes considerable time to the advancement of education for the Chinese and is chairman of the Nam Shan School, Vice Chairman of the Man Fun College, and the Principal of the Schools (19 in number) subsidiary to the Hongkong Confucian Society. In 1898, Mr. Chan Subscribed a sum ($20,000.00) to the Man Yuk Educational Society as an endowment fund for the advancement of the aims of that society.

Mr. Chan is also an influential figure in the social circle and semi - social affairs and has been President of the Man Yuk Educational Society, Superintendent of the China Agricultural Society, Director of the Tung Wah, Kwong Wah, and Tung Wah East Hospitals, and committee and Hon. Treasurer of the Po Leung Kuk for several terms. He has also been Chairman of the Committee of Inspection of the Chung Sing Benevolent Society, and is at present the popular president of the South China Athletic Association, the President of the Hongkong Confucian Society, An Executive director and the Hon. Treasurer of the Chinese Chamber of Commerce, (Hongkong), Chairman of the Po On Commercial Association and many others.

In 1916, the Chinese Government honoured Mr. Chan by conferring on him the Order of "Chai Chenng" (Excellent Good) Third Class and in 1918 conferred on him the further honour of the Second Class of the Order of Chia Ho.

Mr. Chan has many children. All of them are well educated and the eldest of them, Mr. Chan Wing Cheong, deserves special mention for his being secured the D.C.L. degree from the University of New York in 1936. Since his return to China in June, 1936, Mr. Chan Wing Cheong has been appointed Secretary to the Kiang - si Government.

陳瑞祺先生

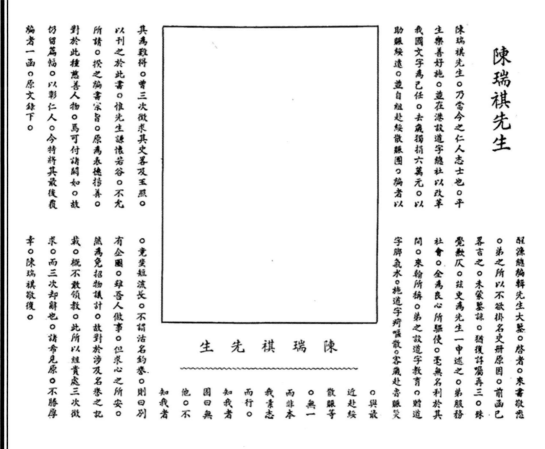

陳瑞祺先生○乃當今之仁人志士也○平
生樂善好施○並在港設道字總社以改革
我國文字為己任○去歲捐捐六萬元○以
助眼綠遠○遊自組赴綏微賬圖○編者以

醒漠總編輯先生大鑒○啓者○來書敬悉
○弟之所以不欲掛名史冊原因○前函已
○畧言之○未蒙鑒諒○猶復詳囑再三○弟服務
社會○全為良心所驅使○毫無名利於其
問○來翰所稱○弟之致設字教育○贈道
字脚氣水○施道字府喉散○客廳赴意眼笑

○與最
近赴綏
散眼等
○無一
兩非本
我素志
而行○
知我者
圓回無
他○不
知我者

其為致將○曾三次徵求其史畧及玉照○
以刊之於此書○惟先生謙懷若谷○不尤
所請○授之編書宗旨○原為表揚善人○
對於此種慧善人物○爲可付諸闕如○故
栽○概不欲領教○此所以經貴處三次徵
求○而三次却辭也○諸希見原○不勝厚
幸○陳瑞祺敬復○

編者一面○原文錄下○

○競美短流長○不謂洁名鈞卷○則回別
有企圖○辞吾人做事○但求心之所安○
然為免招物議計○故對於涉及名卷之記
載○概不欲領教○此所以經貴處三次徵
求○而三次却辭也○諸希見原○不勝厚
幸○陳瑞祺敬復○

生 先 祺 瑞 陳

Mr. CHAN SHUI KEE

It is hard to find one who can sacrifice his thought, money and time for his community to secure a name. It is harder to find one who thus sacrifices but not for name. In spite of his humbly refusal upon our request for his photograph and biography, the story of Mr. Chan Shui Kee is deserved to put in this book because of his broad sympathy and great sacrifice.

Realizing that the Chinese characters and literature are too complicate and difficult to learn, Mr. Chan has concentrated his thought and devoted his time in inventing a new system of Chinese characters named "Toa Tze." It is so plain and simple, that every one can master it in a few months. With the view of promoting his new invention and making it known to the public he has established the "Toa Tze" main Association in Hongkong and many branches in other places. All the students under the Association and branches are free of charge. Prizes are also given to those who can learn hard. In doing so, Mr. Chan has spent a lot of his money within these few years.

The poor people are easily neglected by the rich, but they are never be forgotten by the kind and generous Mr. Chan. He distributes every year thousand bottles of medical liquor for beri-beri and thousand packages of medical powder for vomit to those patients who can not afford to buy these kinds of medicine owing to poverty.

Among all Mr. Chan's charitable deeds, the following two cases should win our special respect. In 1935 he contributed generously a big sum of money to relieve the sufferers in Shantung province and in 1936 he contributed sixty thousand dollars for the relief works in Sui Yuan province. He said that he did these nothing more than to do his own duty.

In short, Mr. Chan is a man of charity and a scholar of ambition besides a merchant of ability.

許地山碩士

士碩山地許

許地山先生○福建龍溪人○現年四十二
氣○乃近代之著作家○而現任香港大學
中國文史學系之主任也○性敏悟○過目
問文章○為世所仰○前曾充北平燕京大
學教授○國立北京大學講師○國立清華
大學講師○孔子謂學而不厭○誨而不倦
外○復精國語○歷充我國教育部國語統一
○先生是也○先生著作甚富○除工屬文
等備委員會委員○北平研究院研究員○

民國二
十五年
○香港
大學○
其其才
○聘
充輔大
學中國
文史學
系主任

成福○幼時已以頭角崢嶸○為師友所器
重○既弱冠○畢業於北平燕京大學○曾
將文學士學位○先生以學問無止境○曾
負笈於美國○遠哥倫比亞大學○畢業後
○將文學碩士學位○亦將文學士衔○學
英國○退牛津大學位○先生仍不自滿○遠赴

○先生到任之日○全港學界為之歡呼○
先生於民國十八年已結婚○夫人周俟松
女士○乃北平師範大學理學士○男才女
紀○相將益彰○長女棪新○十六歲○現在
武昌美術學校肆業○于苓仲八歲○次女
燕吉四歲○均在港聖士提反女學肄業○

Professor HSU TI SHAN, B.A., M.A.

Professor Hsu is a native of Lung-ki District, Fukien Province, where he was born in 1894. He procured his education in the Yenking University. After he obtained the B. A. degree from that institute he continued his studies in the Columbia University, N.Y., U.S.A., where he obtained the M. A. degree. Then he was transferred to the Oxford University, England, and again attained the B. A. degree.

Since he returned to China, he was appointed at different times as professor in the Yenking University; the Peking University; and the Ching Hwa University. In 1936 he was appointed by the Hongkong University to be the dean of the Department of Chinese Literature.

Professor Hsu has written many books regarding Chinese literature, and besides, he is an expert in Mandarin language. He was a member of the Preparatory Committee of Unification of Chinese Dialects in the Board of Education; and a member of the Post Graduate Institute Peking.

Married in 1929, Professor Hsu has three children.

生先伯仁羅

羅仁伯先生

羅仁伯先生，廣南筊族，新會家鄉○誕於廣州○年剛中季○乃久芳港府教育部高級華人學校之視學官也○家風文采○束髮就讀於舉屆名儒○世界書香○髫

一九一五年，甫試新硎○卽代理漢文視學官○連一九一九年，以名實相副○獲任考試委員會委員○及專門學校漢文師範班監之職○一九二○年，眞除正視學官○兼充灣仔官立學校校長○同年至一九二四年，兼任本港教育委員會名譽秘書○一九二二年，調充新界視學官○

一九二五年，內遷代理金港華人學校高級視學官（遵教育委員會委員）至一九二七

齡博通乎我國古學○精長審辭案於育才書院○年甫弱冠○留學英京○致遠金橋○專攻理化○公元一九一二年畢業○且歷學士文衔○迴圓兩易寒裘○不惹惹於自見○發匱陳書○揣摩簡絲○以增益其學問○不精窮其辭鉉○果也不罷則已○

年而實校高級視學官○任職以迄於今○非先生龍猛其祿○與港府敬才善任○吳能致受耶○先生辦事精明○律身廉潔○劉於倫肥辦學○指導勤助○尤為鴝力○故極將全港文學界之完頭○元配江夏氏○已作古男女公子數人○俊秀非凡○長女尤亭亭於王立○迎前兩展盟運俊陳維周之文郎○

一飛冲天○不鳴則已○一鳴驚人○於

Mr. LAW YAN PAK, B.A.

Mr. Y. P. Law is a native of Sunwoi District, Kwangtung Province, and was born in Canton in 1888. He received his early education from private tutors and also attended for a few months at the Ellis Kadoorie School, (or the Honan College) Canton. In 1905 to 1912, he continued his studies in England, where he obtained his B.A. degree in the University of Cambridge in 1912.

In 1915, Mr. Law was appointed assistant master in the Education Department Hongkong. In the following year, he became acting Inspector of Vernacular Schools.

In 1919, he was appointed a member of the Board of Examiners and concurrently Supervisor of the Vernacular Teachers' Classes of the Technical Institute. In the following year, he was appointed Inspector of Vernacular Schools and was acting Head Master of Wanchai Government School.

From 1920 to 1924, he was Honorary Secretary of the Board of Education. From 1922 to 1925, he was Inspector of Vernacular Schools for the New Territtories.

Since 1925, he has been Senior Inspector of Vernacular Schools for Urban Districts, and an Ex-office Member of the Board of Education.

黃炳耀先生

生先耀炳黃

黃先生炳耀○籍廣東台山縣○生於海洋洲烏綠倫島○現年六十二歲○是香江百萬華僑十八領袖之一○當局常資借異○幼時隨父母返港○時為一八八六年也○卒業來為主宰○誠傑出之人物也○

其門如市○而先生益自策勵○以期無負眾人屬望○如何能便利保戶也○如何能追盜公司也○兼顧統籌○未嘗一日精懈○現春秋已高○跨寬有子○仍不自遜○常至公司○主持大較○以匡後進之不逮焉○其辦事精神○良足欽仰○先生不僅能成體育○於商戰稱雄○亦極愛護同群○為社會造福○現任太平局紳○市政衛生局員○香港大學校董會董事等○其殁○其他尚多○不及備述○夫人伍氏○名貴錢○內助稱賢○哲嗣二人○長名迻○字兆良○畢業港大工程科○一九三零年，廣土木工程學士銜○曾任藏本港工務局二年○耀隆克城門水塘助理工程師○一九三三年，史求深造○實習於多文朗公司○將英國土木工程會，及英國建築工程會，認為會員○現充工程師於廣州梅菉鐵路○次于兆榮

卸讀於皇仁書院○中英學兼○均甚豐富○一八九二年再赴烏綠倫島畢業於奧梯高書院○一九○六年始畢業返港○因先生具商學天才○對於經濟一科○不似師承○自有心得○故學成後○卸出而就商○熱營保險事業○受破於水明公司○任事以來○港中僑胞以其記為大眾謀安全○且待人接物○謙虛有禮○咸趨之○於是○雙聲本島○亦商界後起之秀○

Mr. B. WONG TAPE, J.P.

Mr. B. Wong Tape, one of the most prominent merchants in Hong Kong, is a native of Toishan District, Kwangtung Province, and was born in 1875 in Dunedin, Otago, New Zealand.

He came to Hongkong with his parents in 1886 and entered Queen's College, where he passed out Class I in 1892. As there was no University in Hongkong at that time, he proceeded to Dunedin, New Zealand, and completed his education at the Otago Boys High School.

In 1906, he returned once more to the Colony and joined the China Mutual Life Insurance Co., Ltd., where he rose to the position of Secretary in 1909 and became manager of the Hongkong branch in 1919.

Later, the firm was taken over by the Sun Life Assurance Co., of Canada and in turn he became Resident Secretary of the local branch of that company. He became official-in-charge of that firm in 1927 and retired from this executive position in 1934, but retaining his connection with the company as local adviser for South China.

Mr. Wong Tape has been a non-official Justice of the Peace since 1924. He has also been a member of the Po Leung Kuk; Chairman of the Chinese Y.M.C.A; President of the Chinese Club, the Chinese Recreation Club and the Queen's College Old Boys' Association and Vice-president of the Kowloon Residents' Association. He is at president a member of the Urban Council and a member of the Court of the University of Hongkong.

Married to Ng Kwai Chuen, Mr. Wong Tape has two sons. Mr. Eric Wong Tape, his elder son, obtained his B.Sc. degree from the Hongkong University in 1930. Then he became a staff in the Public Works Department and two years later became assistant engineer in the construction of the Shing Mun Dam and Reservoir. He proceeded to England in 1933 and completed his practical training as an engineer with Messrs. Dorman, Long & Co., where he obtained the degrees of A.M.I.C.E. and A.M.I. Struct. E.

His second son, Mr. Irwin Wong Tape, also obtained a thorough education and possesses a good reputation in the commercial sphere.

范潔朋先生

范潔朋先生生

范潔朋先生，粵東南海人。現年中壽普七十。生而不見。少有大志。賦性況毅勇敢。持躬刻苦耐勞。識見超卓。胸懷磊落。平素對於社會公益事業無不出力以赴。壯歲即以傑出之材。受知於兩廣總督。（時維清代，譚公鍾麟總制兩等），派赴扶桑。致查商務。新知益進。責劇勞瘁。民元時曾加入中國同盟會。獻身革命。

被舉為廣州市參事。香港出口爆竹商會主席。澳門兵桑慈善會持籌主席。現承全國經濟建設運動委員會總會籌備處聘充委員。香港華商總會值理。澳門商會主席。鏡湖醫院主席。同善堂值理。鏡湖女校校長。坐德女中校董。又歷掌中鏡湖救傷會總理事。鏡湖護士學校校長。民二五屆大選舉。澳門護僑區監督。今先生年將七旬。猶精力過人。且待人接物。和諧可親。各大社團。咸欲為領袖。各盡棉力。而其熱誠尤為救國。抱愛國熱。用分遴。古之卿以風世。今之招人有千里者。自視太高。折節與人交。以赴扶。立為解救。凡憂力以始安。近日世譯任俠者。報紙稱先生也。亦有求必應。予以救濟。具概慷慨。而先生尤熱心公益。世譯任俠者。報紙稱先生之慷慨。如此也。又矣天下。不拔一毛。先生時為國盡力。而其熱誠尤為救國。前澳陽之變。粵軍出次。如利天下。不拔一毛。

為趙理忠實信徒。討龍之役。措勞扰来。曹長持軍繼邸軍需。逐陳炯之役。又主滇軍旅邸怵軍材。時也百粵江河不靖。復充扰諜於反衛旅保商營。各機關附重長材於東省長公亦。登滇軍總司令部。此民十一以前先生之建樹也。剝使撮脫軍政兩途。從事工商實業。其舉舉大者。在羊石則有亞通造廠之組織。其對於社會公益。慈善。教育。工。商。等事業。均有不好贊勷。曾愛穿黨國之志士。

振躬而起。倡辦兵桑慈善會。敎亡之舉。恢世界巨款六十餘圓以為之倡。藥集十餘萬金。乃各界從血捐。自滙寄之者。亦數萬圓。先所指。舉國同欽。去歲值公桑辰。勸捐懷。以接充賓國防。又保獻機。戰力。勤懇。時慨兩遇。落。僑氏之困苦。有此紀三萬。款迄。澳輸石之漿。以洪中商務之慈。續覺開。可紀我。先生又繼續。勢夾可。軍政商學之開人。可敬也。

論居留号。港。澳。三地。均有不好贊勷。曾愛穿黨國之志士。社會公益。慈善。教育。工。商。等事。不。

Mr. FAN KIT PANG.

One of the most prominent Chinese whose name spreads not only in Hongkong but also in Macao is Mr. Fan Kit Pang. He is a native of Nam-hoi District Kwangtung Province, where he was born in 1880.

Owing to his clever thought and exellent conduct, Mr. Fan was sent by the late General Tam Chong Luen, who was a high official of the Ch'ing Dynasty, to go to Japan to investigate commerce.

Later, he returned to China and devoted himself in the commercial sphere. He initiated the Macao Investment Co., Ltd., in Macao and organized the Ah Tung Knitting Co., in Canton. Besides, he is either stock-holder or partner of many business concerns in Hongkong.

Mr. Fang is a man of board sympathy and every good cause finds him a willing supporter. He was Councilor of the Canton Government; Chairman of the Hongkong Firecrackers Exporters' Association; and Chairman of the Society of Charity of Macao. At present, he is one of the committees of the Financial Construction Campaign of China; Committee of the Hongkong Chinese General Chamber of Commerce; Chairman of Macao Chinese Chamber of Commerce; President of the Kiang-Vu Hospital, Macao; Principal of Kiang-Vu School and Kiang Vu Nursing School, Macao; Besides he is director of many outstanding schools in Macao.

In 1936, during a selection of delegates for the national Congress, which is to be held in the nearest future, Mr. Fan was appointed Supervisor of that campaign in macao by the Chinese Government.

Mr. Fan is a faithful nationalist, and was an important member during the building of the Republic of China.

詩有之○高山仰止○景行行止○雖不能至○然
心嚮往之○余讀朱氏詩○想見其為人○先生名
汝珍○字聘三○亦號隘園○顧高世家也○其高
曾綽堂公○達河公○以經學司鐸○其封翁恐
公○以軍功權座○海岳文宗○久紹家風○陸慎
詢賦○良多世德○學遵庭訓○素受名師○芝蘭

按中國禮俗而制定之○修律大臣卒從其議○宣
統己酉○創定商律○奉派赴各商埠調查商事習
慣○報告凡數十萬言○又以所定各國刑法比較
篇○各國法律○當不宜於中國○不必採用○應
墓修法律○雖時創定民法○先生謂親族承繼兩
素於日本法政大學○列最優等。) 歸國○得奬
記名遇缺補題奏○任京師法律學堂教習○仿續纂

試○奉簡派為貴州省主考○公畢入都○復慕成
十卷逆呈○將供內諸衙○廣成戌科首次舉行法官考
德宗實錄○入直南書房○（纂派編輯德宗御
製詩文○清查內廷書畫圖籍○得奬頭品頂
戴○紫禁城內乘馬,
現有清代詞林輯署等
書面世。) 不求聞達
於諸候○浮海來粵。

史太珍汝朱

就秀。齊集洋池○（弱冠縣試冠軍,與其兄汝
琦,汝湖,汝璟,次第進庠。) 角逐文壇○辭
雄質雅○恥騁鑿苑○食餼膠庠○丁酉與試選拔
○戊戌朝考先發○遙奈卯之年○黈宮折桂○
（應順天卿試,中舉人。) 甲辰之歲○雁塔題名
○（應會試,聯捷成進士。) 屏特詮而校拾遺名
○（殿試欽定一甲第二,賜進士及第,授職翰林
院編修○) 欽為我百粵增光矣○及清廷改寬○
命為如拾荼○及清廷改寬○力爭而止○

士壬,續聘,而先生乃辭之○癸酉,就孔教學
院黃事之聘,為該院院長,宣指聖道,厥功有足
多者○僑僑善誘○晴江學子相馬○慷慨長
征○豈島之傷肥辛矣○又復情敦桑梓○墓記泵
衆○（先生粵之清遠縣人。) 而總其成○陸記自披
龍岡,屢枝勃遽,力爭而止○有欲有成○圓
卑象矣○至情至性○富貴非顧○鄉可期矣○

○以選粹告終○先
生之德己立○而先
生之操守愈不○貞以
幹事○慮以姆時○居
家著述。○（先生於甲
午,庚午,南歸,
年己耳順矣○）于十月得
疾,甫以威時○居
家著述○）

即為我百粵增光不淺○從梅謙博士讀律○三年
學成。) (畢業於日本法政大學。) 從梅謙博士讀律○三年學成○
留學東瀛○（華

Dr. CHU U-CHUN.

Dr. Chu was born in 1869 in Ching-yuan District, Kwangtung Province. His predecessors and father were notable mandarins of the Ching Dynasty. He was under tutor at his early age and his destined talents and intellegence in his studies may be seen from the fact that he procured the scholastic title of Hsiu Tsai when he was but twenty years of age.

In 1897, he began to study law in Kiangsu, and after three years when he had a thorough knowledge in the subject, he was promoted judge of the District Court of Kiangsu.

At that time, the emperor of Ching Dynasty realized the urgent need of reforming the administration of government and commanded to retrench those unnecessary staffs of the government organizations by means of a strict examination. More than four hundred candidates were summoned and Doctor Chu was selected first and the result was that he should be promoted to combine law, a post of high dignity.

Dr. Chu is one who loves studies more than anything and he continued his studies with renewed efforts. In 1903 he attained the degree of Chin-Shih, equivalent to Doctor degree, and later was admitted free scholarship to study law in the University of Law and Politics in Japan. Three years later, he graduated and returned to China. Then he became tutor in the law school in Peking. Since then, he had been holding many important posts in the Chinese Government.

In 1931, Dr. Chu was tutor of Chinese philosophy and literature in the Hongkong University. But he resigned the post in the following year.

Since then, he has been president of the Confucian College.

胡惠德醫師

DR. ARTHUR WAI-TAK WOO

惠德先生，籍原廣東鶴山。生於香海。現年四十有九。故名醫胡爾楷翁之哲嗣也。少時肄業於本港拔萃書院。旋華赴英留學。習法文，及拉丁文。旋進倫敦大學習醫科。以繼父志。一九〇七年，入倫敦醫院實習。初試拔內科臨床醫學優等証書。至一九一三年，而學成。修業期間。一九一一年，中國政府給以駐英華軍上尉軍醫榮銜。同時當地政府復派往倫敦第一師野戰隊第三隊服務凡三載。旋任倫敦醫院眼科醫師。繼充嘉扶散醫院駐院醫師。統理該院內外科及又光科各部。時當歐戰。該院房接收由法運回傷兵之最前段。為供先生多量診斷與施術之良機。任滿。倫敦約之布林敦傳染病房醫院又延之當駐院內科醫師。來裁。倫敦約道產科醫院聘之當駐院副醫。診治內科。既著成約。復研外治。以後選為寶度錫士醫院駐院外科醫師。於一九一六年經考試而兼產婦科。且據選該院產科副教校。厥職向無異諸國外人者。先生以不同種族之新後學。竟能任此。其造詣也可知。且同時兼主該院婦科門診部。及倫敦市工花柳科醫院鏡點駐局醫官。一身數職。局夜間駐局醫官。倫敦約政總氏外科割股用之鈎。而發明胡氏外科割股原理。根應付裕如。尚有餘閒之暇。及把針器。精神飽力。有異尋常。

其時歐戰延長。醫師缺乏。英政府再委為來修復及葉斯域醫院高級駐院醫官。及世界和平。先生復燃煤油富商賂克化剌氏之學額。赴美留學。再求深造。首選紐約產科醫院。繼入約翰哈堅大學醫院。歡後實習於美與醫院。故院察路。再求深造。耳先生治理傷兵之經驗。請其演講「我於外科及婦科之功用。」一九二三年『在中國發生之子宮外孕。』一九二四年『白帶三百醫案。』一九一八年『利華殿氏絨鉗收瑣消毒劑及把針器』對於外科及婦科之功用。一九一六年胡統合著『食管膨脹六醫案』一九一八年『利華殿氏絨鉗及把針器』。故能日進新知。馳名中外。肯晷行經驗所得。廣為著述。三十年來。因研求醫學。足迹遍歐美者四。於銃治癌。及外科技術。凡歷各大都市之醫療機關，如倫敦，完丁堡，維希那脫等地，曾有特別探討。先生學歷。為倫大學內外科醫學士。英國皇立外科學院。及倫敦皇立內科學院。英國皇立熱帶病學院會員。美國醫學會會永遠會員。及維也納美國醫學會員。汎科學院院士。一九二五。連任該科主考。現就醫務所於華人行。一九三四。對於惠德之貧苦病人。不少免費治療。且有銃救治癌病痿在抱者也。

博得醫學大會勳章。駐師故鄉兩稔。乃仍助長才。以承其志。一九二三年。代表荃大總統元洪出席上海外交交通兩部聘為醫事顧問。於一九二二年。驻宮微為名譽醫官。育才濟世。兼而有之。歸國。即任北平協和醫學院產婦科副教授。兼充華產婦科教校。遠未能任此。駐師故鄉兩稔。具有勳勞。慶五等嘉禾章。時港大產婦科教校。夫以一人而身兼數要職。洵屬罕有。現任醫務所於華界跑馬地。對於惠德之貧苦病人。界環鞁。大不乏人。其值得崇科。有如此者。

『一九三五年『伊弗敦庭藥一百醫案』等書面世○他和醫學組織○無不熱烈參加○一九三七年『戒煙血清治療○附一千醫案』等書面世○曹君香港中華醫學會會長○中華醫學會香港分會秘書○復又會長○英國醫學會會員○現任該會監察委員○為香港分會理事，港大醫學會聯兩屆會長○尤以一九二八年任上海博醫會中華及香港分會理事，港大醫學會聯兩屆會長○尤以一九二八年，參與上海醫學會長○為我國醫界最光榮之事○誠以華人膺斯職者○此為創舉○參與上海醫學大會○欲推為大會主席○誠以華人膺斯職者○此為創舉○本由中外醫師值理○批推為大會主席○博醫會之副會長○亦將半百○至於社會公益慈善商界各事業○前歲與中華醫學會合併○又獲舉為副會長○現任香港支委值理○華人慈善會主席○在我國成立○平將半百○本由中外醫師院義務外科醫官○富義務醫官，及主考，與財委會指導所義務總醫師○倡故華人慈善會○一九三〇年叛斜新界贈醫傷院○復任該會副主席○設立巡迴贈醫所十處○計用醫藥護士費式萬餘圓○限取手者過卒○一九一三年，代表華人青年會會長○倡組港紅藥料等往上海紅十字醫院外○造送兩救援院義務外科醫官○申江一二八之役○倡組港紅藥料等往上海紅十字醫院外○造送兩救援組織手者過卒○一手提又光模○造戰事待息○將捐款萬圓撥充中華醫學會建交英理事大會○前任香港華人青年會會長○連任五屆主席○數任倫敦各校基督教聯合值理○一九〇八年，創設英基督教學生會○連任五屆主席○數任倫敦各校基督教所之用○一九〇八年，創設英基督教學生會○現史義務多往紐約之世界基督教學基督教起人○現任值理○聯青社員○聖保羅堂值理○現史義務多往紐約之世界基督教學會基督教服務團贊助員○英國海外倫民會永遠會員○上海大新公司董事○香港金龍酒家董事○香港總會員○基督教服務團贊助員○健瑩慈善社員○聖保羅堂值理○中華聖公會華南區長○一九三六年召集首屆聯會○香港總會主席○華商俱樂部會員○曾任華工時期○自養蕃服○復任輔政司視函○極符貝倫軍高英函華商俱樂部值理○現任值理○聯青社員○聖保羅堂校醫○擔任健康運動○及游泳院○現充等職○一九二五年○香港龍工時期○自養蕃服○復任輔政司視函○極符貝倫軍高英謝○一九三四年○本港舉行治疫運動○港府與其他之揗音台演講○及檢驗工作○現充謝○一九三五年，獲英故皇佐第五銀禧紀念勳章○先生喜接極○及游泳會○及板球會會員○德禮金函教謝○本港啟商慕興君之愛妲○中華游樂會○曹修棠於聖士提反女校○現有于女六人○月女士○本港啟商慕興君之愛妲○體育運動聯合會名譽會長○中華游樂會○曹修棠於聖士提反女校○現有于女六人○者體育○早研創辦，參術，胡球，泉島等有益運勳○現為香港馬會會員○金港學界尤等職○華商俱樂部會員○英國海外倫民會永遠會員○上海大新公司董事○

In 1932 during the Sino-Japanese trouble in Shanghai, when an urgent appeal for medical aid came to Hongkong, Dr. Woo was elected Chairman of the Hongkong Medical Relief Committee. The total subscription raised exceeded $40,000, more than half of which was raised by Dr. Woo himself. Besides supplying money to the Red Cross Society in Shanghai, doctors and nurses, medical supplies, two ambulances and a set of portable X-ray were sent up as well. After the trouble was over, through Dr. Woo's influence, the sum of $10,000 was given to the Chinese Medical Association in aid of the Association Building Fund.

During his student days in England, besides taking part in many sports such as fencing, boxing, tennis and riding, Dr. Woo was also keenly interested in Christian work among Chinese students. In 1908 he founded the Chinese Students' Christian Union of Great Britain and Ireland, which continues its excellent work. He was its Chairman for the first five years of its existence and also served on the Executive Committee of the London Intercollegiate Christian Union. In 1913 he was elected to be one of the Chinese representatives to attend the World Students' Christian Federation Conference held at Lake Mohonk, New York. He was a Vice-president of the Hongkong Chinese Y.M.C.A. and has given many Health Campaign lectures, as well as personal service in examination and guidance for the general health of members. He is a Committee Member of the Diocesan Old Boys' Association and serves as Honorary Medical Advisor to the Diocesan Boys' School, and St. Paul's Girls' College in which connection, with the help of his colleagues, he gives free annual examination to the boarders as well as free vaccination to both schools. He gives also free treatment to the inmates of the Blind Girls' Home. He is a member of the Executive Committee and Hon. Medical Advisor of the Street Sleepers' Shelter Society.

In 1925 during the General Strike in Hongkong Dr. Woo was one of the first to volunteer for service, and later received a letter of appreciation and thanks from the Colonial Secretary.

In 1934 at the request of His Excellency the Governor, Sir William Peel, Dr. Woo broadcasted in Chinese on behalf of the Cancer Campaign and received afterwards a personal letter of thanks from His Excellency.

In 1935, Dr. Woo was honoured by His Majesty, the late King George V with the Jubilee Medal.

Dr. Woo was a member of the Committee of St. Paul's Church and is a member of the Diocesan Board of Finance of the Chung Hwa Sheng Kung Hui (Church of China) for South China. He has also been a member of the Committee of the Mission to Chinese Seamen.

A charter member and Director of the Rotary Club, he is also South China District Governor of the International Association of Y's Men's Clubs. He had the honour of calling and presiding over the first District Conference of Y's Men of South China, which was a great success. He is a builder member of Toc H, a life member of the Overseas League and a Fellow of the Royal Empire Society.

A Member of the Chinese Chamber of Commerce and Chinese Merchants' Club, and past committee member of the latter, Dr. Woo is also a Director of the Sun Company, Shanghai, and a permanent Director of the Kam Loong Restaurant.

Attesting to his interest in and patronage of sport, he is a member of the Hongkong Jockey Club, Hon. President of Interscholastic Athletic Union, and a member of the South China Athletic Association, the Y.M.C.A. and the Chung Sing Benevolent Association. He has been a supporter also of the Chinese Recreation Club, the International Golf Club and the Craigengower Cricket Club. His chief recreations now are gardening and swimming.

香港‧澳門雙城成長經典

Dr. ARTHUR WAI-TAK WOO

M.B., B.S. (LOND), M.R.C.S. (ENG), L.R.C.P. (LOND).

Doctor Woo was born in Hongkong in 1887, and received his early education at the Diocesan Boys' School where he had a brilliant scholastic career. In 1905 he went to finish his education in England. Following in the footsteps of his father, Dr. Woo Yeo Kai, he chose the medical profession. After passing the necessary French and Latin tests in record time, he matriculated into the London University and entered the London Hospital in 1907. In his first competitive class examination he was awarded the certificate for efficiency in Elementary Clinical Medicine.

In 1911 the Chinese Government granted Dr. Woo an honorary commission as Captain in the Chinese Army Medical Service, and from then to 1913 he was attached to the Third London Field Ambulance, First London Division (T), for training in Army medical work, which served him in good stead during the Great War.

In January 1913, Dr. Woo graduated and his first appointment was that of an Ophthalmic Clinical Assistant at the London Hospital, working under Sir William Lister. His next appointment was that of Resident Medical Officer at the Gravesend General Hospital, having charge of both departments of Medicine and Surgery, including X Cabinet This hospital was one of the first to receive the wounded from France at the beginning of the War. When that commission was completed he became House Physician at the General Lying-in Hospital, York Road, London, and from there took up next the post of Assistant Resident Medical Officer at the London Fever Hospital under the eminent physician Sir John Broadbent. Subsequent to this, he was appointed House Physician at the well-known Brompton Hospital for Consumption and Diseases of the Chest.

Dr. Woo then decided to turn his attention to surgery, and in 1916, after the competitive examination, he became House Surgeon to Lieutenant Colonel Sir Alfred Pearce Gould and Mr. Sampson Handley, at the Middlesex Hospital. After that he became Gynaecological Obstetric House Surgeon under Sir Comyns Berkeley and Mr. Victor Bonney, world famous gynaecologists also at the Middlesex Hospital. Before very long he had the distinction of being asked to take the post of Gynaecological and Obstetric Tutor, Registrar, and Acting Lecturer on Practical Midwifery at the Middlesex Hospital, a post previously held only by a Britishor. At the same time he was in charge of the Gynaecological Out-patients and the Venereal Disease Clinic under the London County Council. In conjunction with this work, and for night duty only, he was performing the functions of Resident Medical Officer to the London General Post Office, thus relieving three men at one time for war service.

It was during this busy period that Dr. Woo invented the "Woo" needle and holder for abdominal surgery—a modification of Revordin's in principle. Later, because of the further shortage of doctors as the War progressed, he was asked to take up the post of Senior Resident Medical Officer at the East Suffolk and Ipswich General Hospital, having charge of three hundred military and one hundred and fifty civilian beds.

After the Armistice Dr. Woo became a Rockefeller scholar and left England to take up post-graduate work, first at the New York Lying-in and Post-graduate Medical School, later at the Johns Hopkins University Hospital under Professor Howard Kelly and Dr. Thomas S. Cullen, and lastly at the unique Mayo Clinic in America. Dr. Charles Mayo paid him the compliment of requesting him to address one of the weekly staff meetings which are attended by visiting doctors from all over the world, on his observations of the treatment of wounds with aniline dyes during the War.

Upon his return to China, and for a period of two years, Dr. Woo was, first, Assistant Surgeon to Professor J. Preston Maxwell and later an Associate with him in the Department of Obstetrics and Gynaecology at the Peiping Union Medical College, of the Rockefeller Foundation. At the same time he had full charge of the whole outpatient Gynaecological Clinic. During his stay in Peiping he was made Physician Extraordinary to the President of China, and Medical Adviser to the Ministry of Foreign Affairs and Ministry of Communications, and in 1923 he was asked to be President Li Yuan Hung's personal representative to convey his special message to the Biennial Conference of the China Medical Missionary Association held in Shanghai. Before leaving Peiping he was decorated by the President of China with the Order of the Chia Ho (Excellent Crop) Fifth Class.

Upon his return to Hongkong to take up medical practice, Dr. Woo was appointed lecturer on Gynaecology and Obstetrics at the Hongkong University as well as being Internal Examiner on the same subjects during the period of 1924-1925 prior to the arrival of the University Professor.

On four occasions Dr. Woo returned to Europe and America for post-graduate work, mainly in Radium Therapy and General Surgery. The cities where he made his special studies were London, Edinburgh, Berlin, Paris, Heidelberg, Vienna, New York and Rochester (Mayo Clinic).

Dr. Woo is now a Bachelor of Medicine and Bachelor of Surgery of the University of London, also a Member of the Royal College of Surgeons, England, and a Licentiate of the Royal College of Physicians, London. He has also been a Fellow of the Royal Society of Tropical Medicine. He is a life member of the Mayo Clinic Surgeons' Club, Rochester, and a life member of the American Medical Association, Vienna.

Dr. Woo is now Principal of the Woo Clinic, China Building Hongkong. He opened the Babington Hospital and Sanitarium in 1934 and is its medical diector. The Home is fully equipped, even having radium for treatment of cancer cases and many from the poorer classes have been treated there free of charge.

Dr. Woo's medical writings are:—(Co-author, with Dr. Batty Shaw) "Six Cases of Oesophagectasia" (a paper read before the Section of Medicine of the Royal Society of Medicine on November 28, 1916). "Revordin's Needle-Holder and Needles" (The Lancet, March 23, 1918). "Some Observations on the uses of Flavine, Brilliant Green and Ensol in General Surgery and Gynaecology," 1922. ' Ectopic Gestations in China," (Journal of Obstetrics and Gynaecology, of the British Empire), "Study of three hundred Cases of Leucorrhea," 1924, Evipan Anaesthesia 100 Cases," 1935 Chinese Medical Journal, and "Auto-serum Treatment for Opium Addicts (Observation on 1000 cases) in January, 1937 Chinese Medical Journal.

As well as performing distinguished medical service and keeping himself abreast of the development of medical science, Dr. Woo has also taken a prominent part in matters of medical organization. He is a member of the Supervisory Committee of the Chinese Medical Association, of which he now is a life member. He has been President of the Hongkong Chinese Medical Association, and also Secretary and later President of the National Medical Association of China, (Hongkong Branch) and a Council Member of the British Medical Association, Hongkong and China Branch. He was twice Vice-president of the Hongkong University Medical Society.

In 1928, Dr. Woo received a high Chinese medical honour when he was elected to be the first Chinese President of the China Medical Association. The following year he presided, and delivered his presidential speech, at the 1929 Biennial Conference held in Shanghai. This association was an international medical organization of more than forty years' standing, which later became amalgamated with the National Medical Association of China to form one united organization known as the Chinese Medical Association. In the new organization Dr. Woo was elected to serve for two successive terms as its Vice-president.

Parallel with his medical work, Dr. Woo has taken an active interest in social and other public problems. He has contributed much time, thought and effort to Leprosy, Opium and other evils affecting the Chinese population. He is a Committee Member of the Hongkong Auxiliary of the Chinese Mission to Lepers and a keen worker in the cause of charity.

He is the chief medical officer in charge of the Anti-opium, Ante and postnatal, Birth Control, Sterility, and Child welfare Clinics run under the auspices of the Chinese Benevolent Association. which he founded in 1933 and of which he is now an Executive Committee Member.

Realising the great need for medical service among the villgers in the a New Territories, Dr. Woo organized in November 1930 the first medical clinics in ten different centres, where there were no Government doctors, and later founded the New Territories Medical Benevolent Society. Its total expenditure for doctors, nurses and drugs was over $22,000. At the request of His Excellency the Governor, this society became amalgamated with that of the St. John Ambulance Association to form the New Territories Medical Benevolent Branch of the St. John Ambulance Association. A cheque for $10,000 was handed over to the Director of

林承芬博士

士博芬承林

Dr. SHING FAN LAM, Ph. D.

Dr. Shing Fan Lam was born in Kwangtung Province in 1888. After obtaining a good knowledge in Chinese literature, he went to America to continue his studies in the American Institute of Banking, New York. Many years later, he succeeded to get the Standard Certificate from that institution and there after he was employed by the Anglo-California Trust Company, San Francisco, California, U.S.A., as manager of their Chinese Department. His business ability and wide contact with the Chinese overseas enabled him to be advanced to the position of manager of their Montgomery Street Branch. He was afterwards promoted to be Assistant Cashier, and Assistant Vice-president at the time when he resigned in favour of the Bank of China.

Dr. Lam is a man who is always anxious to learn more, so he made use of his leisure hours and continued with his studies and research work in the Lincoln University, San Francisco, where he procured the degree of Ph. D. in Banking Administration.

The Bank of China, Shanghai, offered an attractive position to Dr. Lam. Knowing that such an experienced technical man is beneficial to a banking concern, the Anglo-California Trust Company, California, where Dr. Lam was working, offered a triple increment of salary in order to make Dr. Lam to stay with their institution. But Dr. Lam was a sort of man who always intends to render himself to serve his own nation, so he refused the American Bank and returned to China where he was appointed sub-manager of the Bank of China, Hongkong.

At present, the bank has established a branch in New York City, U.S.A. and Dr. Lam may be sent to extend service in that direction.

Although Dr. Lam is not a rich man, any occasion that concerns charity he is always doing his best to contribute.

Dr. Lam has four children. All of them obtained a thorough education. His oldest daughter acquired the B.S. degree in Home Economics from the University of Nevada, Reno, Nevada. The second daughter graduated from the University of California, in plant genetics, Berkeley, California. His son is studying mechanical Engineering in U.S.A., and his third daughter expects to study police Administration or Education in U.S.A.

李景康先生

○本港政府紳商之請。亟思挽倡我國國學。遂有官立漢文中學之創設。教育司署因詢長之。遂使主官立漢文師範學校事。亦屈十載。以迄於茲。能循循善誘。沾溉士林。故本港之教育家也。能循循善誘。多出其門。聲稱於馬益著。

李先生景康。字鳳坡。系粤南海人。現年四十五。學貫中西。讀書中西兼善。誠我國富有學問之教育家也。幼在河里松滘鄉私塾肄業。旋資笈香港聖士提反中學。於民國元年。考獲英國牛津大學高等試文憑。中文特著俊異。其時香港大學創辦伊始。乃攻文科。民國四年。以第一屆

先生凡遇教育設施。無不竭力贊助。與吾邑教育界殊。如民十三。在粤省教育會許鎮員。及歷充廣州南海中學校董。偏廷港大馮平山圖書館。偏廷香港孔聖堂幹事值理。偏港南海商會董事。創辦港大中文學院起草委員。港大文學會名譽會員。港大中文學會名譽會員。智其无届致試委員。者也。先生擅詩文。工

創辦南海石門中學校董。偏廷港大馮平山圖書館。偏廷香港孔聖堂幹事值理。偏港南海商會董事。創辦港大中文學院起草委員。絪事○枚徵為江蘇常署。廣東社員。湖南長沙市社湘集社員。江蘇吳縣中國國學會會長。香港國學合作社幹事值理。居位潛心國學○著述甚富○螯嘗散實模詩。

草○七言律法歐陽○及與國大典苓光趙兩太史○陳延庠进士等合編國文模範讀本三冊○吳張谷鄉君合編陽羨風雲圖考○葉公卷虎爲之作序○多藝多才○不愧嶺南名士也○先生原籍鄉夫人○詩款○平仄○紲宝蘇夫人○名蓮贵○上海啥○明女中學學生○男公子六○長毅，尚勇○尚信○素中學○尚治，尚沛，尚平○鲜素小學○尚高○末屆學齡○女公子四○日绮林，已婚○绮姗，则尚幼焉○衔授○均就小學○绮燗，则尚幼焉○

畢業○庠學士銜○民國六年○朱慶瀾任廣東省長○創辦全省保衛團總局○以綏治安○且通民隱○先生被徵為參議○未幾去歲○乃就教席於母校聖士提反中學○畔辭五載○於民十一年○因愛邑內紳商公報○返廣州任南海中學○兼縣立南海師範學校校長○政貨整頓邑校之責○成績卓著○邑人多之○迨香港政府設教育視學官○兼英文視學官○典論会然脆往○民十五年○金○民十三年○應香港政府之聘，衔授○均就小學○绮姗，则尚幼焉。

生先康景李

Mr. K. H. LI, B.A.

Mr. Li is a native of Nan-hai District, Kwangtung Province, and was born in 1892.

He received his early education from a private school of his native village, and later entered St. Stephen's College, Hongkong, where in 1912 he passed the Oxford Senior Local Examination with distinction in Chinese and the first Hongkong University Matriculation Examination. Thereupon he took an Arts course at the local University and graduated in 1916 with a B.A. degree.

In 1917 when General Ju Hing Lan was Civil Governor of Kwangtung, the Bureau of Provincial Protection was established and Mr. Li was appointed a councilor of this institution.

Mr. Li returned to Hongkong in the following year on being offered a teaching post by St. Stephen's College, his alma mater. He held this post until 1922 when he was appointed Headmaster of the Nan-hai Middle School and the Nan-hai Normal School, Canton, on the recommendation of the gentry and the Chamber of Commerce of his native district.

Appointed Inspector of vernacular Schools and English Private Schools by the Education Department in 1924, he returned to the Colony for a second time. In two years he was transferred to the Headmastership of the Government Vernacular Middle School, and that of the Government Normal School, the former institution was founded in 1926 and the latter in 1921.

Mr. Li is a man of broad sympathy and every good cause finds him a willing supporter. In recognition of his success in educational work he was elected a member of the Advisory Committee of the Kwangtung Provincial Education Association in 1924 before he came back to Hongkong in that year. The various social services he has rendered in Canton and Hongkong may be well signified by the following elections and appointments. He has served as member of the school council of the Nan-hai Middle School, Shek Moon Middle School, Canton, Executive Committe of the Confucius Hall; Hon. member of the Chinese Association of the Hongkong University, and Hon. Treasurer of the Hongkong University Graduates' Association, Hongkong.

In 1928 he was called upon together with Dr. Au Tai Tin and Dr. Lai Chai Hsi to draft the scheme and syllabus for the establishment of the Chinese School of the local University, and has served as member of its Board of Examination.

Mr. Li is an adept of Chinese literature and pictorial art. He is a member of the U-Shia Literary Association at Chang-Hsn, Kiangsu Province; member of the Nan-Shia Literary Association at Changsha, Hunan Province; and member of the China National Learning Association at Wu Hsien, Kiangsu Province the last two being the leading societies of men of letters in China. He has published three of his many literary works in Chinese, namely, the Pi Yun Lau Poems, a study of Seven-Word-Line Poems, and a set of three books entitled Model Readers on the Dictions and Styles of Chinese Essayists. For the last work he is a joint editor. Being a connoisseur of Chinese painting he was responsible for the organization of the Chinese Pictorial art Section of the China Exhibition held in the local City Hall in 1931.

Mr. Li has six sons and four daughters; except those who are still young, the others are receiving their education in local schools.

杜其章先生

MR. TOH KEE CHENG

提起「杜其章」三個字○可請「天下誰人不識君」○其愛國愛鄉○名聞寰宇矣○先生字煥文○列號小沅草堂主人○前清秀才○原籍福建泉州清粱鄉○八閩望族○世代書香○杜「少陵」「祁公」之遠裔也○其先君柏森公○舉進士○文武兼資○有上為毅戰○下馬草露布之才○當清之世○排滿歌力○丁亥前後○赴越南○隱於商○與劉將軍水福抗法軍於諒山高平等省○不受清廷命令○而保全銀南關逃防委隆○人至於今稱之○先生生而岐嶷○少年讀書破萬卷○豪俠有乃父風○博愛為懷○有我不入地獄，誰入地獄之

志○且天縱多能○如文學家○書畫家○美術家，藏古家，教育家○政治家○慈善家○音樂家，奉術家○均兼而有之○年未及壯○憤清政不綱○意偏冠○辛亥○浮海外○直往越南○贊翊革命○○功成不居○以齠齔已除○乃逃往祖國○民國建立宜○於民國十六年組織書畫社○以保存國粹為宗旨○杜友遊海內外○象鄉先生尚義桓○財○乃舉為永遠會長○成立迄茲○十餘年矣○

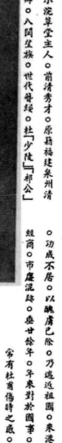

常有杜甫傷時之感○滬陽之變○淞滬之役○○偷淪國殤○開始廣州○諸愛國之士○與日俱積也○先生不徒熱血滿腔○有潛當世○而天性率友○亦著於時○○且屏絕不良嗜好○

書畫展覽會○為宣傳抗致救國盡力之一人○現仍摧進不軌○所謂愛國之忧○與日俱增○香港，澳門等埠之

社務之主持○與報章之佽助○均不稍懈任之○其他國內外各機關社團俗重先生○而以我輩相煩者○亦日益衆○

旅港杜氏宗親會會長○旅港福建商會董事○書畫社學主席○香港文化事業社董事長○非非畫報社社長○中華學術會顧問○留港學生公立采葉義學顧問○大中女子中學監學顧問○培芳女子中學顧問○領袖戌男女中學董事○廣東革命紀念會董事○全國小型足球協會董事○

烈士遺囑學校董事○香港華商總會故金港小型足球協進會正會長○廣州廣戌百義殉救計繁榮香港委員籌委員○廣州城西方便醫院名譽董事等等碩○對於桑梓○尤極關懷○在其故里○力事提倡開學校○建醫院○開公路○集公園○為鄉黨父老所敬重○畢為鄉中紳士○而各界○史抵之為東華醫院總理○保良公局總理馬○先生雅愛音樂○善擒古琴○而於獨奏一

志○且天縱多能○如文學家○書畫家○美術家○文藝界領袖○必先訪謁先生○蓋以先生為書畫港華聞美展○必先訪謁先生○蓋以先生為書畫文藝界領袖○登高一呼○萬山響應○其號召力之偉○足以左右一切○此地適生以本誌為世界交通樞紐○必洽成功之目的○且知先生辦事負責○宜以保存為友盡力○必洽成功之目的○故遣人韜之○先

也○

然華○尤務紀嬰○鐘期未遑○素不自炫○前歲青年會為籌款事○微泉先生登臺報効○始獲聆其第一次書法○奇頭縱橫○有繞樑三日之概○至先生之書法○娟健清秀○有如銀畫銀鈎○真草隸篆○均臻妙境○而楷書尤為壓倒一切○彼對此造○寢饋逾三十年○常獨創派地擇毫一格○其書學案大字○筆力之雄○不可思議○編者於年前參觀廣東全省市展會○書為「忍令上國衣冠淪於夷狄」「相率中原豪傑還我河山」一氣呵成○有虬蛇蜿舞之姿態○觀者莫舉如富○致為觀止○其句如「國破家何在」「存亡當自決」「喚奴來滅」「何以家為」等聯○其讓恤激昂之氣○躍於字裏行間○善書之名大噪○求者遂紛至沓來○惟先生個性特奇○遇聲氣相投者○則連紙墨亦樂贈之○倘遇有未愜○縱萬金亦不能得其隻字○蓋先生之墨蹟○不能以全錢而代偽之也○前年先生漫遊安南○為東華醫院勸捐時○當地官紳恭求其名者○恭求墨寶○戶限為穿○於時堤岸一埠○頗成洛陽紙貴之地○至先生之奉術○閱歷內功甚深○竟能解出境十年期尚未滿之瓊花○足徵其懷有絕技○與眾不顧身之勇○方港先生前夕曾暑遁身于○追隨兩匪於松秀街○交響著壹出○皆遮解出境○與眾不顧身之滿之操慈也○足徵其懷有絕技○而才名籍甚○崇隆○現先生年綸四十餘○而才名籍甚○聲譽崇隆○來日方長○為國家社會人羣謀幸福○正未可限量○于四女四○均是秀出班行○澗源家學○盎德者福大○積厚者流光○理固昭然不爽也○

Mr. TOH KEE CHEUNG

Mr. Toh Kee Cheung is a native of Chuanchiufo, Fukien Province, and was born in 1897.

His fore-fathers were famous officials of the Ch'ing Dynasty, and Mr. Toh, being came from a high stock, is well bred and educated.

He is a member of the Nationalists Party and rendered great assistance to the Chinese Revolution. After the establishment of the Chinese Republic, he declined every position offered to him, but came to Hongkong and mingled himself in the business field.

He organized the Association of Arts and Literature in the Colony and was appointed Permanent President of the organization. During the Sino-Japanese Conflict of 1932, he held an exhibition of painting works in order to raise money to relieve that calamity.

Mr. Toh is very attentive to public weals. He is a member of the Prosperity-scheming Committee of the Chinese General Chamber of Commerce, Hongkong; Director of the Fukien Chamber of Commerce, Hongkong; Chairman of the Fukien Free School; Chairman of the Board of Directors of the Hongkong Literary Enterprise Association; Adviser of many local schools; President of the Tung Wah Hospital; Committee of the Po Leung Kuk; and Hon. Director of the Western Public Hospital, Canton.

Mr. Toh has eight children and all of them are well educated.

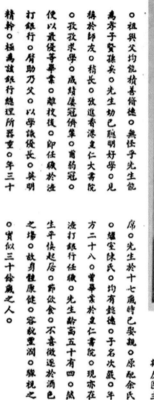

容子名先生

○祖興父均能積善餘德○無怪子容先生能
為孝子賢孫矣○先生幼已聰明好學○兒
猗於師友○精長○致退香港皇仁大書院
○孜孜求學○咸結屢冠儔輩○甫韵冠○
遂以最優等畢業○離校後○卽任職於渣
打銀行任職○先生齡高五十有四○齡
生平慎起居○節飲食○不喜微逐於酒色
之場○故身健康健○容貌豐潤○矍视之
精幹○極為諸銀行總理所器重○年三十
○實似三十餘歲之人○

容子名先生○原籍中山南屏鄉○而世居
於香港○祖諱良○充本港渣打銀行肯任
買辦○父諱憲邦○繼之而為第二任買辦
○先生性情豪爽仁俠○尚能熱心社會事
故譽卷四溢○現已成為港中巨商之一矣
辦○使繼父繳○先生自任職以來○勤以諡
十餘年○無日不克忠克誠○以勤以諡
行中服務多年○籉约甚鉅○遂亦聘充買
痛欲絕○諸銀行以先生才德遂茂○且在
○忽丁父艱○先生極峯○遭此大變○哀

辦房圍主
香港銀行
局董事○
院及保良
東華三
幹事值理
華商總會
並歷任
太平紳士
政府委充
素○故港

Mr. YUNG TSZE MING, J.P.

One of the most important figure in Hongkong is Mr. Yung Tsze Ming, compradore of the Hongkong Charter Bank of India Australia & China.

His grandfather was the first Chinese Compradore who worked in that Bank since its inauguration, and his father was the second to succeed. Mr. Yung Tsze Ming was born in Hongkong in 1883 and was educated in Queen's College. After his graduation, he worked in the Charter Bank, helping his father.

His intellegence and his ability soon came to be understood by the president of the Bank, who made him compradore of the same bank after the death of his father. Since then he assisted greatly in flourishing the business of this outstanding firm.

Mr. Yung is a Justice of Peace of Hongkong and an influential figure in the Chinese community. He held important positions in the Chinese Chamber of Commerce, Hongkong, and was in the Directorate of the Tung Wah Hospital, the Kwong Wah Hospital, the Tung Wah East Hospital and the Po Leung Kuk. Chairman of the Banking Compradore Association. Besides these, Mr. Yung is very popular for his bigness of heart in dealing with charity and social matters.

At present, Mr. Yung's son Yung Chi Yim is also working in the Charter Bank.

馬叙朝先生

馬叙朝先生○廣東省台山縣白沙塘口村人○現年五十九歲○容貌溫良○性情敦厚○乃香港享有信譽之紳商○而現任公有源綢緞莊之總司理也○先生謙冲坦誠○熱心國家社會事業○民國三年○我國大總統為酬報勛勞起見○曾頒給以四等嘉禾章○其在港府所任名譽職務○西歷一九二四年○充東華醫院主席○及太平局紳○一九二六年充團防局紳○一九二八年充團防局紳○其在華人團體所任名譽職務○一九二四年○充保良局總理○一九二五年○充保良局首席總理○一九二九年○又任團防局紳○

歷充華商總會幹事○四邑商工總局董事○及台山商會董事○現任中國經濟建設運動會廣東省分會委員○其在商場所任職務○除今任公有源綢緞莊總司理之外○現尚充四邑輪船公司○及新寧鐵路等董事○一生忠厚○人多敬之○十八時已結婚○現有兒孫及昆弟○

Mr. MA TSUI CHIU, J.P.

Mr. Ma is a native of Toishan District, Kwangtung Province and was born in 1878. Having acquired a good knowledge in Chinese literature, he came to Hongkong in his early age to obtain commercial knowledge. At present, he is the General Manager of the Kung Yau Yuen silk piece store which is dealing with piece goods and silk commodities.

Mr. Ma was Chairman of the Po Leung Kuk in 1924 and 1928, and in 1925 he was appointed Chairman of the Tung Wah Hospital and Justice of the Peace, Hongkong. He was appointed member of the District Watchmen Committee in 1926 and 1929 respectively.

Mr. Ma is also a commanding figure in his own community. For many times he was member of the Board of committees of the Chinese Chamber of Commerce, Hongkong.

He is also Director of the Sze Yap Commercial and Industrial Association, and Chamber of Commerce, Toishan.

In 1924, he was honoured by the Chinese Government with the Order of the Chia Ho (Excellent Crop) Fourth Class.

Besides his vast interest in the Kung Yau Yuen Store he is also Director of Sze Yap Steamship Co., and the Sun Ning Railway.

盧仲雲先生

盧仲雲先生○名家裕○以字行○粵之中山縣上
柵鄉人也○現年五十八歲○乃本港早已成名之紳
商也○生有鳳姿○未弱冠○已畢業於香港皇仁
書院○因成績優異○遂將受該書院之聘○充任
教員○惟先生尚有志於商業○故未幾○即辭教
職○就本港德華銀行之聘○活動於金融界○歐
戰發生○德華銀行停閉○遂轉就我國北方京奉
鐵路委辦○二十五年前○再返港○遂晉荷蘭銀行
充任華總理（即俗稱買辦）○當先生服務於該銀
行已滿二十五年之日○故銀行以先生忠誠勤敏
○二十五年如一日○為酬勞獎勵起見○特致

盛大宴會○遍邀中外紳商○以誠先生○故行總
理○即席贈先生以一古而最有價值之時辰鐘
○稱先生以誠實之商業報告及悠久之服務○以
贊助該銀行○其功用極似此古時辰鐘云○同時
駐港荷蘭領事○亦即席贊揚指先生○謂代表荷蘭
女皇○頒賜先生以寶星一枚○故先生不特名溢
於香港○而在荷蘭國○及爪哇羣島各地之人羣
○亦莫不仰先生之

名卷也○先生歷充
東華醫院及保良局
董事○香港政府於
西曆一九二五年○
曹港充郵政檢查員
○職位重要○尚非
為公家服務○尚非
努力○實不易得此

至於其在商業方面○歷充大新公司○嚴口長
安人壽保險公司等董事○裕興昌業有限公司永
遠監督○現款舉充華商總會值理○香港銀行辦
房園主席○港仔公立醫局副主席○發起人都
令人羨慕○而生平見義勇為○當仁不謙○尤為
當世所敬仰也○

盧仲雲先生

Mr. LO CHUNG-WAN.

Mr. Lo Chung-wan is the Compradore of the Netherlands Trading Society, and a very prominent figure associated with the commerce of Hongkong, Holland and the Dutch East Indies.

Born in Chungshan District, Kwangtung Province, he was educated at the Queen's College. Upon completing his education, he was offered a position in that College as a Member of the Teaching Staffs.

His vocation, however, proved to be mercantile, so he resigned from the College and entered the Commercial Circle.

About twenty-five years of age, he joined the Netherlands Trading Society and has become the Compradore of that very large and respectable Banking Institution.

Upon his completion of a quarter century of meritorious service, he was invited to a large reception tendered by the Bank and which was attended by many prominent people of Hongkong.

In a speech made by the Chief Official of the Bank, Mr. Lo Chung-wan's services were very highly eulogized and he was presented with a very antique and costly Dutch Clock. The high official of the bank remarked that Mr. Lo Chung Wan's good qualities were very identical to that of the clock for in as much as the clock had for a long period given very accurate reports of the time and positions of the moon etc., Mr. Lo Chung-wan likewise had been very useful to the officials and clients of the bank by his supply of very useful trade informations and assistances. The Consul for the Netherlands Mr. M. H. van Schroven spoke very highly of Mr. Lo Chung-wan in his speech, remarking to the gathering that in connection with most excellent services rendered by Mr. Lo Chung-wan, Her Majesty the Queen of the Netherlands was most graciously pleased in awarding him with the very coveted and most Excellent Order of the Orange of Nassau.

Mr. Lo Chung-wan was also in the Directorate of the Tung Wah Hospital and the Po Leung Kuk and also enjoyed the confidence of the Hongkong Government in 1925 when appointed to the important position of Postal Censor which position he very capably held and was suitably thanked by the Hongkong Government.

Besides his many important activities, Mr. Lo Chung-wan is in the Directorate of the internationally known firm of Department Stores, The Sun Co., Ltd., operating Chain Store in China and the huge building in Nanking Road, Shanghai. Director of Ngan How Motor Bus, The Kong On S. S. Co., the National Commercial & Savings Bank, and The Wing On Life Insurance Co., Ltd., and is in the Committee of the Chinese General Chamber of Commerce. Mr. Lo Chung-wan is also the Chairman of the Bank Compradores' Association of Hongkong, a very important and potential financial association in Hongkong.

生先雲靄陸

陸靄雲先生○廣東肇慶府高要縣人○現年五十五歲○容貌秀俊○體姿壯健○性情篤實○乃鳥恩倫燕梳公司港行之華經理○亦新任本港之太平局紳也○幼年時○已受良好家庭教育○精長○進培英學校○繼而進皇仁大書院○攻讀英文○勤奮好學○最為師友所嘉許○年十八已升為守規○

誼校第一班學生○西曆一九〇〇年畢業○二十一歲應日本橫濱鳥恩倫燕梳公司之聘○充任委職○繼調充港行華經理○服務三十餘年○其恆心與毅力○殊非他人所可及○在社會享有盛譽○西歷一九三六秋○委充太平局紳○一九三七○充保良局紳○歷任南華體育會主席○現任該會會長○生平樂善好施○忠誠坦直○實近代不可多得之人物也○長女龐婿姑娘曾在嶺南大學○及北平燕京大學畢業○現正日學美國柯力近大學○以求深造○其餘子女○亦受良好教育○

Mr. O. W. LUKE, J.P.

Mr. Luke is a native of Kwangtung Province and was born in 1882. He was born in a well-to-do family which can afford him to obtain a thorough education. He procured his early studies in the Phui Ying School and later he enrolled in the Queen's College, where he left in 1900.

He started his commercial career in 1903 in the New Zealand Insurance Co., Ltd., Yokohama Branch. He did not remain there long, and a few years later he returned to Hongkong and became compradore of the same company. For thirty three years he was employed under the same firm, and his experience, consciousness and ability are valuable assets to the company. His honesty and innate courtesy endear him to all his business associates and friends.

In different times he has been member of the Financial Committee of the St. John's Ambulance and of many other local educational institutions and Chairman of the South China Athletic Association for a number of years. He was appointed a Justice of the Peace in 1936, and Member Committee of Po Leung Kuk in 1937.

Mr. Luke has many children. His eldest daughter is a graduate from the Yenking University and Ling Nam University and she is advancing her studies in the Oregan University, and Merril-Palmer School, Detroit, U.S.A.

何華生先生。廣東省順德縣人。現年六拾五歲。非特為港地名人。亦南洋巨賈也。君少時。家非素豐。亦能奮志創業。成今日之聲望者。實非偶然。德前清庚子年間。君創設瑞昌號於本港水藥街。僅經營銅銀疋頭耳。耀西代售中門，設立會豐商店。國內之通商大埠。皆有何君之商業。旋由國內而推行於國外。於是創會豐商店於星州。開設三十餘年。營業中西經驗良藥。數年間生意進展。遂分枝會豐分號於呱哇，坺嵐。中國之上海等埠。又在江門，佛山哇。設三昌公司於汕水埠。三益公司於孟嘉錫埠。及大世界公司於八打威等埠。營業西藥。旁及入口土洋什貨生意。亦達物非常。何君一生馳驅南北。策劃經營。歷年迫耳順。猶復精神奕奕。於籌營商業餘暇。致力於社會公益事業。亦粵。本港之慈善機關如東華醫院則為總理。於保良局則歷任值理局鐘。在精武會則為會長。在華商總會則為值理。又為何君本邑之順德商務局主席。及連任三屆司庫之職。其熱心公益。久為港地人士所推崇。其哲嗣耿中君。年少英偉。亦曾任東華醫院總理。及保良局董事。寶後起之秀

西藥品。為在港華人藥業之前茅。港僞而營業日進。發行鸚鵡牌各種超良藥。至今歷三拾七年。久已風行於廣東，廣西。與夫南洋羣島，及荷屬之爪吐各埠。瑞昌之名。遐不屆而走。於是努力進邁。設立五洲藥房於廣州。又創五洲藥房於廣西之南寧，梧州，桂林，柳州。廣東之韶關等埠。又於潮安，及汕頭，厦也。

何華生先生

Mr. HO WAH SANG.

Mr. Ho Wah Sang is one of the most prominent business men in Hongkong. He is a native of the Kwangtung Province and was born in 1872. He was not born in a family which could provide him with a thorough education and yet with his vigorous struggles and unwearying labors, he was able to gain a good position in this commercial sphere.

Thirty-seven years ago, he established the Sui Cheong Co., in Wing Lok Street. It was dealing with piece-goods and later it dealt in retailing of drugs and medical products. For many decades, under the able management of Mr. Ho, it becomes to-day one of the most outstanding business house in Hongkong.

The chief manufacturings are the famous different kinds of "Parrot" branch medicines, which are welcome not only in South China but also throughout the Malayan Peninsula and the Dutch East Indies. Branches were established in different important ports to represent its products.

Mr. Ho is not only a prominent business man, but also a social magnate. He has been the chairman of the Tung Wah Hospital: a member on the board of Committee of the Po Leung Kuk, and the Chinese Chamber of Commerce: Chairman of the Chin Wu Athletic Association and many others.

Mr. Ho has many children. His eldest son, Mr. Kung Chong, is a smart young man who has been chairman of the Tung Wah Hospital and director of the Po Leung Kuk.

馮耀卿先生

馮耀卿先生

即一九一五年○美國三藩市巴拿馬世界博覽會開幕○先生充我國粵省出品委員○既沐美雨○復析歐風○從而接近各地廠商○用謀銷國登陸○果能如願以償○倂於今日地位○氏六○卽一九一七年○彼為擴張海外營業起見○乃分設支店於香島○業務進展○史一日千里○柳先生不徒遠有術也○而眼光與思想○均屬超人一等○觀其能改良雅貨中之什器○藤器，葦器等○以博取優厚之代價○從而吾惠桑梓○倅貨苦工人○得免失業○此誠我國際出之材也○柳先生個性音度橫過太平洋○今

馮先生伯塽，字耀卿○廣東鶴山縣人○現年中壽晉七○前香江皇仁書院之尊案生○性聰頴，勤讀書，試輒前列，曾考獲該院免費生序利信學額○今粵港利豐出入口莊之總幹事也○生而岐嶷○少有大志○當恁我國商戰不兢○基於故步自封○傷鄰愈起豆逃○將受天演淘汰○乃舊念以商業救國○遠學成而廣州貨興磁莊甚其村○廷主出口部事○時公元一九零四年也○越二年○先生念資興佳營磁器一案○未足以應外人需求○乃與李君造明另組利豐號○以承其乏○營謀大綱○注重雜貨出口○十二年間○佳著展其長○份偏促如帳下駒○未免逞其身手○馳騁於世界市場○竊以為憾○迨民四，

辯非少壯諳華○獨膺膺長男償償長征○遠遊歐美各國○則其志趣之有異乎人○已可想見○其賢內助林楚貞女士○知書絕學○四德俱全○現有男公子凡五○名漢偉，漢杜，漢興，漢邦，漢彥○女公子凡三○名虎華，虎棠，虎露○均受相當教育○而長男漢偉，次男漢杜，兩君佐父分任粵港要職○年少老成○才長貨長○虎父無犬子○將門無弱兵○信然○強○

Mr. FUNG PAK-LIU.

Mr. Fung Pak-liu is a native of Hok-shan, Kwangtung Province, and he was born in Canton fifty six years ago. He was educated at Queen's College, Hongkong, and after graduation joined the Po Hing Co., in Canton in 1904, as manager in the export department. This firm dealt mainly in porcelain and earthen wares. Under his able management for twelve years, he considerably advanced the prosperity of the firm.

An opportunity was given to him in 1915, when he was appointed as a Committee Member in charge of the products of Kwangtung Province to be exhibited at the Panama Exposition. It was during this period that he visited many famous American and European factories.

On his return to China, he established an Export and Import firm under the name of Li & Fung in Canton, in partnership with Mr. Li To-Ming. A Hongkong Branch was opened not many years after the establishment of the Canton Head Office. This firm proved a success and before long it became and still is one of the most famous business houses in Canton and the Colony.

Married to Lam Wai Ching, Mr. Fung was blessed with eight children. Two of the older sons are holding important positions in the firm, and the others are receiving their education at various schools.

劉德譜先生

德譜先生○廣東省寶安縣人○年四十有九○為作古閩人嶺聲奇島之劉公緒伯哲副○現為本港油蔴地物舶有限公司之總理也○生於豐厚家○而無紈綺習○其慈愛之大才○不屑屑於牽句○以為我國積弱

生先譜德劉

孔聖會值理○中華聖教總會值理○佛學會理○中南中學校董○西南女子中學校董○養中女子中學校董○華商俱樂部會員○華商會所會員○五陵會會員○平湖紀幼勞學校董事長○平湖念婦賢醫院董事長○至商業經營○於主油蔴地物舶公司事外○且任德信銀號董事○平湖城興公司總理○夫人曾文儀女士○蓬於國學○乘出名門○男公子鎮國○年會七○畢業於拔萃男書院○女公子恭儀○年十七○攻讀於拔萃女學校○

退也可知○吾甚其人○嘉其志○尤慶我國商界有此卓犖奇才○故樂為之記○先生忠孝累子天性○早年服勞黨國○曾發中央政府寵錫三等嘉禾章○對於貢獻本港社會○史能善體親心○秉承遺教○前任保良公局值理○港府特委電報檢查員○華商總會值理○現充寶安商會值理○

在乎德貢○慈洽其株○爾業是尚○故僅舉案於育才書社○卻出而角逐於德求第二市場○富奇港華英教育代理物業銀兩有限公司司理○繼乃周旋於我國唯一商埠○充上海昌成洋行司理○中間服務於宗邦革命源地之廣東○任全省酒稅局總辦○少壯特期○已展長才○貽盛譽於拔萃女學校○

於港滬粵○則今日有此地位○其記述

Mr. LAU TAK PO.

Mr. Lau Tak Po is the eldest son of the late Hon. Mr. Lau Chu Pak, C.M.G.

Born in 1887 he was educated in Hong Kong and on graduation commenced his business career as manager of the Anglo-Chinese Educational Co., Ltd.

He subsequently became Shanghai manager of the Hong Kong Mercantile Co., Ltd., where his ability and business acumen greatly assisted the prosperity of the firm.

On appointment as Superintendent of the Kwangtung Provincial Wine-Tax Bureau he returned to Canton.

In 1923 he promoted the Hongkong & Yaumati Ferry Co., Ltd., and became managing director of this important concern.

Married to Miss Tsang Man Yee he has a son and a daughter.

Mr. Lau who is the recipient of the 3rd class Chai Ho, Order of the Excellent Crop is an important member of the Community and amongst other position he is President of the Buddhist Association, Vice-President of the Chinese Confucian Association, the committee of the Tak Shun Bank, the managing director of the Chun Hing Co. in Ping-woo, the committee of the Sai Nam Boy & Girl School and the Yeung Chung Girl School, the chairman of the committee of the Ki Kui Loo School and Nim Fu Yin Hospital in Ping-woo, member of the Chinese Club, the Sports Club and Chinese Merchants Club, a former Committee member of the Po Leung Kuk, Chinese Chamber of Commerce, former Hon. Censor and a committee member of the Po On Chamber of Commerce.

羅文顯先生

生先顯文羅

羅文顯先生〇粵人〇於西曆一八九六年〇生於香港〇父諱長榮〇乃已故著名港紳〇家庭富裕〇故先生得受教育機會較多〇未弱冠〇已畢業於香港皇仁書院〇卽攷進香港大學〇攻讀三年〇於西曆一九一八年華業〇且厚學士榮銜〇學問文攷〇予名德政〇年纔三齡

〇於西曆一九二七年已結婚〇夫人林忠姬女士〇甚有淑德〇現已有子女三人〇長女佩瑛〇次女佩珩〇均肄業於梅芳女校

〇戀遠有無〇磐卷信用俱佳〇一九三四年〇升任渣甸洋行華總理之職〇生平品格清高〇誠怡忱成〇熱心社會事業〇歷充香港太平局紳士〇華商總會值理〇五陵會值理〇洋行辦房聯合會主席〇及廷

薪公
司童
事〇
平時
喜運
勁〇
網球
尤擅
〇故
健兆
健捷
壯健

Mr. M. H. LO, J.P., B.A.

Mr. M. H. Lo is one of the commanding figures in the commercial sphere of Hong Kong.

A native of the Kwangtung Province, and born in 1896, Mr. Lo is a member of a very well known Chinese family in Hongkong, his father being the late Mr. Lo Cheung Shiu, J.P., a prominent and well respected resident.

Mr. Lo was educated at Queen's College and in 1915 entered the commercial Course of the Hongkong University, and left in 1918.

In 1934 Mr. Lo was appointed Compradore of the Princely Hong of Jardine Matheson and Company, Limited. His experience, conscientiousness and natural ability are valuable assets to the firm, whilst his transparent honesty and integrity, and innate courtesy endear him to all his business associates and friends. He is a member of the Committee of the Chinese General Chamber of Commerce and the Sports Club, Director of the Hongkong Engineering and Construction Co., Ltd., and Chairman of the Compradore Association. He was appointed a Justice of the Peace in 1936.

Mr. Lo's favorite sport is tennis. Married in 1927 he has two daughters and one son.

陳鏡湖先生

陳鏡湖先生，廣東番禺縣河南寶崗鄉人。現年三十有八。少懷大志，氣宇不凡。幼肄業於廣州寶英中學。深得校長教員之贊許，而以高材生試必冠其曹。在平常誠于師友，如是四年，而居於信者，仍以誠信鉅賈爲己任。

生先湖鏡陳

Mr. CHAN KENG WOO.

Mr. Chan Keng Woo, general manager of Yat Kee in 4, Lyndhurst Street, is a native of Poon-U District, Kwangtung Province, and was born in 1899.

He acquired his education from the Wang Ying College, Canton, and after his graduation he came to Hongkong and was appointed as General manager of the Yat Kee, a dealer in curios, pearls, jewellery and head ornaments. His business acumen and his ability to distinguish the true jewellery from the false have allowed him to further his business, and to-day Yat Kee possesses a good reputation amongst its line.

Mr. Chan pays an immense interest in sports and athletic affairs. He is Hon. President of the Inter-schools Sports Association, Hong Kong; Chairman of Chong Nam Athletic Associaton; Chairman of the Advisory Board of Chin Wu Athletic Association; and committee of the Poon-U Chamber of Commerce, Hongkong.

Married in 1920 to Lau Ling Sang, Mr. Chan has two children.

顏成坤先生

顏成坤先生○籍廣東潮陽○年三十晉七○美丰儀○優品格○具冰雪聰明○富國家思想○持躬尚道○篤學早見影○建業有方○從商己始於弱冠○吾華之傑出人物也○依早歲曾致力教國工作○追隨孫總理有年○復以革命將屆成功○之港別開發展○時九龍方面○交通事業○尚來晉及○爲造福僑胞計○公元一九二三年○創

廢不以要礙相加○蓋仰慕先生之爲人○而其背靡過也○彼性素更○計前後所居贊劇○有如下列○且其中不鮮熱於處任者也○

（一）體育○華人體育協進會主席○兼任體育會副會長○學界運動聯合會會長○南華體育會名譽會長○第六屆中華全國運動大會名譽顧問○兼香港區代表國總領隊○第十一屆世界運動大會男校校童○英華女校校童○（二）教育○英華書院校童○民生書院校童○汕頭港商義學校童○

（三）教育○中華基督教青年會副會長○香港青年會副會長○中華基督教合一堂主席○

（四）慈善○東華、廣華、東華東院、三院統一首屆主席○廣華醫院顧問○建築東華醫院募款委員○雅麗氏醫院值理○兒童保護會執行事值理○優生學會值理○（五）公益○華人俊備警察財政委員○一切統一院務交集○剛啟有值得表揚者○則當其主席東華三院時代○剛啟

廣州濟時中學名譽校童○

此外更於一九三三年再向香港方面努力建設○改組為香港有限公司○與電車公司分道揚鑣○同人鳥其勇於任事○公推為董事主席○兼監理○而各行商號○與商業機關○無不以大業者○遂爭相延攬○故歷任大光粮館董事主席○嘉華人壽保險公司董事主席○新亞酒店董事○華商總會會值理○湖州八邑商會會童○利思堂畢業生

組中華汽車公司於半島○十載服勞○人咸稱便○至一九三三年○

有值得表揚者○則當其主席東華三院時代○統一院務交集○復遷粵省及華北各地水災○救民數百萬○敕敕待哺○情實可憫○先生病療在抱○被瀾爲懷○立蒙巨款四十餘萬○分送各方賑濟○獲救吳榮○至今稱頌○堪責僑界○特委省太平局紳○以約大衆者○而欲約施政○亦能盃庭○少年老成○堪責僑界○特委省太平局紳及國防局紳○而欲約施政○亦能盃庭○寧非淑配黃女士亦梅○坚約翰敕傷隊值理○○公益○華人俊

體育，教育，教會，慈善，公益，各社團○亦有賢名○

生先坤成顏

Mr. NGAN SHING-KWAN, J.P.

Mr. Ngan Shing-Kwan is one of the most prominent personages in Hong Kong. He is a native of Tsao-Yang District, Kwongtung Province, and was born thirty seven years ago.

He obtained a thorough education from a local college, and after he was graduated, he became a faithful follower of the late Dr. Sun Yat Sen and his service was highly appreciated.

In 1923 Mr. Ngan initiated the China Motor Bus Company in Kowloon, and a decade later he secured the bus franchise from the Hong Kong Government for the whole Island of Hong Kong, and the Company was then re-organized under the name of the China Motor Bus Company, Limited. Since then Mr. Ngan has been the managing director of the Company, and beyond doubt, as long as it is managed by Mr. Ngan, its prosperity reached the apex.

Mr. Ngan is an influential figure in social affairs. He is the chairman of the board of directors of the Tai Kwong Newspaper and Printing Co., Ltd., Committee of the Chinese General Chamber of Commerce, Hongkong; Director of the Chiu Chow Chamber of Commerce, Hongkong; and adviser of the Rice Merchants' Association and the Chiu Chow Residents' Association. He was also the Chairman of the Ka Wah Life Assurance Co., Ltd., and Director of the New Asia Hotel Ltd., in 1934.

Mr. Ngan is also very attentive to the athletic and educational world and the followings are posts which he has held or is holding.

Athletic.

Chairman of the Hongkong Chinese Amateur Athletic Federation, Vice-president and Chairman of the South China National Athletic Association, Hon. President of the Hong Kong Inter-Scholastic Athletic Union, Hon. Adviser of the 6th Chinese Sports Meet and Chief Delegate of the representatives of Hong Kong and Coach of the Foot-Ball team which represented China in the 11th World Olympiad.

Educational.

Committee of the Ying Wah Boys' College, the Ying Wah Girls' School, the Mun Sang College, the Hong Kong Merchants' Free School in Swatow and Hon. Director of the Chai Sze College in Canton.

Religious.

Chairman of the Sixth District of the Kwong Tung Synod of the Church of Christ in China, Vice-president of the Chinese Y.M.C.A., Hong Kong; and Chairman of the Hop Yat Tong Christian Church, Hong Kong.

Public Welfares.

First Chairman of the Tung Wah, Kwong Wah and Tung Wah Eastern Hospitals; Advisor of the Tung Wah Hospital; Chairman of the Kwong Wah Hospital; Member of the Tung Wah Eastern Hospital Building Fund Committee; Committee of Alien Memorial Affiliated Hospitals; General and Executive Committee of the Society for the Protection of Children; Executive Committee of the Hong Kong Eugenic League; Vice-patron of the St. John Ambulance Association; and Member of the Financial Committee of the Hong Kong Police Reserve (Chinese Company).

Moreover Mr. Ngan is a Justice of Peace, Hong Kong; and Member of the District Watchman Committee in 1932.

陳符祥先生

生先祥符陳

陳符祥先生〇粤之台山水南鄉人〇幼讀於鄉〇身修國學〇年十八〇素偏習商〇來港三年〇自覺學歷尚淺〇爲求深造〇念一歲負笈中江〇考進南洋公學〇修業僅一年〇同粤轉考入嶺南學堂〇肄業四載〇輟學後〇再來港經商〇料理退尤及出入口貨〇前後凡五歷寒暑〇嗣由四邑輪船公司〇選派出遊日本〇檀香山〇英國〇古巴〇墨西哥〇秘魯〇智利〇柯根廷〇巴西〇及西印度等處各大都會〇考察商務及航務〇歷時十三閱月〇返港後〇遂蒙季公煜堂上海聯保水火險有限公司〇任總司理〇遠誌二十有二年〇經營銀業〇

民十三〇倡設陸海通有限公司〇任總司理〇而陸海通人壽保險有限公司〇陸海通旅館〇陸海通飯店〇陸海通銀行〇以次成立〇尚港府註冊〇營業獨立〇各有專司〇耀西開設六國飯店〇及礄敦酒店〇以上各種事業〇均賴先生蓋有碩到〇方底於成〇除上述外〇曾任中國郵船公司〇廣東銀行〇新寧鐵路公司〇四邑輪船公司〇平安公司等董事〇其對於各社團〇各學校〇亦肯貢獻〇前任東華醫院總理〇香港華商總會〇四邑商工總局〇旅港台山商會〇香港基督教育年會〇董事或值理〇現任廣州嶺南大學〇香港嶺南分校〇梅芳中學〇西南中學等校董〇先生富國家思想〇有乃父風〇贊勷革命之捐輸〇前後約七千餘圓〇其他依助公益慈善事業〇歷年不可勝計〇當選萬金〇用是名滿國內〇前廣東省長公署〇廣西省長公署〇台山縣等〇咸重其人〇禮聘之爲參議〇先生年十六時〇娶譚氏女爲室〇閱三年〇譚氏去世〇續娶朱氏〇現共育男女九人〇長女齊其〇次女齊華〇均菲華女校高材生〇一適張〇一適梅〇長子伯純〇次子伯紹〇三女梅性〇現已就商〇三女梅性〇讀於菲仁書院〇四子伯昌〇讀於嶺南大學附中〇五子伯騏〇讀於西南中學〇四女梅芳〇讀於飛利科學校〇曾修業英皇學校〇

Mr. CHAN FU CHEUNG.

Mr. Chan Fu Cheung is a native of Toishan District, Kwangtung Province, born fifty-eight years ago.

He was educated in his native village till he was eighteen years old and then he came to Hongkong to practice business. Finding it is difficult to look for a high prospect in this complicate society without a thorough education, he proceeded to Shanghai in 1900 and continued his studies in the Nanyang College (now University of Communication). He returned to Kwangtung in the following year and entered the Ling Nan College, Canton. Four years later, when he left the college, he came to the Colony again and mingled himself in the commercial sphere. He transacted imports and exports and concurrently dealing in exchange business. For five years he was in the position until he was chosen by the Sze Yap Steamship Co., to investigate navigation in the Western countries. A year and a month later, Mr. Chan returned to the Colony and with the co-operation of Mr. Lee Yok Tong, one of the local prominent merchants, he established the Shanghai Fire & Marine Insurance Co., Ltd., where he holds the position of manager up to the present time.

In 1924, Mr. Chan organized the Luk Hoi Tung Co., Ltd., and after its inauguration, he established the following business in successive order:— The Luk Hoi Tung Life Assurance Co., Ltd., The Luk Hoi Tung Hotel and Restaurant; The Luk Hoi Tung Dispensary; The Luk Kwok Hotel and the Nathan Hotel.

Besides the above mentioned, Mr. Chan has been in the capacity of either director or committee of the following organizations:— The China Navigation Co., Ltd., (defuncted); The Bank of Canton, Ltd; The Sun Ning Railway Co.; The Sze Yap Steamship Co.; The Ping On Co.; The Tung Wah Hospital; The Chinese General Chamber of Commerce, Hongkong; The Sze Yap Commercial and Industrial Association; The Toishan Chamber of Commerce, Hongkong; and the Chinese Y.M.C.A., Hongkong. At present, he is director of the Ling Nan University, Canton, and its branch school in Hongkong; the Mui Fong College and the Sze Nan College.

Mr. Chan is an enthusiastic nationalist. He has contributed not less than seven thousand dollars to assist the Chinese revolution, and large amount has been contributed by him to accomplish philantropic and charitable affairs. He is so popular that he has been appointed counsellor by the Kwangtung Government and the Kwangsi Government.

Married when he was sixteen, Mr. Chan has nine children. All of them have obtained good education, and his eldest son is at present practising business in Hongkong.

李自重先生

李自重先生

自重先生○來粵台山人○李公理堂之哲嗣也○現年五十五歲○幼研國學○十載寒窗○年十七○隨其尊人之羊石○實地研究電學於電力公司○翌年○赴日學武○胡漢民○汪精衛等○諸人○結交甚篤○翌年○馬君武○先生亦參與其間○辛丑○王寵惠○鄧慕韓○胡衍鶚○注重○劉成禺○服從三民主義○先後加入中國革命同盟會○叛立廣東獨立協會於橫濱○先生與於癸卯○孫總理開設革命軍事學校於東京青山○先生與於

至於公益慈善事業○其亦不特一二而已○尚義且樂為人之急○其慈念熱誠○人咸敬愛之○所有香港童軍總會主席○華體育會主席○鐘聲慈善社○保良局總理○東華醫院總理各善舉○先生亦熱誠任其事○翕走捐輸○如此者已尚義同胞○德時○嘗倡修築省港公路○公餘之暇○亦請其踐履躬親○其慷慨樂助之熱忱○為數甚鉅○如三四許人○慈念所及○出自至誠○故其熱心社會事業○亦素為邦人所欽仰○壽嚴如山○有子女多人○均中英俊美○品學兼優○他年發展○必有望焉

仲賢等十三人從之遊○銳志研求○留為國用○乙巳八月○奉總理命○與馮自由返國○兩人共宜聯絡港澳等三地同志之資○遵任入會主盟我國以完成革命之機○尚待時而革命志士○皆由香九龍敢進光漢學校○教材教法○在本港九龍敢進光漢學校○希冀步地拓展教育○則任用兵事訓練先生欲推進體育運動○故先生此舉為軍事議員○兵足以自固存已○乃有道有識之士○曾認先生此舉○甚善○自足以為倡○亦樂於贊助甚著○成績於焉甚著○自足以為模○亦有望育才之組織○道有識亦樂於貢獻

配於體育軍訓一道○何吉甫○其權智○勵志為興學○史為興學○有才識○聘先生任○均禮聘先生為校長○率其聘請各校教席○其他各校○如康然取得○粵省微有間言○競心正是聞名○阻止○粵省先生迫於失望而退其軍國民教育之度○當光漢學校退於廣州○同志兩人○先生逃於失望而待辦○癸戌以三月廿○二十餘年○而其軍國民教育之度○攻學營署之役○胡漢民等諸先生○屢任香九龍退○攻學營署之役○伍者攻學營署○菜堆之○其義長度支○生不忍坐視○教育不振○遂以四載教育之俊○均念邦交○故教育清廷○其他各校○均聘先生為教席

水火險素計多所列其非宜廣東保全現欵各從前所倡伊始效力可知其列非宜廣東水火險素計多所列其非宜廣東保全現欵各從前所倡伊始效力可知其列非宜廣東

繼續材料業廣告多所先生在銀行現欵有戲劇○可退出上海聯理之故○司理華共謀政○司理華共謀政○司理華共謀政

營理庫家商會一九二二年極廿四年深湛之本集港當久金華為司庫○营業○营業○营業

廣東經濟學○極廿四年深湛之本集港當久金華

Mr. LEE CHI CHUNG.

Mr. Lee Che Chung is the oldest son of the late Mr. Lee Yok Tong, one of the most prominent personages of Hongkong. He is a native of Toishan District, Kwangtung Province, born in 1882.

He was taught in a school in his native village till he was seventeen years old, and then he went to Canton and acquired practical knowledge in the Electrical Power Co., Ltd., which was initiated by his father.

He proceeded to Japan in the following year and learned the craft of military - training.

At the end of the Ch'ing Dynasty when the late Dr. Sun Yat Sen started revolution, Mr. Lee, who is an enthusiastic nationalist joined into the party. In 1901, he became a member of the Kwangtung Independent Federal Association, Yokohama, which was organized by Dr. C. W. Wang. Two years later, when the late Dr. Sun Yat Sen established the Revolutionary Military Training School in Tokyo, Japan, Mr. Lee was one of the members of that institution.

He was under the instruction of Dr. Sun, and returned to Hongkong in 1905 to ally with those revolutionary members in Canton and Macao.

By that time, Mr. Lee established the Kwong Hon School in Kowloon with the main object to furnish the students with, high education and military training. His object was favorably appreciated by the Chinese community and many schools such as the Tai Yok School, the Yok Ying School, the Chi Yung School, the Ho Kut Po School, the Mok Lai Che School, the Lai Chi School, and the Ellis Kadoorie School, by which he was offered respectively the position of a teaching staff. Mr. Lee returned to Canton and became a student in the Public Medical College, when he was twenty four.

After the Chinese Republic was established, Mr. Lee returned to the Colony and set himself in the business field. He was Treasurer of the Bank of Canton, and later promoted to the position of assistant manager. He was connected with this bank for twenty - four years until it was re - organized in 1936. At present, he is general manager of the Shanghai Fire & Marine Insurance Co., Ltd. Besides this, he has been president and treasurer of the South China Athletic Association; director of the Shui Fung Cotton Co., Hankow; the On Lok Yuen Co., Ltd., Hongkong; and the Hong Lin Life Assurance Co., Ltd.

During the famous Sino - Japanese Conflict in 1932, Mr. Lee contributed a great amount of money to relieve the calamity.

Mr. Lee has many children and all of them have obtained a good education.

聞申嶽先生

聞嶽先生，字申嶽。浙江寧波府鄞縣人。現年五十有六。少時讀書家鄉。繼而學習商業。念一歲來香島。創設恆興成分莊。經營川漢麥縣南北雜貨生意。追

○英倫德孷洋行港行華經理○曹承釺建築中環救火會大樓，卑島酒店○城門石榴背前後兩水塘，及昂船洲大藥庫山洞等處工程。此在本港之建樹也○其於星加坡○廣州○汕頭○各方面○亦有不鮮貢獻○在星洲任丕雷華經理○迪曾承釺港自有華商總會○建築電地郵政局，工務局，及新山水塘建築工程○故星洲海軍港港工場之為總代表馬○為僑港江浙商會出席代表，現任江浙商會主席○

今三十又三矣。前戚以本港為交通樞紐○史自立順記字號○身辦出入口貨業務蒸蒸○大有進展○先生信用昭彰○長袖善舞○歷年所幹俱大事業○卓然可觀○如上海美華銀行港政府股束註冊人配价氏○公于二人○長友麟○字徽俊○從事○旅港寧波泉商公會會長○廣州寧波會館主席○汕頭寧波同鄉會名譽會長○足加城三江會館名譽會長○香港各省客幫聯合會代表○其他等等○不及備述○敘次友麟○字徽明○

香港分局○駐港浙江銀行副理○兼理港政府股束註冊人○德國地亞士洋行軍裝代理人銀業○均頭角峰港○有聲香海也○

Mr. WEN SYN YOAH.

Mr. Wen Syn Yoah, proprietor of Messrs. Shun Kee and Hang Hing Sing, prominent business houses of the Colony, is a native of Ningpo, Chekiang Province, and was born fifty-six years ago.

He received his early education in his own town. When he was twenty-one years of age, he came to Hongkong and established himself in the business field. He initiated the Hang Hing Sing, dealing in drugs and general merchandise. Later, he operated the Shun Kee, dealing in the same particles and imports and exports in addition. Through his perseverance and hard-working, the firms advance to the climax of success.

Through his business career, Mr. Wen has come into close contact with many other lines. He is a representative for the shareholders of the Mei Hua Bank, Shanghai, to register in the Hongkong Government; Assistant manager of the Chekiang Bank, Hongkong branch, Contractor in the construction of the Central Fire Brigade Building; the Peninsula Hotel, the Reservoirs in Sek-lau, Shing Mun, and the tunnel of Ngon-shuen-chow; Compradore of the P. Louis Co., Singapore; Contractor in the construction of the main building of the General Post Office, and the Public Works Department, Singapore; and the construction of the reservoirs in Johore Bahru.

Mr. Wen has been elected as representative for Shanghai laborers in Singapore during the construction of the Naval Base there. He has been a committee of the Chinese General Chamber of Commerce, Hongkong; and delegate for the Kiang-Che Chamber of Commerce, Hongkong, of which he is at present chairman; He is president of the Ningpo Association, Hongkong; Hon. president of the Ningpo Association, Swatow; and Hon. president of the three Kaings Association, Singapore.

Mr. Wen has two sons. Mr. Wen Ching Ming, his elder son, is now managing the Shun Kee, and Mr. Wen Chao Chin, his second son, possesses a good reputation in the commercial field of Hongkong.

生先嶽申聞

香港・澳門雙城成長經典

68

黃省三先生

我國自絕海禁○門戶洞開○趨新慕外之徒○歷不知來是尚○機械物質○肥欲注茲○猶可說也○文化藝術○舍短從長○中魁楚也○依籍廣東番禺○現年五十六歲○品清高○志淡泊○學宗孔孟○日以讀史自娛○衎紹岐黃○惟期醫學濟世○古人所謂不爲良相○亦作良醫○先生讀書得間○殆已三復斯言○抱負不凡○慨然以活國自任○其期許也深○其用功也苦○故卒歲窮○貽名代良醫○港粵○與似卷京滬之陸氏仲安○南北馳映○名重公卿焉

黃省三先生

亦佳事也○若解心異族文明○舉數千年來先氏貽留可貴可珍之國粹○如固有之醫學○如土產之藥材○亦不加愛護○任受摧殘○良足惜己○我國懸壺問世者○且先生宅心慈善○對求醫者○雅重情感○不較酬勞○特捐介自持○不隨流俗○非富貴所能浼○處武所能屈○重視氣節○老而益堅○惟讀書人○能存本色○是真名士○別樹高風○先生之醫術○固值表揚○先生之節操○尤當效法也○縱多不學無術之流○豈乏讀書破萬卷○而代從事三指活人者○黃省三先生，此

Mr. WONG SING SAM.

Mr. Wong Sing Sam is one of the well-known Medical Doctors with Chinese method in the Colony and in South China

He is a native of Poon-U District, Kwangtung Province, and was born fifty-six years ago.

He had obtained an excellent knowledge of Chinese literature before he began to pursue the Chinese medical course. His high talent and great learning have made him very successful in practice of medicine. He has earned a good reputation not only in Hongkong but also in many places.

Mr. Wong is a quiet and wonderful man. He is a man of emotion and generosity, He cannot be possibly hired by money; but his kindness has always made him to give free service to many poor patients. Unlike other Chinese medical doctors, he does not advertise and not even putting on a sign-board. His office is exactly a common residence and no passers-by can know that it is the office of a famous medical doctor.

曾寶琦先生

曾寶琦先生○廣東寶安縣人○現年四十九歲○乃本港安和商號之總理也○父諱展材○原為安南華僑名商○先生幼曾隨父南渡○稍長○四鄉攻讀漢文○十四歲來港○即在堂叔所設之安和號○幫助乃叔營業○克勤克謹○極為各方所信仰○民國三年○乃叔棄世○先生遂任總理之職○除安和之外○另有合股生意多處○

故經濟充裕○信用昭彰○歷任本港華商總會值理○賓安商會委職一九三三年副主席○又因熱心好義○服務社會○故一九三二年被推充任東華醫院總理○一九三三年起港府委充保良局紳○一九三六年被推充任孔聖會副主席○於一二八德受時先生慷慨捐輸○其愛國之心○至為熱烈○而平時為慈善公益○解囊輸出之款○已不可勝計○廿六歲時○已結婚○夫人文氏○生三子四女○長子鏡坤○十五歲○次柱興○十三歲○三洪光○才四歲○長女愛枝○已適陳氏為室○次銀枝○三燦枝○四靈枝○均在港中僑校肄業○

Mr. TSANG PO KI.

Mr. Tsang is a native of Po On District, Kwangtung Province, where he was born in 1888. His father was a prominent Chinese merchant of long residence in Indo-China, and Mr. Tsang was brought there to receive his early education in his minor age. Later, he returned to China and then came to Hongkong, when he was but fourteen years of age.

He began his career with a low position in his uncle's shop. By his exerting struggles and unwearying intelligence he was promoted gradually, and finally, upon the death of his uncle in 1914, he was promoted as general manager of the shop, which at present stands distinctively amongst its line of business under the name of Ah Yung, Shipping and painters.

Besides this, Mr. Tsang is also partner or stockholder of many other firms.

Mr. Tsang is usually highly populated for his kindness and generosity. As long as charity concerns, Mr. Tsang is quite sure to help with his best part.

He is a member of the Committee of the Chinese Chamber of Commerce, Hongkong. In 1932, he was appointed Chairman of the Tung Wah Hospital and in 1933, he was appointed a visiting Justice to the Po Leung Kuk. At present, Mr. Tsang is also vice-president of the Hongkong Confucian Society.

Married in 1914, Mr. Tsang has seven children. They are receiving their education at local schools.

鄧肇堅先生

肇堅先生○百粵南海九江人○年纔三十晉六○乃已故紳商鄧公志昂之哲嗣○鄧天福銀號之司理也○性裏爽任俠○遇有求助者○必不使人失望○故所營商業日興○善於運用金錢時間之損失○在所不計○而對於公益事業○尤盡力以赴○故中西人士○同致敬仰○以為朱稔先生者告○亦競省志青年○開風興起○社會多一熱心人物○即為同群增進無量○先生曩任紙業聯安公會主席○籌建軍款逾三萬二仟圓○一九三五年五月六日○英前

MR. TANG SHIU-KIN

人俱樂部新會所華人義務司庫○建築香港仔兄弟工藝院籌款值理○孔聖會義務司庫○東華醫院籌款專員○研究本港婢女制度委員會委員○任保良局總理○一九二四年○任東華醫院年尊○委充港大校董○一九二八年○任東華醫院主席○及東院基委主任○一九二九年○港府以其精明幹幹○特委為太平紳士○一九三二年○港府委其賢於教育○委鄧志昂中文學院名譽副會長○東華醫院永遠顧問○新界元朗博愛醫院駐港執行委員○雅利氏醫院董事○廣州方便醫院董事○保良局首總理○又崇蘭醫夫人○在本港設萬國婦女會○建設女童軍總會幹事值理○兄童游樂場會幹事值理○孔聖堂義務司庫○童子軍會會長○兼財政委員○聖約翰十字救傷隊財政委員會主席○九龍汽車公司主席○華僑商信託管理地產委員會主席○南華體育會會長○精武體育會會長○宜安焬梳公司總理○新界物船公司司庫○百家利公司董事○新界焬梳公司董事等職○

皇賞以銀禧紀念勛章○是歲十月三十日○史美謀奇代表英國聖約翰救傷隊總部○頒以 The Venerable Order of St John of Jerusalem Rank of "Officer" 勛章○年來港中教育慈善機關○商業鉅肆○莫不以得先生尤任委職為榮○計現任者○如九龍城公立義學校長○梅芳女中校董○香港大學志昂中文學院名譽副會長○東華醫院永遠顧問○雅利氏醫院董事○廣州方便醫院董事○華商總理○赤柱志士提反學堂校董○新界屏山達德學校校長○

三月十三日○貝督夫人代表女童軍英建總會○以其籌款建設 Jaublianda Hut 之功○錫以獎章○紀其籌款建設之功○一九三四年元旦○英建賜以 M.B.E. 榮銜○同時港府委為圍防局紳○又本港創建貝夫人健康院○先生肯捐鉅金○以之倡○為向外勸募○按先生現方少壯○建立事功○當仁不讓○已如上述○想將來造福於僑胞者○史無涯涘也○

Mr. TANG SHIU-KIN, M.B.E., J.P.

OFFICER, VENERABLE ORDER OF ST. JOHN OF JERUSALEM.

Mr. Tang Shiu-kin, native of Kau Kong, Nam Hoi District, Kwangtung, aged 36, son of the late wealthy merchant, Mr. Tang Chi Ngong, is the manager of the Tang Tin Fuk Bank. He is of liberal disposition and generous. He never disappoints anyone who comes to him for help, and even when he has to sacrifice his time and money he does not mind. He always exerts his full energy on undertakings beneficial to the general public thereby gaining the admiration of both Chinese and Europeans. He is enjoying higher and higher reputation in the course of his life. His good work for the community is stated below for the information of those who do not know him. It is hoped that ambitious young men will follow his good example, for every additional enthusiastic worker for the community will help much to promote the welfare of the people.

Mr. Tang was the Chairman of the Luen On Chinese Native Bankers' Association; Hon. Chinese Treasurer of the Committee for the building of the Cheero Club; Member of the Committee for raising funds for the Aberdeen Industrial School; Hon. Treasurer of Confucian Society; Special Officer for raising funds for the Tung Wah Eastern Hospital; Member of the Committee on Muitsai, appointed by the Hong Kong Government; Director of the Tung Wah Hospital (1924;) Director of the Po Leung Kuk (1927) and Chairman of Directors of the Tung Wah Hospital (1928) when he was also Chairman of the Committee for the ceremony of laying the foundation stone of the Tung Wah Eastern Hospital, by the then Governor, Sir Cecil Clementi K.C.M.G. In 1929, he was appointed Justice of Peace, and in 1932, Member of the Court of the University of Hong Kong and Chairman of Directors of the Po Leung Kuk. He was responsible for the contribution of $10,000 for the establishment of the International Women's Club, founded by Lady Southern and a similar amount for the erection of the Sandilands Hut, the Headquarters of the Girl Guides in the Colony. On March 13th, 1933, Lady Peel on behalf of the Girl Guides Headquarters in Great Britain presented him with a Badge of Thanks for the good work he did in raising funds for building the Hut. In 1934, His Majesty the King conferred upon him the decoration of Member of the Most Excellent Order of the British Empire for his distinguished services. In the same year, he was appointed a Member of the District Watch Committee by the Hong Kong Government For building the Violet Peel Health Centre, he took the lead by contributing $10,000, and was instrumental in raising the sum of $32,000. He was a recipient of His late Majesty's Silver Jubilee Medal in 1935. On October 30th the same year, His Excellency the Officer Administering the Government, the Hon. Mr. N. L. Smith, on behalf of the St. John Ambulance Brigade Headquarters in Great Britain, decorated him with the Venerable Order of St. John of Jerusalem, Rank of "Officer".

Educational, charitable and other institutions and commercial organizations consider it an honour to have Mr. Tang among their important officials. At the moment, Mr. Tang is the Managing Director of the Kowloon City Public Free School; Member of the Council of St. Stephen's College, Stanley; Director of Tat Tak School, Ping Shan, New Territories; Member of Council of the St. Paul's Girls' College; Director of Mui Fong Girls' Middle School; Hon. Vice President of Tang Chi Ngong Chinese School of the University of Hong Kong; Member of the Advisory Board of the Tung Wah Hospital; Member of the Advisory Board of the Pok Oi Hospital, Un Long, New Territories; Member of the Executive Committee of Alice Memorial and Affiliated Hospitals; Resident member in Hong Kong of the Executive Committee of the Fong Pin Hospital of Canton; Executive Member of the Committee of the Chinese General Chamber of Commerce; Executive Member of the Committee of the Society for the Protection of Children; Executive Member of the Committee of the Street Sleepers' Shelter Society; Member of the Children's Playgrounds Association Executive Committee; Member of the Chinese Temples Committee; Hon. Treasurer of the Confucian Hall; Hon. Treasurer of the Taipo Rural Home and Orphanage; Member of the Finance Committee of the Boy Scouts' Association; Member of the Finance Committee of the Hong Kong Police Reserve, Chinese Section; Chairman of the Finance Committee and one of the Trustees of the Headquarters of the St. John Ambulance Brigade Hongkong; Committee Member of the Chung Sing Benevolent Society; Committee Member of the South China Athletic Association; Committee Member of the Chin Wu Athletic Association; Managing Director of the Kowloon Motor Bus Co., (1933) Ltd; Chairman of the Directors of the China Merchants Industrial Administration Ltd; Director of the I On Insurance Co., Ltd; Treasurer of the Kwan On Insurance Co., Ltd; Director of the Bakilly Co., Ltd; and Director of the Hong Kong and New Territories Ferry Co., Ltd.

Mr. Tang is young and energetic and is a man of achievements. As stated above, he is never behind others in doing good for the general public. It can be foretold that in his great future he will yet do much to promote the welfare of the Chinese residing in the Colony.

香港・澳門雙城成長經典

72

陳蘭芳先生

陳蘭芳先生○粵之東莞人○現年五十三歲○初在鄉城創立陳泰記號○製造爆竹烟花○行銷國內外○此為先生發軔之始○民國五年○遂蒙港政府特准○在旺角開設廣萬隆公司○獨家設廠製造○爆料花旗，新金山，荷蘭，南菲洲，及南洋

業前途○蒸蒸日上○內地知名省，佛，等城○均有支店設立○仰食者數萬人○合港澳粵同業計之○無出其右者○然先生曾不以此自足○復以振興爆業為職志○發亞電船○行走澳門，石歧，冰使○先生於商務紛紜之下○對於社會公益○如無不為○為無不力○觀其歷任本港東三院總理○華商總○保良局紳○九龍樂善堂童○

○會值理○孔聖會副主席○鐘聲慈善社社長○約翰救傷隊名譽隊長○東莞工商總會副主席，及司庫○党邑東義堂主席○澳門商會值理等職○可謂賢者多勞○

又在旺角以個人名義○創辦義學一間○專收同邑失學兒童○免費辦案○其熱心平民教育○概可想見○先生和平忠厚○樂善好施○遇現方亮歡○擇于千金○毫無吝色○深復社會人士之同情○故能信孚退過○凡所經營○無不一帆風順○成為港中有數殷商○或且稱之為爆竹大王○良非侈效也○

蓑島一帶○烟花爆竹○刷以銷場日廣○求過於供○復在九龍城碼頭角北帝街七十號○自行建築工廠一間○容積較大○常僱男女爆工逾千人○民國十五年○為展拓業務○增設廣興泰，精祥公司○三廠於澳門，廣興隆泰記一廠於佛山○均係撥力鉅地興建○共可容納男女工人四千餘名○至是而規模大備○營

○近出品推銷○且普及哥林埠等埠○

Mr. CHAN LAN FONG.

Mr. Chan Lan Fong, King of Firecrackers, is a native of Tungkoon district Kwongtung province, and was born in 1884. Immediately after he had finished his school days, he started his business career and initiated the Chan Tai Kee Firecrackers manufacturing Company in his native town. As the products of his factory are excellent in quality and cheap in price, they are welcome and purchased by most people in many places.

In 1916 it was granted by the Hongkong government to establish the Kwong Man Lung Firecrackers Manufacturing Co., Ltd., in Mongkoktsui Hongkong. It is the only concern in the Colony to manufacture all kinds of Firecrackers, Flashlight Crackers, Fireworks and etc. Since then his business has become so prosperous, that his products are exported throughout South China, Indo-china, Dutch E. Indies, Malaya, Siam, South Africa, Philippines, United States America, and Australia.

A few years later, Mr. Chan established and constructed a large manufacturing building in 70 Pak Tai Street in Ma Tau Kok District Kowloon city and employed more than one thousand of male and female workers there. With a view of extending his business Mr. Chan established in 1926 the Messrs. Kwong Hing Tai, Messrs. Kwong Hing Lung and Messrs. Jing Cheung in Macao; and Messrs. Hing Lung Tai Kee in Fatshan. All buildings of the above-mentioned companies were constructed with his own money, this keeping busy the wheels of industry and making happy about five thousands of workers. He has also established many branches in many places in Kwongtung province. It is said that more than fifty thousand people depend upon him to earn their livings.

Mr. Chan is very prominent in the community. He has held many important positions in different social and benevolent Associations. He is always generous in giving his money to do charitable deeds and has established a free school under his name in Mongkoktsui Hongkong.

劉景清先生

劉景清先生○籍系粵海東官○公元一八八七年十月五日○誕於本港○年十五○攻讀於西營盤建家書院○(今易其名曰書院)一九零五年畢業○即轉皇仁書院○遂攷得港府官學生○一九零七年○以優等卒業○翀歷充港府清淨局○任太平山症房結詳員○旋服務港府政水師○油麻地警署○新界之屏山，上水，警署等機關遷事○

司自任總經理外○兼任淘甸燕梳公司駐當洋面燕梳○香港火險燕梳○兩公司港局代理○粵行經理○景譽日彰○益為中西人士所敬重○先生素性博愛○贊助公益○慈善○教育○諸事業○廉不力與財俱○如創推善毒之光除○(先生憫倫肥況淪於紅九○不惜屢十數月之光除○而成推善毒會○)熱心教育也○(先生主席港色東義學堂數年宜，欵有徐裕)對於堂科之義學十間○學生五百餘○屢付將助束黨商會貢花籌欵外○並指示其女公子於奂桃

助束黨商會貢花籌欵外○為黨色東義學○東華醫院○孔聖會○貢花籌欵其四次○共籌花籌欵之特准○年中可將款三千金左右○使束義學經常有全埠錦票部主任○又游藝大會錦券部主任○充其如為黨商會南遊服務募捐也○充善社籌欵勁萬金○其至足為人稱頌者○至今猶膾炙於人口○

職省與五年○均能勝任愉快○僉為上游所器重○廣東陸軍測量學堂○暨粵東女子師范學校○聞其賢○恭其材○禮聘之四粵堂英文教席也○先生遂辭職港上○芟身教育界○以結粵貢歉於州人○時間兩拾○復展香港○初受職成以○如安公司○公安公司○萬祥源行○○公泰行各號○公泰洋交涉之責○海英公司○值是一九二二年○海員大罷工○曾為彼此同業建立不鮮事功○甚為各所稱許○然坎坷未得實兩○切池中物耳○今則大展鴻猷足○除劉海洋船務公

生先清景劉

誌為華其服務於各社團所任委辦如下○廉充僑港黨色束義學主席○現任奇港推善促進會會長○僑推束黨工會總會副主席○鏡涛慈善社副社長○約翰紅十字會會董○奇港華僑教育會會董○香港九龍女子中學校董○中華教育會會董○孔聖會值理○華商總會值理○如行中學校董○西南中學校董○領島女子中學校董○志德醫院駐港董事○石龍惠育醫院名譽理事長等○夫人袁氏靜儀○如夫人陳氏趙如○鰛源○女公于奂桃○男公于兆棋○

氏燕貞○男公于兆棋，鰛源○女公于奂桃○

Mr. LAU KING TSING

Mr Lau King Tsing was born in Hongkong on 5th October, 1887, his parents being native of Tungkoon District. He was educated at the Sai Ying Pun Government School (now the King's College) and laterly at the Queen's College, Hongkong. After he had graduated from the Queen's College in 1907, he was immediately employed in the civil service for a period of five years. He resigned his position from the Hongkong Government, as he was offered a post on the teaching staff both in the Kwangtung Military Surveying School and in the Yuet Tung Girls' College in Canton. Two years after he came back to Hongkong to start a commercial career. He was Secretary for foreign business in the Cheung On Rice Guild, the Kung On Rice Guild, the Hoi Ngan Rice Guild, the Man Cheung Yuen Hong and Kung Yuen Hong. During the famous strike in 1922 he rendered efficient service and great assistance to the above mentioned concerns.

Mr. Lau is at present manager of the Hoi Yeung Shipping Co. and Foreign Secretary to the Po Tai Co. (Rice Guild). He is a Representative of the Hongkong Fire Insurance Co., Ltd. and the Canton Insurance Office, Ltd. both here and in Canton for native business.

Mr. Lau is well known privately and publicly for his social and charitable activities. He was for two years Chairman of the Tung Yee Tong Educational Institution which supports ten free schools with a roll of over five hundred students and was also Director of the Tung Wah and Affiliated Hospitals (1936). He is at present President of newly formed Anti Heroin Society, Vice-President of the Chung Sing Benevolent Society, Vice-Chairman of the General Chamber of Commerce and Industry of the Tung Kun District, Patrons of the Hongkong Chinese Teachers' Association and of the Hongkong and Kowloon Chinese Educational Association, Vice-Patron of St. John Ambulance Association, Committee of the Chinese General Chamber of Commerce and of the Confucian Society, Hongkong.

Married to Miss Yuen Ching Yee, Mr. Lau has two sons and a daughter all of them are receiving their education at the Sai Nam College Hongkong.

歐偉國先生

歐偉國先生，粵之中山籍○生於澳洲雪梨埠○封翁諱彬○久商於澳○名利兼收○歸國後○歷任上海先施公司總理○乃我國之大實業家，兼大慈善家也○先生幼承庭訓○品質純良○精長英京○四歷寒暑○新知閱歷○兩有進益○一九二五年，近滬○充上海先施公司前席秘書○學博如先生○當然勝任愉快○第剖難而用牛刀○遲成大器○良駒未逯伯樂○有屆高材○迨一九二九年，為我國金融鉅子總理廖理上海商業儲蓄銀行之陳光甫賞識○聘充該行襄理○以資幫助○是為先生啟身銀行界之始○迨一九三四年，報長上海商業儲蓄銀行香港分行○乃為先生肥卷香爐島之時○一九三六年，香港廣東銀行復業○放時堂事長宋子文，以非得資望高位○整烜験宏富者○充當司理○則業務難期發展○遂擇聘先生任之○羽毛思滿○且千青雲○將見敏布鴻猷○為我僑胞號冲集團放一具彩也○先生責任○謙和有禮○謙悒尚義○酷肖其先人○對於社會公益之勤助○當仁不讓○現被選為香港中華基督教青年會會長○中華慈善會會長○中華聖公會香港粵教區財政部司庫○上海聖約翰大學同學會香港分會司庫○一九二一年，有室○娶瑪利女校女士○曾進學於廣州真光女校○後卒業於港江聖瑪利女校○才德俱備○現有兄女數人○均施良好教育○

○先修業於香港聖保羅書院○繼攻讀於聖士反學校○中英學識○一日千里○將冠○隨父履中江○考進當時最著名之學府聖約翰大學○數年苦勵○三育兼優○畢業時期○街廣學士○一九一八年，回港○即能舒展其長○充先施公司秘書○任職凡三載○一九二一年，調陞先施公司倫敦分行司理○每於業餘○不作○司伶敦分行商業，及財政○計留

生先國偉歐

Mr. DAVID, W. K. AU, B.A.

Mr. David W. K. Au, son of the last Mr. Au Ben, a prominent merchant in China and one of the founders of the Sincere Co., Ltd., is a native of Chungshan, Kwangtung province and was born in Sydney, Australia, in 1898.

He was brought back in his minor years to Hongkong where he took his first studies in St. Paul's College. He did not stay there long and Completed his high school education at St. Stephen's College. Later, he proceeded to Shanghai and continued his studies in St. John's University, where he procured his B.A. degree in 1918.

Starting his business career as secretary to The Sincere Co., Ltd., Hongkong in 1918, Mr. Au was promoted manager of the Sincere Co., Ltd., London, in 1921. He stayed there until 1925 when he was transferred to Shanghai and became chief secretary to the branch there for four years. In 1929, he was employed by the Shanghai Commercial and Savings Bank, Ltd., as assistant manager. Since 1934 he was manager of its branch office in Hongkong. He has been appointed manager of the Bank of Canton Ltd., Hongkong, since it was re-organized in 1936.

Mr. Au is very active in social affairs. He is president of the Chinese Y.M.C.A., and consurrently, president of Chinese Benevolent Association. He is treasurer of Diocesan Board of Finance of the Chinese Episcopal Church, and St. John's University Alumni Association, Hongkong.

Married in 1921 to Frances Louie who is a graduate from St. Mary's Hall, Shanghai, and they have three children.

郭贊先生

郭贊先生○籍原東莞○生長香江○現年三十有四○為已故殷商郭公少流之第二文郎○其慈贊○穎奇才○翩翩風度○矯矯不羣○洞世佳公子也○童年畢業於拔萃書院○繼進香港大學政商科○為志求自立○不甘以分份于自居○一九二四年○毅然報請○供藏於法國東方滙理銀行○任事五載○閱歷洽深○至一九二九年○遂進○任華經理○今日港中華滙業懋彝於銀行界者○贊繁有徒○然以少年大槪如先生者○未易多覯○則足知其人之才智非等閒矣○先生克承父志○對於公益慈善事業○均有效力○一九二五年

○充特務警察○一九二七年○政編為後備警察華隊○服務多年○旋退後○仍任該隊財政委員會義務幹事○兼司庫○一九二八年○任東華醫院及東院總理○精武體育會副會長○一九三三年○任保良局總理○其他如洋行財房聯合會連屆值理司庫○華人游泳會兩屆主席○拔萃書院舊生會值理○三水工商會董事○港大生宿會籌備會幹事○兒童工藝院籌款值理○聖約翰救傷隊會董，及財政委員○保良兄童會贊務，均其歷年貢獻於社會者○先生除為東方滙理銀行推進金融業務外○於溝通香港越南兩地商務○多所贊助○故一九三六年○越南政府特以龍佩寶星○先生遠遊興趣○赤餘有其尊人○一九二六年○曾旅行新大陸各埠○迨來觀贊城舉行之美國一百五十週年立國紀念展覽會○至東瀛三島○荷屬東印度○菲屬菲律濱等處○均曾留遊其間○於新知授益○史形豐富矣○淑配為陳君原伯之女公子○結婚於一九二九年。

郭贊先生

Mr. KWOK CHAN.

Mr. Kwok Chan, a native of Samshui, Kwangtung Province, was born in Hongkong in 1904 and is the second son of the late Mr. Kwok Siu Lau. He is employed as Chief Compradore of the Banque de l'Indochine, Hongkong.

He was educated at the Diocesan Boys' School, and had commercial training at the Hongkong University.

He joined the Banque de l'Indochine in 1924, and was Chief Compradore in 1929.

Mr. Kwok devoted much time to charitable work and public activities. In 1925 during the General Strike, he served with the Special Constabulary, and in 1927 onwards, when the Police Reserve (Chinese Company) was formed, he continued to be an active member for many years. He resigned from the Force, but was asked to act as Hon. Treasurer and Secretary of the Finance Committee of the Company.

In 1928, he was Football Secretary of the Chinese Athletic Association. In 1930, he was elected director of the Tung Wah and Eastern Hospitals and Vice-president of the Chin Woo Athletic Association. In 1933, he became a member of the Committee of the Po Leung Kuk.

Among other activities, he served on many occasions as Hon. Treasurer and member of the Committee of the Compradores' Association; twice Chairman of the Chinese Bathing Club; committee member of the Diocesan Boys' School Old Boys' Association; director of the Samshui Chamber of Commerce, Hongkong; joint Hon. Secretary of the Hongkong University Women's Hostel Building Committee; member of the Organizing Committee of the Aberdeen Industrial School; Vice-president and Finance committee of the St. John's Ambulance Brigade and Association; Hon. Treasurer and member of the Executive Committee of the Society for the Protection of Children; member of the Hongkong University Alumni Association; member of the Committee of the Street Boys' Association; member of the committee of the Chinese General Chamber of Commerce, Hongkong; and many others.

For his untiring effort in promoting business relationship between the Colony and Indochina, the Emperor of Annam conferred on him the Order of "Chevalier du Dragon d'Annam".

He also loves travelling, and in 1926, visited Canada and United States, and visited the "Sesqui-Centenal Exposition" in Philadelphia. He also travelled in all parts of Java, Japan and the Philippines.

張兆棠先生

生先棠兆張

張兆棠先生。粵之新會人。畢業於廣東陸軍速成學校，及北平陸海軍軍需學校。民國十五年，任黃埔軍事政治學校駐理科教官，兼隊長。值北伐軍興○胡充國民革命軍總司令部總理處財政科長。簡軍北伐。而湘，而贛，而鄂，而浙，而蘇。遊歷數省。飛駒抗來，備極辛勞。及國民政府奠都南京。性任國軍總部總理處副處長。旋派駐漢口事。綜故民以前所歷。固一原幹誠信之理財家也。有聲於軍需界，銀行界○質良有效。故民現年四十五。正有為之時。服務於黨國社會之日方長。誠不可多科之材也。

○任慈理分處長。及四集團軍成立。卽任故軍總部總理處處長。軍餉之經其手收支者。凡數千萬。曾依法報銷。交代清楚。不苟分毫。因之極為李公德部，白公健生，所器重。遠廣西銀行成立。與白君志鵬，分任香港廣西銀行副總理。現任充駐行總理○旅港甚○今年復社數年。信券籍空公司西南航妻兼充廣西童

Mr. CHEUNG SHUI TONG.

Mr. Cheong Shui Tong is one of the most outstanding personages amongst the Chinese banking magnates of Hongkong. He is a native of Sun-wui District, Kwangtung Province and was born in 1892.

He was educated in the Military School of Kwangtung and the Munition School of Army and Navy in Peking.

It 1926 Mr. Cheong was appointed a teaching staff in the Whampo Military and Political School Kwangtung, and concurrently he was captain of the main troop.

Later he became an important figure in the Financial Department of the National Army, following the troop went northwards. Two years later Mr. Cheung was appointed Assistant in the Managing Department of the National Army in Nanking, the new Capital. Before long, he was promoted manager of the sub-department in Hankow.

It was not until the 4th National Army was founded that Mr. Cheung was appointed Chief of the Managing Department of the troop. Thousands of dollars of munition were devised and raised by him at that time; so when he resigned from the post, he was highly recommended by his superiors for his ability and consciousness.

The Bank of Kwangsi established in Hongkong in 1930 and Mr. Cheung was appointed Sub-manager of the organization. In the nearest past, he was promoted manager of the same institute.

In short, Mr. Cheung is not only an adept of Financial administration but also a smart man in politics and in military affairs.

簡熾南先生

熾南先生○南海良沙海鄉簡公規初之第五公子也○幼就傅廣州○喜與同學精研典籍○努力上進○常銘勤有功三字於座右○師器重之○及長從父來港習簡○勤樸誠實○敏事慎言○其尊人亦以克家令子目之○識者原不烏其為年少老成也○先生仍持自勗勉之○專心練習○不棄午而對理○於木業已有相當經驗○從

名巷校長○近年農村破產○嘆撗其眉○婦笑于室○先生惻然愛之○盃謀有效之救濟○除盡力賞助外○復導以雙珠之方○使其循序漸進○故鄉農播以復興其業務者甚眾○斯二者先生造福桑梓之功也○民二四年○先生組織榮泰祥有限公司於香港○年當中外各植木料○故購銷木○規模廣大○同人素仰其為人忠實○有識宏遠○舉為董事兼總司理○先生亦不貧泉坐○矢慎失勤○銳力辦事○且待人接物○皆主公正和平○故○尤能推城相與○其對於同素也○業務蒸蒸日上○故民二一年杉木行商會舉為司

使萊萊學子○徒載不輟○鄉人慕德之○乃舉為整理南海第六區小學○聘賢督教○悉除惡習○○慶衍益斯○有此美滿家庭○可謂積厚而流光矣○富後○必以提倡教育為始○遂於民二一年等故碎一介商人○惟國家觀念獨重○常言碎我國於昆仲凡十有二○兄友弟恭○怡然相愛○德配劉氏○現有男公子六○女公子二○祥呈麟趾○于斯可見○先生以年甫而立之人○具此題著才能○其將來發展○正未可限量也○先生理○今歲集本行商會選為正主席○其擁戴之誠

生先南熾簡

Mr. KAN CHE NAM.

One of the most prominent Chinese lumber-merchants in Hongkong is Mr. Kan Che Nam. He is the son of the late Mr. Kan Yew Cho, and a native of Nam-hoi District, Kwangtung Province, where he was born in 1907.

He obtained his early education from a school in Canton, where he stayed for many years until he was employed as an apprentice in his father's Timber Co., in Canton.

His father died in 1934 and the lumber-yards which he possessed were re-organized. Consequently, Mr. Kan was appointed General Manager of the Wing Tai Cheong Co., Ltd. With his business acumen and experience, Mr. Kan advances the business and to-day, the company is reputed as one ___ ___ be most outstanding firms in the Colony.

Mr. Kan is usually very ___ ___ ___ing with social affairs. Furthermore, he is very much interested in educational a____rs. In 1933, he was appointed Honorary Principal of a primary school in the sixth District of his native town.

Married in 1925, Mr. Kan has eight children. Except those who are still young, the others are attending local schools.

謝雨川先生

謝雨川先生

謝雨川先生。廣東番禺縣第一區市橋鄉人。現年三十八歲。思想新穎。體魄堅健。聲譽優良。又香江商場中之表表人徒。

充總司賬之職。及一九二五年。始歷本渠美最時洋行之聘。充入口部華人大寫及總司賬之職。盡忠守職。歷十年如一日。遂於一九三五年。升任華人總經理之職。對於社會事業。不遺餘力。曾任南華育會參事。歷任華人體育協進會執行委員，兼副主席。及華人游泳會值理。棄義務總幹事。加入設會為水泳會員。又充華商總會會員。通濟公會會員。旅港番禺會所水泳會員。歷任對當埠會委員。平生所好。乃游沐一道。無分四季。無間寒暑。堅心練習。故其體能甚壯也。於一九一九年。已與某女士結婚。現已生三子。長廣榮。次廣煁。現在廣州培正肄業。三廣圻。均年幼。待親來港。

生平提倡體育。物也。幼已異凡兒。愛讀書。弗運勁。十一歲。便進香港聖約瑟書院。專攻英文。迨歐戰發生。始返廣州暫住。翌年再來港。蟬進聖保羅書院。時兩屆一九一五年也。越兩載。畢業於聖保羅。英文學練。善為精深。乃進商場。以謀自立。曾在商業洋行。及港兩華洋行。

Mr. TSE YU CHUEN.

One of the most prominent personages in the commercial sphere of Hongkong is Mr. Tse Yu Chuen. He is a native of Pun-U District, Kwangtung Province and was born in 1899. Having attained a good knowledge in Chinese literature, he entered the St. Joseph's College at the early age of eleven. He remained there until 1914, when Hongkong was heavily effected by the World War, then Mr. Tse returned to Canton. He came back to the Colony in the following year and continued his studies in the St. Paul's College. Two years later, he graduated from the institute and entered the business field.

He started as accountant in the Hongkong Trading Co., and later he was sent to the branch office in Shanghai holding the same post. As that position was not the intrinstic destination of Mr. Tse, so he returned to the Colony in 1925 and employed under the Melchers & Co., one of the most outstanding business houses in the city. At the beginning, he was but chief clerk and chief Book keeper of the Import Department. He worked on honestly and eagerly, discharging duties to every satisfaction. For ten years, he stuck fast in the position and in 1935 he was promoted as Compradore of the firm.

His experience, courtesy and industrious management endear him to all his business associates and friends.

Mr. Tse is publicly known for his social activities. He has been a member of the committee of the South China Athletic Association and Hon. Secretary of the Chinese Bathing Club, and executive Committee of the Chinese Athletic Federation. He is member of the Chinese Chamber of Commerce, Hongkong; Chinese Merchants' Association; and Pun-U Association.

Married in 1919, Mr. Tse has three sons.

左達明醫博士

左達明醫博士

左達明醫師。廣東南海人。現年三十一歲。乃留英醫學博士。香港著名醫師也。少年時已倜儻有大志。審語人曰。不

街。然先生猶以為未足。再遊英國攻化甫盧大學研究數年。又得博士學位。D.M.R.E.。近國後。曾充廣州光華醫科專門學校校長。兼任外科及X光線診斷法教授。連充光華醫院院長。活人無

數。卷之者。輒以華陀比擬也。先生於醫術既精妙。在英時當有關於醫術著作。校刊於英國醫生理學雜誌。待諸一

為良相。亦為良醫。初遊學東最著名之嶺南大學。苦攻數載。畢業後。再貨笈英國。進愛丁堡大學。專攻腎科。畢業時已得醫科學士學位。後因服務勤謹。又蒙該大學醫科博士榮，及醫術深湛，

時。近年先生在港組織左氏醫院。昆仲分任。名譽極佳。現任中華醫學會肺務病組委員。夫人劉氏。乃廣州培道女中高材生。現已有一于名維鴻。年僅四歲。而天真活潑。甚可愛也。

士博醫明達左

Dr. TSO TA MING, M.B. Ch. B., M.D. (Edin), D.M.R.E.

One of the most famous physicians and surgeons in Hongkong is Dr. Tso Ta Ming. He is a native of Nan-hai District, Kwangtung Province and was born in 1906. He pursued his early education in the Ling Nam University, Canton, and after he graduated he continued his studies in the University of Edinburgh, Scotland, where he passed his Medical Course with the M.B., CH.B. degrees with Honours, and the M.D. degree.

Dr. Tso procured his D.M.R.E. degree from the University of Liverpool, England.

Dr. Tso has been putting on his own practice since he returned to the Colony and not long ago, he has established the Tso's Clinic where he is co-operating with his brother.

Dr. Tso was president of Kwang Wah Medical College, Canton; professor of Surgery and Radiology of Kwang Wah Medical School, Canton; and superintendent of Kwang Wah Hospital, Canton. He is a member of the Committee in Tuberculosis, Chinese Medical Association. In 1930, Dr. Tso was contributing editor of the British Journal of Physiology in England.

Married in 1932 to Lau Mong Ha who is a graduate of Pui To Girls' School, Canton. They have a boy whose name is Tso Wai Hung and is four years of age.

黃訪書先生

黃先生訪書，號漢生，蔣縣南海人。生而岐嶷，選清光緒壬寅（一九〇二年）粵制軍陶勤宣公模，易廣雅書院為兩廣大學堂（後史政為兩廣高等學堂）。援補生一百六十人，卒業第一而先生年最少。凡百性兼證，已享其印。旣次乙已（一九〇五年）西林岑公春蒞之名。然負通二○名卽粵籍考之已郅新各科學而者然，雖游學預科館之功也。先生復役焉。趙年，是館政組為兩廣方帑得父。

其間。

務滬廣華公學。粵國立中山大學。省立第一女子師範。省立第二中學。大中學。市立第一職業學校。教忠中學。民念中學。游於其門者。和堂春風。〇其游學子。不能校彼一堂。然而先生學子。〇不鋤厥多士。則其其理其精力以刷新百科書教典籍新科書。〇薈萃百教其科學科典籍。〇鍊其生平。則其功此救教教光大而用者文化。〇五先生〇所服務之功力教育。〇（一九三六年）〇而廣與巴馬萬國博社圑。〇如一九一四年。我團參與巴覽會。廣東出品協會聘為教育級設計委員。〇言欲服務教育。〇如一九一四年中華國貨展覽會籌備委員。廣東分會氏十七（一九二八年）中華國貨展覽會籌主任。

委員員。廣東省。聘為出品展覽會籌備委員委員長。〇西湖博覽會展覽籌備委員。〇為廣州市展覽會設計委員。〇為教育品設計委員。〇言其書籍。〇法有『英文前置詞用法』等。英語會話』。〇英文科詞大辭。『英語前置』等洋洋大觀。〇均以先覺自任。〇之研究』。等英文著作。〇話有『英文科之精神文。英語週刊中之精神文。傑作。均以先覺自任。

古高等專門學校。彼繼續下進。至民元華業。南海中學公益女子師範等校教居。然先生念如無涯。增其學問。果也風能傾，四氏氏十五年。（一九一五至一九二六）應上海商務印書館之聘（一九二七年）茹克廣州商務印書館分館副主任。（同時得英文編輯及事務郵撰誠述氏姓。六〇任英文部編輯。兼兩校英語週刊。理〇員克如先生之試管賃所評撰撰六〇為何如耶。

〇均為教育界人。女弟佩珍及女校長夫人辭治陳氏。於師範。壓任母校校長。今仍服務於師範資。若狀若富者。往往夫今公子六人。士安。咸玫詩於廣州市初中以小學幼女士佩珍。〇長於學問孔老之言以家庭教育多方面心之行。〇一有所發明其賢不肖相去。

然此往往在先生從家事。數十年如一日。〇其賢不肖相去。

似此為熱南北江。先生從事教育。數十年如一日。〇為何如耶。

殊。由港學日退而名燄嘌。趙公之歈一敢。〇育才者侗。諸侯者作。〇用之無汋。〇祝管賃所評撰撰六〇理。〇賃克如先生之。

生先書訪黃

Mr. Hanson F. S. Hwang.

Mr. Hwang is a native of Nan-hai District, Kwangtung Province. He obtained his early education from the Kwong Ngah High School in Canton. Two years later, he transferred to a preparatory school which afterwards re-organized under the name of the College of Foreign Languages. He remained there until 1912 when he was graduated.

Realising the advantage of Education, Mr. Hwang devoted himself to the educational circle. He was a tutor in the Sze Mun High School; Nan-hai High School; Kong Yick Girls' Normal School; Sun Yat Sen University and many others.

From 1915 to 1926, Mr. Hwang was employed by the Commercial Press Co., Ltd., Shanghai, as editor of the English Editorial Department. Concurrently, he was instructor and assistant manager of the Commercial Press Correspondent School. He was also a co-editor of the English Student and the English Weekly, both of which were Anglo-Chinese Magazines issued by the Commercial Press.

In 1927, Mr. Hwang was transferred to the branch office in Canton, and in 1936, again appointed as manager of the branch office in Hong Kong

Mr. Hwang held important posts in different exhibitions, such as the Panama International Exhibition; the Chinese Products Exhibition; the Sze Hu Exhibition; and the Exhibition of Canton.

Literarily, he has written four books in English language. Namely, "The Use of Prepositions", "English Commercial Conversation" "Similarities Discriminated" and "How to Paraphrase".

Married in 1919, Mr. Hwang has six children. They are educated in Canton.

馬國英先生

馬國英先生○別號批三○學之台山縣白沙富洞
堡平陸鄉人○父諱經典○次拿大殷商○憤清政
之不綱○富有革命思想○孫總理嘗赴諸埠籌餉
○賴其幫助至多○今過其居○猶見封翁與孫公

樂觀嚴威○用足備受師尊器重○益為桑梓敬重
○民十三○學成辭里○以先覺自任○即鄰辦富
洞學校○充永遠校董○榮鄉塞樹人之基○隨於
是年冬，來港營商○展其抱貨○開設廣找陸金
山莊○自任總司理○果然貨殖多龍○人羨陶公
偉略○交遊日廣○共仰蓁子高風○矧少年得志
○對人態度謙謙○且綠遠世情○辦事徐理井井
○關身市慶○能提
財重義○接近社會
○喜得敵解紛○其
他關於國家大計○
本港公益○靡不謀
恤輸將○量力以赴
○至熱心興學○則
有前台山縣劉縣長
共勵之文○及充名
譽校董於本港南中
中學之舉○各同鄉

社團儀其人○英不倚重○現任廣州台山會館庶
素管理委員會委員○僑港四邑商工總局董事○
僑港台山商會董事○香港四邑物袖有限公司董
事○先生年緣三十晉六○而有此建樹○淘足侍
吳○德配黃瑞芳女士○賢而知書○女錦珠○讀
於港羹中女中○于民鈴○亦賦牡聰慧○前途可
嘉○

合揆之遺照也○先生東性況敦○年少老成○立
身向學○克俊克勤○且能紹述父志○平發靈術
○不因請書時期○精志定國運動○當蚌素台山
縣立師範之日○每贊勖業務於課餘○救國不尚
空譚○力行期諸實踐○有足多馬○馬氏留台學
會○前此未有也○先生開其先河○且主其事○
富洞閱書報社○歷來所無也○先生實居始創○
嘉○

Mr. MA KWOK YING.

Mr. Ma Kwok Ying, native of Toishan District, Kwangtung Province, was born in 1901.

He obtained a thorough education from the Provincial Normal School of Toishan, and when he graduated from the institute in 1924, he returned to his native village and initiated the Lui Tung School. Hitherto he has been Permanent Director of the school.

Late in winter of the same year, Mr. Ma came to Hongkong and established the Kwong Jip Lung, an imports and exports agent.

His late father, Mr. Ma King Tin, who was a prominent merchant in Canada, was a zealous patriot and helped a great part in the building of the Chinese Republic. Mr. Ma Kwok Ying himself is a faithful nationalist and he followed the foot-prints of his father. He has rendered his service to the Chinese Government.

He is a man of broad sympathy and every good cause finds him a willing supporter. He is the founder of the Ma's Alumni Association in Toishan; originator of the Lui Tung Library in his native village; member of a committee taking charge of the Property of the Toishan Guild, Canton; Hon. Director of the Nam Chong College, Hongkong; Director of the Toishan Chamber of Commerce, Hongkong; and director of the Sze-Yap Steamship Co., Ltd., Hongkong.

黃卓卿先生

生先卿卓黃

讀孟氏書○至天之將降大任於是人也○必先苦
其心志○勞其筋骨○餓其體膚○空乏其身○行
拂亂其所為，一節○而知英雄發迹○皆自寒微
○大器晚成○古今一樣○用述黃卓卿先生之事蹟

歲月○及慶多大人事○迄無適閒者○迄託先生
經理○轉瞬售缺一空○誠足驚人○誠足驚人也
○近世有稱之為南中國木業巨擘者○殆指此也
而彼不以利就名成○沾沾自滿○前後創設
黃榮記機器鋸木廠於港澳粵各地○計達八九家
○中英政府，與各大商行，興築宏偉工程○如

別工夫○獨極力研求○以臻獨到○

○以投亞聖之名言○先生字卓卿○粵之順德籍
山人也○年登花甲○唐衍盆斯○生性聰明○綽
鋁不露○少年英俊○壯志從商○初，隻身來港
○進九龍貨倉○任管理之職○守法奉公○不取
○小位○克俊克勤○深得上峯與社會人士器重○
○有才有識○很速西人木商某氏無育○隆會風雲○
○將時則駕○羨某商積存巨量木材○曾廉不售○

集木行商會主席○建造行商會主席○黃族聯親
會主席○尖沙咀街坊學校校長○德明中學校董
等○聞不日更由其個人捐辦黃卓卿義學一所於
尖沙咀附近○以嘉惠失學之貧氏子弟○最近又

於公益贊助○恆具熱誠○教育提倡○尤為盡力
壓任廣華醫院總理主席○杉
木行商會主席○

祖國言○若北平之頤和園
○暨各省之鐵路○在香江
言○若工務司署○九廣鐵
路○各大船塢○九龍倉橋
○招商局碼頭○上海滙豐
銀行香港分行等○可知先
生經有經驗○所選皆美木
良材矣○洵七迢顧○歡案
宏開○先生之志願能償○
而先生之功業亦爰艾也○欲

採用木料○非先生之商店
莫屬○舉其犖犖大者○在

秋妻先保良局總理○其譽譽可見矣○

Mr. C. H. WONG.

Mr. C. H. Wong is one of the prominent merchants of Hongkong who has achieved success through combats against hardship and difficulty. He is a native of Shun Tak District, Kwangtung Province, and was born in 1877.

He was not born with the proverbial silver spoon in his mouth and therefore could hardly procure a thorough education. When he was but a boy, he was employed in the Kowloon Godown and Wharf. He stayed there for many years and later he began his activities in the lumber line.

A certain European who was manager of a lumber firm had a stock of timber, which he could not find a patron to purchase the lot. Consequently, he confided the matter to Mr. Wong, who showed his business acumen with the fact that the stock was entirely sold out within the shortest span of time.

Since then, his name began to spread in the commercial sphere. Mr. Wong has established, under the name of Wong Tong Kee, altogether nine Saw-mills in Hongkong, Canton and Macao.

Many of the magnificient structures in Hongkong and in China were contracted or supplied by Mr. Wong. Such as the I-Ho Yuan Garden in Peking, which was to be frequented only by the Royal Family of the Ch'ing Dynasty before the Chinese Revolution; the Rail-roads of various Provinces in China; the building of the Public Works Department, Hongkong; the Rail-road of Kowloon Canton Railway; the various famous Docks; the piers of Kowloon Wharf; the Wharf of China Merchant Navigation Co; the gorgeous edifice of the Hongkong & Shanghai Banking Corporation; and many others.

Mr. Wong is Chairman of the Kwong Wah Hospital, Chairman of Fir Merchants' Association; Chairman of Lumber Merchants' Association; Chairman of Chinese Contractors' Association; Chairman of Wong's Club; Principal of the Tsim-sha-tsui School, Director of Teck Meng College, and member of Po Leung Kuk Committee. Mr. Wong has proposed that in the nearest future a free school will be established with his own expenses.

香港華人名人史略（一九三七）

蔣法賢醫師

DR. F. I. TSEUNG

法賢醫師○港故商蔣銘波哲嗣○蔣廣東新會人○生長於香港○行年三十有四○誕應天泉○早有神童之目○曾肄業於育才書社○繼肄業於立仁中學○旋攷港大○以才華卓絕○將廣東省府學額○骨校割醫○性既聰明○志尤篤學○計其在立仁及港大肄業期間○成績優異○獲奬甚多○如庇理羅士，佐頓，何福等學額○其最著者也○民十四○卒業於港大○廈內外科醫學士銜○隨尤國家醫院○為安得臣教授助手○任故職十八閱月○對於生理化學及糖尿病○有高深之研究○曾著有「生理化學檢驗對於糖尿病診斷及治療之重要」一文○當供破國家醫院時○兼應付門診部○日常陷症○便逾百人○查遷後○卽在港開業○仍以糖尿病及理化學等科○展其特長○民廿三○環遊世界各國○觀摩醫學○益求深造○曾在愛爾蘭威爾遠醫院○倫敦醫院○陸律立后屋科醫院○兒科醫院○及奧京維也納醫院等處實習○回港後○卽與胡惠德醫師合作○趙公之暇○致力於社會慈善公益事業○尤具熱心○為普及公衆衛生及預防方法○伕人人有醫學常識起見○常在青年會，及擂音台演講○富任救中華醫學會及聯青社時○貧責與男女青年會聯合○組殘全港健康運劫數次○遊在聯育社舉辦衛生教育研究班○訓練人才○倖賢指導傷肥日常衛生工作之責○復與同志辦新界贈醫會○歷任表楊司理兼司庫○遊故會與坐約輸教傷限合料成堅約輸新界贈醫會○又充司理○且加入教傷限為永遠會員○又義務醫官○一二八滬戰時○曾參與組織香港滬戰救護團○並任故團義務秘書○最近在華人慈善會指導之下○對於我

經及從生工作○極力提倡○蓋醫師不特為故會瓣科○且現任司理兼義醫師也○他如宿會義務工作等○無不竭力參加○計醫師服務于各社團者○有如下述○中華醫學會水遠會員○倫敦英國醫學會會員○倫敦醫學會會員○中國太平洋學會會員○歐美日學生會會員○香港扶輪會會員○曾任港大醫學會德士學校代表及幹事○又遠任三屆義務司庫○港大俱樂部幹事○香港中華醫學會副會長一次○義務司庫兼義務○英國醫學會奇港分會四屆理事○為普香○中華醫學會奇港支會秘書兼會計○民十九○港府委充醫務管理局員○兩屆共六年○又是年至民廿三○任柬華醫院局員○香港教港聯育社艒科人○一任幹事值理○三任副社長○四邑工商總局董事○現任新會商會童事○華商總會值理○商業通濟公會三屆副會長○鐵慈慈善社名譽董事○大埔農化孫兄紀念副社長○奇港中華醫學會理事○女青年會義務醫師等職○奇伕代表選舉開票監警員○西南中學○及聖保羅女校校醫○女青年會等職○均龍歷著賢勞○醫師公餘○不事剛應○或博覽中西文學○或作戶外旅行而已○

× × × ×

Dr. F. I. TSEUNG, M.B., B.S. (Hong Kong)

Dr. Tseung Fat Im (prefers English rendering F. I. Tseung), was born in Hongkong in 1903. He received his early education at Ellis Kadoorie School and later at Queen's College. In 1920 he passed his Matriculation Examination and entered the University of Hongkong with the Canton Government Scholarship studying medicine. Both at Queen's College and at the University he had received numerous prizes and scholarships notably the Belilios, Jordan and Ho Fook Scholarships. He graduated from the University in 1925 with the degree of M.B., B.S. He was then offered the post of Clinical Assistant to the Medical Unit working under the late Prof. Anderson at the Government Civil Hospital for a period of eighteen months making a special study of Biochemistry and Diabetes Mellitus and had written an article entitled "Diabetes Mellitus—The Significance of Bio-chemical Tests in its Diagnosis and Treatment." At the same time he was in charge of a large morning out-patient department at the Government Civil Hospital. Since vacating that post he had devoted himself to private practice specialising in Biochemistry and Diabetes. In 1934 he had a world tour visiting medical clinics in Europe and America and also had postgraduate study in Rotunda Hospital, Dublin, London Hospital, Queen Charlotte's Maternity Hospital and Infant's Hospital, London and also in Vienna. Since his return to Hong Kong he entered into partnership with Dr. Arthur W. Woo.

Besides his attention to medical practice Dr. Tseung is well known in all societies and philanthropic organizations in which he invariably serves either as executive officer or committee member.

Realising the importance of mass education in Public Health and Preventive Medicine in China, both at the Hongkong Chinese Medical Association and at the Y's Men's Club he was actively responsible for the organization of Health Campaigns in conjunction with the Chinese Y.M.C.A. and Y.W.C.A. and under the auspices of the Y's Men's Club he was responsible for the organization of a Health Education Class, for the training of a group of intelligent young men to give periodical health talks to the masses. So enthusiastic was he in this work that his lectures were frequently heard either at the Y.M.C.A. or at the Hong Kong Broadcasting Station.

In 1930 when the New Territories Medical Benevolent Society was formed he was one of the founders and Hon. Secretary and Treasurer until the amalgamation with the St. John Ambulance Association to form the St. John Ambulance New Territories Medical Benevolent Branch and is still now Joint Secretary to the latter. He is also a life member and Divisional Surgeon of the St. John Ambulance Association and Brigade.

In 1932 during the Sino-Japanese trouble at Shanghai he was one of the organizers of the Hong Kong Medical Relief Committee and served as its Hon. Secretary.

In 1926 he was graduate representative and for three terms he was Hon. Treasurer of the Hong Kong University Medical Society. He was for three successive terms Hon. Secretary and Treasurer and once Vice-president of the Hong Kong Chinese Medical Association and is at present serving as a member in its Council. He had served at the University Club and Hong Kong University Graduates' Association as a member of the Committee. For four successive terms he has been serving as a member of the Council of the British Medical Association, Hong Kong and China Branch representing the Chinese. He was Hon. Secretary and Treasurer of the National Medical Association of China, Hong Kong Branch. He is a life fellow of the Chinese Medical Association, a member of the American Medical Association of Vienna and also a member of the Fellowship of Medicine, London, England.

In 1930 he was appointed by the Hong Kong Government as a Member of the Medical Board, which post he has held for two successive terms of three years each.

From 1930—1934 he was Hon. lecturer to the nurses at Tung Wah Hospital and for three years he was himself financially responsible for the running of a free medical clinic under the auspices of the Chinese Buddhist's Association.

He was a charter member of the Y's Men's Club of Hong Kong and has been continuously serving for five years on its Board of Directors, having been once its Director, three years its Vice-present and now its President.

In an honorary capacity he serves as Physician to the Si-Nan College, St. Paul's Girls' College and Chinese Y.W.C.A.

Outside his medical sphere he serves as a member of committee in various local organizations such as the Sze Yap Commercial and Industrial Association, Sun Wui Commercial Society and lately was appointed to the General Committee of the Chinese Chamber of Commerce. He has been for three terms Vice-president of the Chinese Merchants' Association, a post which he is still holding. He is an Hon. Director of the Chung Sing Benevolent Society and also assistant secretary to the Tai Po Rural Orphanage.

Recently at the Hong Kong Oversea Chinese Election of members for the coming National Congress at Nanking he was appointed one of the supervisors for the voting papers.

Incidentally it may be mentioned that he is a member of the Euro-American Returned Students' Union, a member of the China Institute of Pacific Relations, and also a member of the Rotary Club of Hong Kong.

He has many other public activities notably Volunteer to the Hong Kong Street Sleepers' Shelter Society etc. Besides his busy practice, Dr. Tseung has devoted most of his spare time in social and charitable works.

He is still single and his hobby is hiking and reading, as well as collecting of old Chinese literature.

陳鐵一先生

MR. CHAN TIT YAT

梅芳中學校長陳鐵一先生。廣東番禺縣人。年縂三十八歲。一身備歷前，粮，軍，政，學，五途。各有建樹。曾享盛名。誠多藝多才之士也。先生平受良好教育。弱年畢業於本港聖保

羅書院。文在商界。有為到銀。卽有鐵之號。嘗辦水怡昌瓜哇糖压。經營兩載。兼任新聞界編輯一年。復歷充奇闢有限公司華人縂經理。及華南茶業公司縂經理。泰山人壽保險公司。及宏利公司華南縂經理等職。交遊日廣。信用日怒住。社會人士恒以年少老成稱之。先生篤於學。持棗越年之餘。糟不勝讀。日必抽暇兩小時。以從事於揣摩政治經濟等書。對於

孫縂理遺敎。尤有心得。民十二。入國民黨蔣。民十五。衆本港衆工風潮。乃近廣州。開始政治活勸。復大著遠登子推擧。贊措乃不起於人口。長以先生對於國家貢獻。不作浮浮泛泛之語。讀者堅約翰眼港難。兼第一屆主席主任。奇港華僑敎育會創科人。兼第二乃心儀其人。均有慕前輩之懇。時長廣州公育會創科人，兼第二安局者。為錢大鈞先生。仰先生幹練精明。育會主席。全港學度祝敎師敎沈之才。認為不易得之才。特聘之任敎局機要三四屆執行委員會主席。先生嗜游泳。

秘書。以資贊助。迨衆（贊習中西各術八載警備司令。亦請參保司章）。日本武士道柔術而已。復髹）。擅時樹。而於人科學。持統學。病理學尤令部機密工作。及錢氏有特別專長。曾在京滬粵各地監徵考犯任北路縂指揮。領兵北理學。及在各大醫院考案病理學。伐時。復髹遠指揮部機某名領敎者不少。一級品評。均無效服委秘書。運籌凱慨。決學之博可可知。民廿五。我國政府擧行第一至民十七。其遂梼陳耀國民代表大會選擧奇港特別區代表。先生將獲永先生。長國民革命第大多數公民擁衆投衆還擧區代表人。勝千里。君與有力焉。堊更。及歷任各社會工作具有成績。蓋非一軍。春念長才。電召推荐若此。乃選衆結果。成績不殊。蓋至兩名北上。委駐粵軍旅長。望重。卽公民旅長。及廣州行歸。寶續求可保敎耶。先生與吳献坤女士（梅經理處辧公處上校主所居為。乃聘任一敎育家。馬將德高芳女中學校長）結婚於民十二。卽公元一九二任第一軍對埠留守主任。張港警備司令部參三年。璧合珠聯。尤稱佳偶天成。現育有女三鎮。武漢警備司令部參謀長。均能勝任愉人。長女支虹。現年十四。長于萬崇五歲。次快。先生更身軍旅。歷任多年。追入政途。亦于萬崇。先虹則非業於梅芳女子中學初中摩繁缺。如廣東廣州市公安局秘書。兼特務委部。兩于則俱肄業於梅芳幼稚園。員。英德等縣縂經理等職。清化佛區保衛局局長。南韶連韶處處長。上海市公安局特務委員等。可知干前其邪。固無往而不利也。先生創梅芳中學男校於香港。立己立人。久旱衆

Mr. CHAN TIT YAT.

Mr. Chan, born 1901, is a native of the Pun-U District, Kwangtung. He is one of the most famous and popular Chinese gentlemen now in the colony.

After receiving a high education, he began his business career. He first managed the Wing Yee Cheong Co., dealing in Java sugar. Then, for a year, he was editor of a news-agent. After this, he became, in different times, the Chinese manager of the Hong Kok Advertising Co., Ltd., General Manager of the South China Investment Co., and Manager of the Hongkong branch of the Tai Shan Life Insurance Co., (Shanghai).

However, Mr. Chan was still not contented with his success. He was regularly devoting an hour or two every day to improve himself by reading books on politics and economics and the teachings of the late Dr. Sun Yat Sen.

In 1923, he became a member of the Kuomintang, and during the General Strike in 1926, he went to Canton where he began his political activities. Though unknown to the people there at first, he soon attracted much attention by his wonderful articles appearing in different newspapers giving his views concerning the Strike and the chaotic political conditions of the country.

Meanwhile, Mr. Chien Ta Chun, the then Commissioner of the Bureau of Public Safety at Canton, came to know of the rare talents and ability of Mr. Chan and at once made him his private secretary. Then Mr. Chan gradually became known to many political and military magnates of the country especially when his brother-in-law, Mr. Chan Chi Cheng became the General of the First Revolutionary Army. He was therefore afterwards transferred from one important position to another which he filled with credit and satisfaction.

In recent years, Mr. Chan came back to Hongkong and devoted most of his energy to the work of education. He is now the Headmaster of the Mui Fong College, which under his able management, is rapidly becoming one of the most famous schools in the colony.

Mr. Chan is a man of broad sympathies, and every good cause finds him a ready and willing supportor. He has been the Committee member and Scout Master of the South China Athletic Association, Committee member of the Pun-U Chamber of Commerce in Hongkong, and the founder, and Chairman for the first year of the Supervising Committee and Chairman for the second, third and fourth years of the Executive Committee of the Chinese Teachers' Association. Besides these, he is also a member of many other social organizations.

Mr. Chan is skilful in swimming, Chinese Boxing, Jujitsu and riding, besides being an expert in palmistry and Phrenology.

Very recently, Mr. Chan was nominated by the Chinese Community of Hongkong for the election of delegates for the First Congress of China to be held in the near future.

Mr. Chan married to Miss Ng Man Chee, headmistress of Mui Fong Girls' College, in 1923, and he is now the proud father of three children.

吳敏墀女士

敏墀女士。粵之高要縣人。為遜清御史吳柱丹孫輩之第三女公子。陳君頷一之夫人。亦即梅芳女子中學校長也。現年剛不惑。幼已秀髦過人。且篤於學。風聆庭訓。具有師承。早有不

柱。不亞鬚眉。會乃兄配慕烈士。承　孫總理革命工作。由德學成歸國。創造魚需及炸皆。參加復患國運之淪亡。殉致於廣州。遂創梅芳學校於香港。呂為吳烈士紀念。覺精頷乃兄之隆緒。勞於任事。亦呂仲生平之素願。女士為人志苦而行專。

漢，余仕棠，鍾佐廷，林永芬，蕭吉琳，陳樹棠，郭占南，麥寶梯，陳泉和，李宗濂，胡耀賢，黃新彥，何世金等。當分任校董。且現已獲香港伽校向教育部備案董員會成立。復將南華款委員會及中華文化基金會撥時高中部物理儀器全套。彌值敘千元。賞開香港伽校受該會獎勵之先河。敘近退行籌建新式校舍矣。女士於百忙中。史拘開料理社會慈善事案。曾任南華會女子部正主任。○香港教員聯會主席。及育青年會少女團主席。籌建香港孔聖堂委員。現任香港華伽教育會執行委員。南華會女子部學務主任。香港反對蓄婢會值理等職。○一二八之役。組織校員生組義勇軍出動救護傷兵。女士開愛。即分遣該校教傷隊及敘護傷生出勤救護為各慈善圍體光。且撥校舍一部以收容難民。組織傷應以籌醫藥。著理港督修頓夫人特賜以大銀杯一座。劉公嗣志私四字紀念之。○女復提供應。尤喜寫育。○高奇華先生曾囑索乙幀。則女士之畫學深造可知。其刻苦耐苦為該校也以梅名。○站本此志。而女所以起其創科學校也以梅名。○女士為增益見及發展校務起見。敘近又橫渡太平洋赴其國致容。行見其將觀摩所得。為我國教育界增幸福焉。

敘品耐劳。擬其創梅芳女中至今二十載。不足之時。復課恐出其私篋以奔之。不足則出就校外教席以挹注之。○卒能如願昌償。○創科之初。學生不過七人而已。○或逸經常不能維持。環境惡劣。呂人事羞。及中經一度工湖之影○○四次遷校之折屈而復呂成績優越。遐年增加至五百餘人。○校舍由斗室而至巨廈。○學級由初小而至高中。且業科幼稚園馬。○時至今日已料高中華業第六屆矣。○其設備之週詳之歐密。蔚為粵島女校冠。○我黨圍委人坐本港名先生曾面索乙幀。則女士之畫學深造可知。○創科學校也以梅名。○站本此志。而女所以起其流。○嘉女士之能廣育人才。○無不樂為助為。如李明揚，孫科，朱家驊，孫哲孫，陳耀承，胡文虎，葉恭綽，郭幼廷，周琢年，鄧肇堅，洪興錦，陳行祥，賴際熙，岑光樾，溫商，李耀

柳進士之日。再求深造。負笈甲江。呆呂成績最優華業於啓秀甲西女校。今人妹羡女士之博學多才。飲乾為科偷表半。史誚何衫兩件天揭厚。寧知女士今日有如計遠就。學之師。敘恤乎憂圍之損疾。矯於母教之不健全。○審諸人生不幸而為女子。以芊躬之軀而守土。龍救千戈而守土。亦嘗偬教育呂救亡。志氣之不

MISS NG MAN CHEE

Miss NG MAN CHEE.

Miss Ng Man Chee or Mrs. Chan Tit Yat is the third daughter of the later Dr. Ng Kwai Tan, a high official of the Ch'ing Dynasty. She was born thirty nine years ago in the Ko Iu District of Kwangtung.

After receiving her early education in her native village, she went to study in Shanghai where after some time she graduated from one of the most famous schools.

Miss Ng's ability is a great source of envy to many of her friends but it has been due to the many years of hard work and concentration while she was at school.

She realised very clearly the fact that in order to become helpful wives, good mothers and useful citizens of the society, a lady must possess a good education to help her along. With this point in view, Miss Ng, after equipping herself with the necessary knowledge, cherished the idea, even at her early age, of establishing a school where she could help others by giving them an adequate education. Just at this moment the death of her brother, the late Mr. Ng Pui Ki, who sacrificed his life while serving his country, still more strengthened her resolution to carry out her dormant idea. Thus in 1917, she established the Mui Fong Girls' College with a two-fold purpose in memory of her late brother and to offer the Chinese girls a new home of education.

The college was but a small one at the beginning, but Miss Ng spared no effort to make it a success. After many hardships and struggles, she has succeeded in keeping it running for nineteen long years and making it one of the best Chinese Schools in Hongkong to-day. Under the able management of Miss Ng, the college has won the confidence and respect of many prominent persons in Hongkong, in China and elsewhere. With the ready help of these prominent persons the Board of School Directors have proposed to erect a new school building, and the girls students will find a most up-to-date school in the Mui Fong Girls' College before long.

Outside the school, Miss Ng is very keen in social activities. She has been taking part in many different social organizations and is at present member of the Supervising Committee of the Chinese Teachers' Association, Superviser of studies of the Ladies Division of the South China Athletic Association and Committee Member of the Hongkong Anti-muitsai Society.

She has a kind heart and takes a keen interest in the welfare of her fellow being. To the sufferers of the destructive storm at Swatow and of the horrible Sino-Japanese Conflict at Shanghai, she gave her assistance heartfully. When the disastrous as Tank explosion happened in Hongkong in 1934, Miss Ng immediately sent out her school Nursing Division who were the first to arrive at the scene to take care of the wounded people. She also took a number of the poor sufferers back to the school and supplied them with food and clothes. She fully deserved the beautiful silver cup which Lady Southern presented her as a reward for her kind and ready assistance. She has sailed for America to investigate the system of education while this biography is written.

林銘勳先生，原籍粵之新會蘆涌牛環。生文於香島。現年三十五歲。乃我國體育界之優秀份子。而本港九龍汽車公司之主要人物也。第聰明性覺。饒尚武精神。長讀於皇仁書院。數年

生先勳銘林

書一席相邀。先生雖年少而材多。惟方竟顯。游刃有餘也。共和公司，因營業不前。竟方開歇。乃專心效志服務於九龍公司焉。時半島地方建設。任具雛形。交通事業。未臻發達。故九龍公司之辦始也。屬於試辦。規模甚狹。迨一九三三年，公司改組。且爭得港府批准專利之權。先生乃膺任總秘書。主持一切。以遠於今。彼素擅運動。對於球類。游泳。御車，操舟。技術。素加研究。廢一不精。復肯獻身社會。擔任各捷球隊青年會籃球隊隊長。奇港足球總會之東方體育會代表。南華體育會籃球隊隊長。五陵會主席。華商總會值理等

苦幹。三育並進。於一九二零年華業。卽業學從商。初就礦於港環球保險公司。當打字員。鑽研大眾輪船公司。充任書記。閒歷日深。學誼益富。華美實業公司。受其才能。聘掌文案事務。九三年之久。後應其友鄧君次乾之約。組共和汽車公司。遂代理企理士他公司之汽車。合及其附屬應用品。同時九龍汽車公司。亦以設

先生富國家觀念。無時而不切齒於外敵侵略。以祖國空防辦弛。飛行人材缺乏。不惜自購一概。痛下苦工練習。捨偏見請實事。救國不尚空譯。淘不愧今之志士矣。先生於一九二五年。與畢業廣州柔濟醫院之吳雅英女士結婚。現育子女各二。長男肄業廣州嶺南大學香港分校。餘亦在求學中。

Mr. LAM MING FAN.

One of the most prominent merchants in Hongkong is Mr. Lam Ming Fan of the Kowloon Motor Bus Co., Ltd. He is a native of Sun-Wui District, Kwangtung Province, and was born in 1902.

He obtained a thorough education from the Queen's College, where he was graduated in the year 1920.

Mr. Lam began his business career with the post of a typist in the Liverpool & London & Globe Insurance Co., Ltd. A few months later, he worked as a steno-typist in the Admiral Line. He attached to the post for about two years and then turned out to work as Correspondent in the Hongkong Excavation Pile-Driving & Construction Co., Ltd., (formerly Chino-American Industrial Developing Co.)

Three years later, he resigned the post and co-operated with Mr. C. K. Tang and established the Republic Motor Co. of China dealing in Motor Car accessory parts and representing products of the Chrysler Motor Co. The firm did not prove a success to Mr. Lam and a few years later it was closed.

In 1920, the communication of the Kowloon Peninsula was not so well developed. Though the Kowloon Motor Bus Co., had long been established, it possessed only a narrow scope. Mr. Lam was secretary of the company then. After his own business proved a failure, he devoted his main interest in the latter. Until 1933, when the company re-organized and procured the monopoly from the Hongkong Government, Mr. Lam began to put into action his scheme of improving and expanding the business. To-day, the prosperity of the firm reaches the climax.

Mr. Lam takes a great interest in sports. He has been Captain of those famous basket-ball teams such as South China Athletic Association and the Chinese Young Men Christian Association. He likes swimming, and such like games. His interest in aviation is very much, so three years ago, he bought a training-plane and learned the craft of it.

He is the Chairman of the sports Club, committee member of Hongkong Chinese General Chamber of Commerce, & Member of Numerous Clubs & Associations.

Married in 1925, Mr. Lam has two boys and two girls. They are receiving their education in local schools.

何天生醫師

本港著名醫師何天生先生。東粵惠陽人。現年四十二歲。其先祖有大志。作遠行。商於歐洲荷國京城。遂家焉。其先父諱容。生長荷蘭。為該國名商。歷居是地凡六七十年。先生亦誕於斯。長於斯。受教育於斯。以天資之穎悟。益濯溉乎文明。童年已為異邦師友所器重。稍長。念人不可無專門學識。以為將來建業基礎。遂在荷國習醫。並於一九一八年，負笈英國。進蘇格蘭愛丁堡大學。專攻醫科。以期深造。三載精研。遂登堂而入室 。卒畢其業 。且獲 L.R.C.P. & S. 學銜。於一九二二年。忽動故國之思潮。買棹言歸。省識家園之面目。旋來港以所學貢獻於僑胞。慨然以濟世為己任。開業以來。活人無算。現求醫者。戶限為穿。其聲譽亦日益超矣。先生喜運動。擅舞蹈。故身體碩壯。恍若少年。且能曉五國言語文字。於一九二五年受室。其夫人黃氏。為美洲智利國留學生。才德並茂。堪稱璧合珠聯。現育子女凡六人。

何天生醫師

Dr. HO TIN SANG, L.R.C.P. & S.

Dr. Ho Tin Sang, one of the outstanding physicians in Kowloon and Hongkong, is a native of Wai-yang District, Kwangtung Province, but was born in Dutch Guiana, Surinam, in 1894.

His ancestors had long been living in that country and his father was one of the prominent Chinese merchants there. Dr. Ho studied medicine in Holland and when he had passed the Medical Course he proceeded to Scotland and continued his studies in the University of Edinburgh where he attained the L.R.C.P. & S. degree in 1922. He can speak five kinds of language of different countries.

At the end in 1922, he returned to Hongkong and put up his own practice. His experience and skill have given remedy to many fatal diseases and thus won a good reputation in the Colony.

Dr. Ho married in 1925 to Wong Chi Kin, who was graduated in Chile, South America. They have six children and except those who are still young the others are educated in local schools.

蕭遠嚴先生

蕭遠嚴先生○華之潮陽縣宋溪鄉人○現年四十有八○與蝸木哥才○如效高尚義○富國之商人也○幼時讀書故里○勤學異常兄○十六歲就賈○

香江○少年志摩○人以老成日之○當時返清末葉○史治不修○中原豪傑○相率圖謀革命○先生報國情殷○毅然加入○追事機成熟○遠返汕頭○號召民軍○揭竿起義○卒龍光復潮汕○任

蜜謀反正○克忠潮梅先鋒隊大隊部軍需處處長○大功告成○以天職已盡○退海隅○隱於商○遠至現在○專營米業○行昌號其子劍兼任司理者也○先生察係商外人治下○而愛國愛羣之熱誠○與日俱積○當米港一二八之役○集合同鄉籌款地嚴○大著賢勞○民二五，獻機壽辭以充實國防○任善辦員於米業商會○捐主席○成立後○任首二兩屆扶委主席○現充香港華商總會值理○旅港潮州八色商會董事○組香港米業商會○充等均鋒辦兩任○旅港潮州同鄉會執行委員○米業

商會教委，兼訓解部正主任等職○先生於念四歲間交宝○夫人鄭氏○同邑金浦鄉人○現育男公于四○女公于一○長男栢坤○幼讀於鄉○次男栢照○專業本島智中學○三男

頰你安隊部為引稱長○時蔣廉任退的冠耳○趙栢遠○四男栢修○均球業本島香江中學○女玉

三載而素眠改寮○粵省龍氏勤退務區○先生復賞○方退故鄉小學○一家之內○樂也融融○

Mr. SIEW YUEN NGAN.

Mr. Siew Yuen Ngan is a native of Chao-yang District, Kwangtung Province, and was born in 1889.

He obtained his education in his native town, and when he was but a lad of sixteen he came to Hongkong to practise business.

At the end of the Ch'ing Dynasty the policy of the then Government reached its worst and most of the patriots schemed to revolt. Mr. Siew joined into Revolution and went to Swatow to play his activities. Finally, the revolution was successful and the Republic of China was firmly established. Then Mr. Siew became a staff in the Bureau of Protection in Swatow. Three years later, when President Yuan Shih-kai plotted the restoration of a monarchical government, Mr. Siew, who is a faithful nationalist, became Chief of the Munition Department of the Van-guard on the revolutionalists' side.

After this matter was absolutely settled, Mr. Siew resigned every position and returned to Hongkong.

He established a firm under the name of Hung Cheong and deals in rice business.

Mr. Siew is very active in social affairs. He is one of the founders of the Hongkong Rice Merchants' Association and was for two terms chairman of its Executive Board. At present, he is committee of the Chinese General Chamber of Commerce, Hongkong; Director of Swatow Chamber of Commerce, Hongkong; Executive Committee of the Chao-Chow Association, Hongkong; Executive Committee of the Hongkong Rice Merchants' Association, and many other social organizations.

Married when he was twenty-four, Mr. Siew has four sons and a daughter. Except the eldest son, the others are still attending schools.

辛玉銘先生

辛玉銘先生，蔣原樸乾之縣○剛届中年之年○賦社惠善○熱心教育○倚肥感欲物望○里業交稱善人○幼讀於鄉○長商於港○當鑒我國人之無商業道德○往往失信○以累其業○辛敢功敗垂成○吳龍

佩其有信○然則後之置身閻閭○欲悟其業者○堪資借鏡○先生本其懷抱○致力各種公益事業○當仁不讓○歷任香港崇正工商總會董事○及會長○中山倚商會所值理○與董事○及附設義學校長○曾尤任東華三院首總理○鏡舉惠善社社長○現任中山縣六區水豊學校校長○香港聯福行有限公司庫○華商總會值理等職○尚憶甲戌年間○東華醫院籌慈善互助社欲多故貢獻尤殷社第一屆鳥彩執行委員會

枕叔○故對於信用二字○有若書之坤而銘諸座右焉○甫出問世○即受少年老成之目○住譽日進○萬見知於外商屆臣氏洗水公司○壁亞知亞出品洋行○現港中上下兩環○以水福二字作店歡○互相辉○大德無私○仰臍雅乾○繁我遐恩○觀者○即先生多年叛設之商號○為上列兩家代理，及總理之銷埠也○營謀益晉○人方羨欲之多材○業務興隆○我猶

為崇德報功○本線緒平原之義○特贈像而為之贊○曰，為善之樂○端在好施○辛公謀悦○中外咸知○熱心公益○見義勇為○互助善舉○鴉力難持○籍華巨欲○救難恤災○德配黃銀女士○內助賢○現已有另公子三○女公子五人○

辛玉銘先生

Mr. HUNG YOK MING.

Mr. Hung is a native of Chungshan District, Kwangtung Province and was born in Hongkong. After he had obtained an adequate knowledge from a local school, he started his business and established a firm, under the name of Wing Fook, representing products of A. S. Watson's Co., Ltd., and Asiatic Petroleum Co.

His confidence and business acumen soon enabled him to approach the throne of success, and to-day he becomes one of the most prominent merchants in the Colony.

Mr. Hung, though usually very busy with his own commercial tasks, plays an important part in social affairs, he has been president and director of Tsung Tsin Industrial and Commercial Association; committee of Chungshan Chamber of Commerce, Hongkong; and principal of its subordinate school; president of Tung Wah, Kwong Wah and Tung Wah East Hospitals; and Chairman of Chung Shing Benevolent Association. At present he is Treasurer of Luen Fook Hong, Ltd., and committee of Chinese General Chamber of Commerce, Hongkong.

Married to Wong Ngan, Mr. Hung has three sons and five daughters. His eldest son pursues studies in the Far Eastern Aviation School and the other children are studying in local schools.

盧榮傑先生

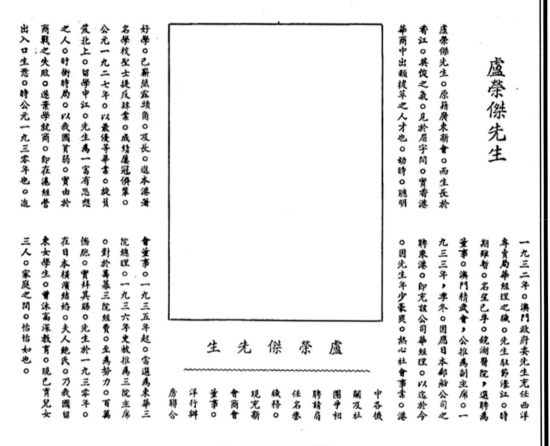

盧榮傑先生

生先傑榮盧

盧榮傑先生○原籍廣東新會○而生長於香江○英俊之氣○見於眉宇間○幼時○聰明

華商中出類拔萃之人才也○因先生年少氣盛○熱心社會事業○港

一九三二年○澳門政府委先生充任西洋年貢局華經理之職○先生駐節港江○時期較暫○名望已孚○銳湖醫院○選聘為董事○澳門精武會，公推為副主席○一九三三年○李冬○因鷹日本郵船公司之聘來港○即充該公司華經理○迄迄於今

中名儀
關友社
團爭相
聘請肩
任名卷
綏務○
現充新
會商會
董事○
洋行辦
房聯合

好學○已斯羨露頭角○及長○進本港著名學校聖士提反球棄○成績屢冠儕輩○公元一九二七年○以最優等畢業○拔貢笈北上○留學中江○先生為一富有思想之人○時衡時局○以我國貿易淪亡○乃我國商戰之失敗○遂棄學就商○即在港經營出入口生意○時公元一九三零年也○追

會董事○一九三五年起○當選為東華三院總理○一九三六年史被推為三院主席○對於籌募三院經費○至為努力○百萬傷胞○實科其賜○先生於一九三零年○在日本橫濱結婚○夫人跑氏○乃我國東女學生○曹沐高深教育○現已育兄女三人○家庭之間○怡怡如也○

Mr. LO WING KIT.

Mr. Lo Wing Kit is a native of Sunwoi District, Kwangtung province, and was born in Hongkong in 1907. He came from a well-to-do family and had sufficient means to obtain a thorough education. He attained his primary studies in Hongkong and later he studied in Shanghai for a short period. Finally, he returned to the Colony and continued his studies in the St. Stephen's College. He remained there until 1932 when he graduated from the institution and in 1930 he started his commercial career in Shanghai as importer and Exporter. His conscientiousness and honesty enabled him to set a foundation in the business sphere, and two years later, he returned to Macao and was authorized by the Portuguese Government as the monopolist of opium in that city.

He returned to Hongkong in the following year and became compradore of the world-famed Nippon Yusen Kaisha Steamship Company. His experience and natural ability are valuable assets to the firm, and his integrity and innate courtesy endear him to all his business associates.

Mr. Lo is very active in social affairs. When he was in Macao, he was director of the Kang Wu Hospital and Vice-Chairman of the Chin Wu Athletic Association. Since 1936, he was appointed president of the Tung Wah, Kwang Wah, and Tung Wah East Hospitals. He is director of the Sunwoi Chamber of Commerce, Hongkong, and also of the Compradores' Association Hongkong.

Mr. Lo married in Yokohama in 1930 and has two daughters and a son.

楊蔭浩先生

生先浩蔭楊

香港華人名人史略（一九三七）

楊蔭浩先生○原籍粵東番禺○生長於香港島○年僅三十有八○搜貨雄才○服膺總司理○壯歲而有老成之練○辦事富有朝氣○社會人士○交相稱許○以為楊氏積德○現方力謀擴張○蒸蒸日上○是凡數推○誠此路寫之兄也○致就懋營○素先生不特守成○且能創業○昔人謂生子當如孫仲謀○何所見之不廣○耶○先生個性謙恤○又復尚善○對於社會事業○恆祝己力○多所贊勳○現之人○己得如許造就○其將來貢獻於吾人者○寧有限量○我國商界○誠摯而出此奇材○異域青年○何修而發斯橅杭○先華商總會等機關會員○以年未屆乎不惑

于貢○無統格習○寫裝弦高○少英俊○曾肄業於港中聖保羅書院有年○中英文學問○甚為豐富○先生以學資兒效用○使無延樹○好多亦以為○乃不俟學業○蔣而就商○現任香江著名科館之宏記也○先生德祀源氏○以賢淑稱○

Mr. YEUNG YAM HOO.

One of the prominent merchants in Hongkong is Mr. Yeung Yam Hoo. He is a native of Kwangtung Province and was born in 1900.

He obtained his early education at St. Paul's College, Hongkong, where he remained many years until he attained a thorough knowledge in English language.

After he left his school, Mr. Yeung devoted himself in the business field. Though stared with a low position, he could easily approach the destination of success by means of unceasing effort and carefulness of work. At present, he is general manager of Wang Kee Co., Ltd., one of the outstanding business houses in the Colony.

Mr. Yeung is a member of the Chinese General Chamber of Commerce. Hongkong.

Married to Lo Yun Ling, Mr. Yeung has many children.

葉大楨醫師

師醫楨大葉

葉大楨醫師，行聘鶴山。乃廣東宋生族。生於奇島。為是地良醫。濟世有心。活人無算。誠醫界後起之秀也。湖先生誕於公元一九零二年。現纔三十晉六○當

齡攻讀於本港聖保羅書院○雙廣州嶺南大學○一九二二年，既冠受業京○學道專門○肆業醫科於倫敦大學○覺成一醫之長○將來造福人類○下惟歉哉○有志竟成○遞一九二八年，而發將○倫敦皇家內科醫學院扶照士○及英國皇家外科醫學院院員○翌年，史屑倫敦大聖士提反學堂○于永艱○三齡○

學內外科醫學士街○乃歸港開業○斯時也○先生齡未屆子而立○人位以年少框之○造企抗沉疴○遂聲鶴起○而先生臨症不芍○益為偽胞所器重○乃先生仍不自囿○一九三三年遊英時○再遊聖巴多羅馬醫院研究○今則業已大翅○名勁公卿○

去癒，軍委長夫人宋氏止於天南○紆尊莊港○踐門求醫○則其邊指知

何○必有趑出乎尋常萬萬者矣○彼於業徐○亦能致力社會○一九三○至一九三一年○充香港青年會董事○一九三五年，晉任故會副會長○又為聖約翰救傷隊永遠會員○及外科醫生○尊配陳氏慈芳○現育公子二○女佑成○五癒○讀於

Dr. YIP TAI CHING, M.B., B.S.

Dr. Yip Tai Ching, one of the most prominent physicians and surgeons of Hongkong, is a native of Hock-shan, Kwangtung Province, and was born in Hongkong in January 13, 1902.

He received his early education from the St. Paul's College. Many years later, he proceeded to Canton and continued his studies in the Ling Nam University.

Having graduated from the University, Dr. Yip proceeded to London, England, in 1922 and took up the Medical Course in the London University.

In 1928, he was admitted as member of the Royal College of Surgeons of England, and concurrently, licentiate of the Royal College of Physicians of London.

Dr. Yip graduated from the London University in 1929, and obtained the degrees of M.B., and B.S. Returning to the Colony in that year he started his own practice.

From 1923-1929, Dr. Yip studied in the St. Bartholomew's Hospital of the London University.

Dr. Yip is one who interests in public welfares. He was director of Chinese Y.M.C.A., Hongkong, in 1930; and in 1935, he became Vice-president of the same organization. He is also a life member and divisional surgeon of St. John's Ambulance Association, Hongkong.

Married to Chan Wai Fong in 1922, Dr. Yip has two children. The elder one is a girl and is receiving her early education in the St. Stephen Girls' College.

楊少泉牙醫師

師醫牙泉少楊

楊少泉先生。字祖復。鐵城之下恭鄉北山鄉人。○誕於濱江。受於奇海。已屆弱冠。始履家鄉。○現年五十有九。本港久享盛譽之牙科醫師也。○先生喜讀書。尤勤於學。幼隨母居港中。○教會設立之中文書館。及其他國學皆修科。攻讀七八年。章乃大進。乃將習繁行文。方期中英合璧。竟以丁母

之黃色人種。而能為牙醫先進之白色人種服務。則先生之名符其實可知。而先生仍不自滿。○故嘗於間○乃向牙科函授學堂○索錄課程。例必持功○件扰准及格。○一九一四年。○蒙港府頒行牙科社冊例持功○翌年再復上海美國牙科學堂之華葉文憑。○先生重於才。○而齋於德。○如勉力圖上進。○且讀力圖之。○則是學指模。而服務社會。○醫劇歎性不不辭。○沾理家庭。○兄女均此教育者。○有如下述○前任中華國內佈道會副會長。○中華堅公會港基督教聯會副會長。○香港堅羅堂值理。○港基督教聯會副會長。○香港面待道會值理。○堅保羅堂女士。○港基督教聯會副會長。○提反堂值理。○中華基督教會港九牧師。○及堅保羅堂公理。○堅保羅女書院幹事。○兼月報副刊。○理。○平民義學委辦。○兼理青年會副會長。○理。○大光報館內佈道會值科○青年會副會長。○及體育部委辦。○前會長。○香港住客持值會理會事。○中國海會會長。○人游沐會會長。○反對蓄婢會發起人兼會長。○華人游沐會值○港北山楊氏公益社社長。

理。堅公會議副值理員。○中山僑商會所值理。○中山北山山鄉鄉政殊持會長。○現任堅祿堂當值理。○反對蓄婢會幹事值理。○基督教嘉興會副會長。○中華國內佈道會香港值理委辦。○駐港基督教青年董事。○香港基督教青年會香港值理委辦。○楊氏公益社值理季幹事。○先生配室黃氏。○細室黃氏。○緦室陳氏。（原任小學教師）均己故。○現氏下子女兒十一人中鈞。○現由廣州國綫對佗畢業生陳紹儀女士。○主持家中餉。○先生注重體育。○為冬字李泳之○泳沐之○與太極拳。○其之所到。不問冬著寒暑。○叛始人。故齡將耳順。而精神穀然不遜青年也。

愛報諸而工。故非符己。至十九歲。愛業於當特名醫徐善亭之門。○越兩年。適唐公紹儀南下。倡其師之館。為山海關鐵路學堂招生。○泉佐應考。以叔俊獲選。○詎料入校半年。因圉匪之亂。○令諜近港。一再挫折。有志竟成。亦足傷己。○先生知不能與物爭衡也。○復從徐師遊數載。○卒倚其秘。乃自設醫館問世。時公元一九零六年也。○以技術俊良。人咸信任。迄一九一二年。○本港陸軍醫院哥頓何宏君。○重其材。特立合約。○聘其為陸軍士兵科理齒郡。○以牙醫後學...

Dr. YEUNG SHIU CHUEN.
(REGISTERED DENTIST)

One of the most prominent dentists in Hongkong is Dr. Yeung Shiu Chuen. He is a native of Chungshan District, Kwangtung Province, and was born in Macao in 1878. He was bred up in Hongkong, where he pursued his Chinese Studies in missionary and other schools for many years. Later, he turned his course to English studies. Deprived of the loving care of his mother at the age of sixteen, Dr. Yeung was compelled to earn his own living. When he was nineteen, he worked as an apprentice under Dr. Tsui Sien Ting, who was a famous dentist at that time. Three years later, he had the opportunity of continuing his studies in the Shan-hai-kwan Railway College. This was soon ended when the uprising of Boxers in 1900. He returned to the south and worked under Dr. Tsui, the dentist.

In 1906, he started his own practice in Hongkong. His skill and good-work was Soon commended by most of the inhabitants. He was offered to a contract by Lt. Con. F. Gorden Hall of the Royal Army Medical Corps to consult all dental cases among the army. In 1914, he was licensed by the Hongkong Government as a Registered Dentist, and in 1915 he obtained a diploma from the Shanghai America Dental College, Shanghai, (L.C.S.)

Dr. Yeung is a man of broad sympathies, and every good course finds him a willing supporter. He was Vice-chairman of China Home Missionary Association, Hongkong Branch; Standing Committee of Diocesan of victoria; Vice-chairman of Hongkong Chinese Christian Union; Chairman of Hongkong Harbour Mission; Member of St. Stephen's Church Vestry; Treasurer of St. Paul's Church Vestry; Vice-chairman of Yeung Men Christian Association, Hongkong; Committee of Physical Department, Y.M.C.A.; Director of a free-school under the management of Y.M.C.A.; Committee of St. Paul's Girls' School; Director of Tai Kong Newspaper & Co., Ltd.; Committee of Hongkong Tenant Protection Association; Chairman of Chinese Swimming Association; Chairman of Chinese Bathing Club; Founder and Chairman of Anti Mui-tsai Society, Hongkong; Chairman of Fan Hing Christian Association, and manager of a monthly magazine issued by that association; President of Pekshan Kong Yick Association, Hongkong; and Chairman of Pekshan Home Police Maintainance Association.

At present, he is standing committee of St. Paul's Church Vestry; Reader of Diocesan of Victoria; committee of Chungshan Chamber of Commerce, Hongkong; Member of a committee taking charge of rice-affairs of the Chungshan Chamber of Commerce, Hongkong; Executive committee of Anti Mui-tsai Society, Hongkong; Vice-chairman of Fan Hing Christian Association; Vice-chairman of China Home Missionary Association, Hongkong Branch; Director of Hongkong Chinese Christian Union; and committee of Pek-shan Kong Yick Association, Hongkong.

Married in 1905, Dr. Yeung has eleven children and all of them are well educated in local schools.

趙鶴琴先生

趙鶴琴先生○老儒醫也○現歷春秋○六十有七○粵之新會縣三江鄉人也○少從名師呂拔湖遊○夙工駢儷○深知造詣○既長○欲精一技以為世大之扶梃○遠歐美醫學東漸○乃修業廣州博濟醫院○後旋院因留學教嘉約翰君逝世告停頓○竟虧一簣之功○未届畢業而退學○轉習國醫於長壽寺僧醫席○有眼時○則從事著述○歷年所撰成之諸義○有全體解剖○兄科胎生學○雜症擇要○疹症○傷寒論○生理學○方藥○兒科○婦科○脈學○方藥○診斷○眼科○凡十二種○其有功於國醫界甚良○非非港鮮也○先生綜覈本色○自少至老○不厭儒生本色○對於扳棋附勢者流○尤深惡痛絕○然先生亦非徽物怙才○抱人千里○有說打破階級觀念○蓋欲待人○向無貴族平民之劃分也○至其醫德○亦有足稱○遇貧人就治○非惟診金分文不取○抑且施贈醫藥○曹不稍吝○故曹將港粵人士好感○譽滿粵垣○如夫人三○曰徐美珂○均由先生以活人之術教之○既集大成○遂出其所學以壽世○先生以香國醫者○多自秘其術○不肯易得諸人○遂為最大之缺點○忍力矯此弊○乃於遜清光緒三十年○創辦廣東中醫研究所○時主粵政者為岑公春煊○及王公人文等○多其就學○准予設立○計開辦後○學生畢業○凡念一屆○泊遷海隅○繼續努力○亦進本港教育司備案○逸今第六公子名榮民○現題壼山石○遊習西醫於光華醫院○其餘子女多在各校讀書○

生先琴鶴趙

芹○為刖涮博○更尚黃炎○闡溪阶沂○諸名醫領敎○既集大成○遜出其所學以壽世○先生以香國醫者○多自秘其術○不肯易得諸人○遂為最大之缺點○忍力矯此弊○乃於遜清光緒三十年○創辦廣東中醫研究所○時主粵政者為岑公春煊○及王公人文等○多其就學○准予設立○計開辦後○學生畢業○凡念一屆○泊遷海隅○繼續努力○亦進本港教育司備案○逸今第六公子名榮民○現題壼山石○遊習西醫於光華醫院○其餘子女多在各校讀書○

Mr. CHEW HOCK KUM.

Mr. Chew Hock Kum is one of the most well-known medical doctors with Chinese method in the Colony. He is a native of Sunwui District, Kwongtung province, born in 1870.

He was educated in his native village and when he was grown up he entered the Poh Tsai Hospital Canton after a competitive examination. Unfortunately, the principal of the institute died before he was graduated and he was compelled to leave the hospital without passing his final test. Then he learned the medical course in Chinese method and after many years constant studies, he started his own practition in Canton.

In 1904 he initiated the Chinese Medical School in Canton and in 1925 he removed the school to Hongkong where he is now managing the institution with unweary efforts.

Mr. Chew is not only famous for his skilful treatments but also for his literary works. He has written twelve kinds of books regarding to Chinese medical treatments. Furthermore, he was in the capacity of Resident medical doctor of many schools and government organizations in Canton.

Mr. Chew has seven sons and nine daughters. All of them are well educated and two of his sons are following in his footprints to take up the medical course.

吳志澄先生

吳志澄先生○名城波○以字行○廣東中山縣山場鄉人○現年四十七歲○乃香港商場中上等人才也○幼在鄉塾攻讀漢文○聘師爲其才器○十二歲丁父艱○十六歲隨兄來港○受業於港中已

故名儒季賜碩老師○漢學益進○十七歲攷入皇仁書院○年修英文○二十三歲○以資俊等畢業○中西學問斐然可觀○閱年就其樂公司之聘○

宪任職員○後改就法國郵船公司及太古船澳職○均歷三年之久○乃應先施公司之聘○由書記長至爲監察助理○服務凡七年○故公司

以其才幹不凡○工作勤敏○擬調往星嘉坡埠○

吳志澄先生

宪旗公司分行司理缺○但先生不欲遠離洋行○且不願水客人顧下○遂出而自行創設華資洋行○經營三載○生意原有蒸蒸日上之勢○不幸香港大罷工風潮○發生於西曆一九二五年○當時香港商業停頓○先生迫將該洋行出讓他人承辦○但該聘先生充任司理○在職凡三年之久○乃

出而再創光俊公司○專營攝影機具○兼代表歐美各大工廠產品○生意發達○聲聞佳○壓充華商總會董事○值理○倉港練髮足頭代表○值理○中山商會董事○兼第五屆主席○港料坊聯合會值理○通濟公會董事○均先生充任司理者○有二事○自別以爲快慰者○潔身自愛○絕無不良嗜好○且生平媒先生夫人言○先生一生尚

一則爲臂力於商業通濟公會之發展○今日故盛藥造品物○生意發達○及進進勤勤○爲社會稱道者○先生之力也○一則爲竭力於諧佳集之敎育○因先生家庭甚大○以一人之力○維護全家○規模甚爲獨子○今日佳集五六人均長大成材○亦先生之力也○其太夫人現年八十四歲○性極慈祥○先生奉侍唯謹○孝悌可嘉○

Mr. NG CHI CHING.

Mr. Ng is a native of Chung Shan District, Kwongtung Province, where he was born in 1890. A few years' early education pursuing Chinese knowledge in his own village enabled him to obtain a fair result in the subject. When he was sixteen, he was brought to Hongkong by his brother in order to continue his studies as well as to further his knowledge. In the following year, he entered the Queen's College and there he stayed until he was twenty-three when he graduated.

In the same year, he started his business career as a staff in the Clark & Co. Then he turned to work in the Messageries Maritimes, and afterwards in the Taikoo Dock. Three years later he worked in the Sincere & Co., Ltd., a famous universal provider, as a clerk. With his ability and intelligence, he was promoted gradually to the position of assistant superintendent of the firm with a long service of seven years. Finally the terminate selection of him as manager of the Singapore branch office forced him to resign on account of his unwilling departure from Hongkong and concurrently his ambition to establish his own business.

He founded the China Mercantile Co., and with his experiences he furthered the business in the utmost extent. The famous Strike of Hongkong in 1925 effected him heavily and he was forced to sell the business. The new partners found him very useful in the future promotion of the business, so he was offered with the position as manager of the firm. In 1928, he established the Kwong Tat & Co. dealing with photographic instruments and at the same time, as representative of different European and American Textile manufacturers. His experience and his abilities enable him to make the firm one of the most prominent commercial plants in Hongkong.

Mr. Ng is also very active in social affairs. He has been a member of the committee of the Chinese Chamber of Commerce; Chairman of the Tung Chai Association; delegate of Chinese Piece goods Association; director of the Chung Shan Association and a few others.

香港華人名人史略(一九三七)

蔡惠鴻先生

蔡先生惠鴻。南越鎮城人。現年三十二
為本港體育界之領袖也。性聰敏。而善

場。在各行中。有邁人之建樹。居重要
之地位。如前任中華煤業有限公司董事
（凡五年）也。如現克奇港油蔴地小輪公
司。及九龍汽車公司董事也。其措極退
取。純有朝氣。宏於造就。不謀老成。

吾知來日方
長。先生必
有爲人之
展耳。先生
富愛羣觀念
。常獻身公
共團體。民
二一〇曾任
東華醫院總
理。現克奇
港中華體育
協進會委員

長。齊港中華體育會委員長。華商總會
值理等職。彼為新生活實行家。無不良
嗜好。喜偶體育。雅擅足球。求學時期
。任頒大足球隊代表。港粵人士。曾領
袖其絕技者。原不知其為此中健將也。

讀書。少年絕愛高深教育。修業於廣州
嶺南大學。雖出身豐裕家庭。人嘉其刻
苦自勵。力求上進。未嘗以紈袴子弟例
之。彼學成後。不徒克紹先人遺業。且
龍發揮其天才。出而馳騁於遠東第二市

蔡惠鴻先生

Mr. CHOY WAI HUNG,

Mr. Choy Wai Hung is a native of Chungshan District, Kwangtung Province, born in 1905.

He was descended from an excellent family and therefore was able to obtain a thorough education at the Lingnam University, Canton. After many years' hard efforts and struggles, he graduated from that institution. Then he came to Hongkong and settled himself in the commercial sphere.

He was Director of the China Entertainment Co. Ltd., and is at present director of the Hongkong Yaumati Ferry Co., Ltd., and of the Kowloon Motor Bus Co., Ltd.

Mr. Choy is very active in social affairs. He was president of Tung Wah Hospital in 1932 and is at present Chairman of the Board of Committees of the Chinese Athletic Federation, Hongkong; Chairman of the Board of Committees of the Chinese Athletic Association, Hongkong; and committee of the Chinese General Chamber of Commerce, Hongkong.

Soccer is the favorable hobby of Mr. Choy. During his school days he represented the Ling-nam University to play in Hongkong.

李焯權會計師

李焯權先生○粤中山良鄉人○生长香港○現年二拾有九○港中之唯一華人會計師也○父國趨○少商澳洲○現任香港永安有限公司董事之職○母蕭氏○泰出望族○深得孟母遺風○教子有方○故先生早年卽飽受家庭教育○民拾叁○卒業於香港皇仁中學堂○旋負笈澳洲○入聖約翰大學○同時實習於澳洲著有聲譽之劫打公衆會計師行○迨加入為澳洲會計公會會員○及英國商業公會會員○對於會計一科○富有經驗學識○用氣考列澳洲昆士蘭省會計大試第二名○為我僑胞生色不少○先生以我留學澳洲僑胞之泛無聯絡也○又從而組織留學生會○以團結之○至今仍為該地人士所稱頌○民念三○返自澳洲○卽本所學○設會計事務所於香港永安銀行三樓○遊開辦商業會計學院○以養成商業會計人材○基於我國舊式簿記之複雜○恒以改良中式簿記為己任○所撰『改良中式簿記大綱』一書○行將脫稿付梓○書中要義○詳述粤省原有簿記之制度○與乎從事改良之方針○本港公司現例○亦無不分條刊入○將來公諸於世○當大有神益於商場○刷自香港開埠以來○華人會計師之將稅查稽中西賬目者○以先生為第一人○民國二十五年春○先生為謀聯絡同業之感情○利便同業之切磋起見○倡組華人會計師公會○枇推任該會首屆主席○先生曾任永安銀行查數員○及充英國商業公會、澳洲會計師公會、兩機關之駐華南總代表○窒集閩港同業○開慧善疏舞醫大會二次○一為籌款以助兒童保護會○一為籌款接也○全於體育一門○先生尤提倡不遺餘力○故對於港中小足珠賽○曾畧次報劾賬物○其熱心可見○夫人郭貴容女士○乃乩敦澳洲華僑○前奇山銀行總經理鄭公泗金之女公子○賢淑柔和○匹配先生○怡成佳稿焉○

師計會權焯·李

THOMAS LE C. KUEN, A.A.A., A.I.I.S., F.C.I.

Mr. Thomas Le is the first and the only Chinese "Incorporated Accountant and Auditor (Aust.)" practice in Hongkong. He is the son of Mr. and Mrs. Lee Gock Chew, a well-known merchant and one of Directors of the Wing On Co., Ltd., of Hongkong.

Mr. Le was born in 1908 in Hongkong. He received his early education at the Queen's College and thereafter went to Australia where he studied for his Accountancy professional qualification. For some years, he was articled to Messrs. Porter and Porter, a well-known firm of Accountants in Australia. After passing his final examination, Mr. Le admitted as membership of the Association of Accountants of Australia (Incorporated) the Institute of Incorporated Secretaries and of the Institute of Commerce (England).

Upon returning to Hongkong, he established his own practice at Wing On Bank Building under the name of Thomas Le C. Kuen & Co., and as a matter of fact he is the only Chinese Incorporated Accountant who is authorised by the Governor in Council to practise as Part 1 Auditor for both Chinese and English firms.

Mr. Le is a keen advocator on reorganization of Chinese book-keeping and accounts. He has written a book in Chinese on "Improvement of Chinese Accounting System" which is in the course of printing.

Besides his professional activities, Mr. Le is the president of Association of Chinese Accountants and Auditors of Hongkong. South China representative for the Association of Accountants of Australia, the Institute of Incorporated Secretaries, and the Institute of Commerce (England). For some time, he was also principal and Lecturer of the Accountancy-Secretarial Institute, founded by him in 1933.

陳福善先生

陳福善先生

福善先生○原籍粵東番禺縣○公曆一九〇四年生於中美洲○巴拿馬欣商陳公寧基第四公子也○其兄福田為美術家○其弟律紀，福添，福澄，福童齡○就讀香江○敏而好學○富有藝術天才○年十二○且擅英文美術書法○每試必列前茅○近國○能為人作英國各種古體字帖○卒業後○為山頓爵士賞識○以其律師樓之高級席位相屬○先

民國廿四年○實習期不過十數月○以有好奇心○復背加研究○卒有偉大之收穫○先生之居○面山背水○如在畫圖中○發種種妙景○以天然風景○就地寫生○取之不禁○用之不竭○故其所作之畫○均有捐到○山頓爵士夫人見而激賞○特介之加入香港美術會為會員○而該會藝術展○先生屢應徵列選○旋舉為該會董事一席○華人從未參指○至先生始開新紀錄（該會董事一席為我國增光不少）○

民廿四○先生親應肯貝士打酒店舉行其個人畫展○開本港畫界之先河○由山頓爵士夫人主持開幕○到會者眾○腎都德俊爵士夫人為行開墓○腎寫且畢其扇聯佳作○史寵庶○止英抱○以菲金題去○鍚爵士夫人為行開幕○史家游○以重金購去其列佳作○是年曆緞舉行○史家游○現自

生感恩知遇○亦願以中特之學�通題○詎料今日之成名○在依而不在耶○先生七年前○尚未豐心習畫○亦未曾有畫術指明人○其學校之面校○今則一躍而為本港藝界聞人○其成功之速○委非聰明紹頂不可説○須具有獨立社○方可語○俄容云「美術之發展○非其宗作○則屬其天才」○斯言也○以品後學也○先生自賞○若救遇學校○則周所得○以晶後學也○先生以學無止境○欲求進步○

創其宗作○非先生自賞也○先生自賞○若救遇教校○則周所得○以晶後學也○先生以學無止境○欲求進步○相接○而先生大忙矣○先生尺牘頭○史進一步於客氣風景之描○朝夕努力○並辦香港藝術研究社○及業宗主持○其宗主○又因多取畫材○黃宗岩，等個人畫展○時多已借出○先生倡藝術之進○如發表其所著「一九三六年美術請而演諸也○如發表其所著「一九三六年美術畫展討」一文○說中西各根也○而原聞體悟烏馬○無不扶輪大雅○

刀作油畫為最出色○查先生以刀作油畫○始於筆○鋼筆○無不別樹一幟○尤以用粉彩○水彩○粉畫是務也○故深得各界賞識○

Mr. LUIS JOSE CHAN.

Mr. Luis Jose Chan is a native of Poon-U District, Kwangtung Province, and was born in 1904.

Though he was born in Panama City, he was brought back to Hong Kong when he was very young. He is at present to be considered as Hongkong's own artist.

He was not at first interested in drawing, but at school he was attracted by Old English Characters. He began collecting different styles of English Lettering, characteristically inventing fancy forms for himself. As a matter of fact, he did not attend any arts school but entered for a course at the Press Art Correspondence School of England.

For some months he drew and sketched in black and white. Then, needing colour, he changed the course to water-colour.

By good fortune Lady Shenton became interested in his work and introduced him to the Art Club. In 1934 Mr. Chan held the first one-man show given by any member of the Art Club.

Early in 1934 he began experimenting with the palette knife. He brought back from a month's holiday in the North about forty pictures and the most of these were executed in Peiping.

In October 1936, he held his second one-man show, which was opened by Lady Caldecott, with great success. His Excellency the Governor wrote a Forward in the catalogue of the exhibition and bought many of his pictures.

Mr. Chan is one of the four founders of the Hongkong Working Artist's Guild, a society of artists organized a little over a year ago.

劉樹聲先生

劉先生樹聲○字君任○粵之東莞人○學海名流○藝林碩彥也○少耽風雅○善工書○叔叔有花卉夫人○對之尤有欽崇○除向西洋名女畫家容臣夫人○國畫思潮○陳諸會中○曰研究西洋畫○私人又似其國畫及蜀奈一情飛躍○以鉛筆覺外○富時中西報章○均紀其事○而介紹其佳紹○或刊油畫到前綫去○或刊國畫悲賢之或史有爲之出個展者數年如大光報是也○先生大雅扶物○不忘國敵○偶展覽日

洲支加高大學藝術科○受華盛頓美術大學教藝術序○乃贊揚藝術○提倡教育爲己任○創立萬國美術科學院○藝花藝術學院○香港華僑美術美術專科學院○萬國函校

生先聲樹劉

會○志賢女子中學○均任主持○治事之徐之拉○雅集文人○切磋砥礪○蜜俯馮師粹○李鳳公○張谷雛○李景康○傅菁祥○聚工伙諸名流紐士○申書畫合作社○同人衆其任社刊編粹○奇港華僑教育者會○以先生育效力文化事業○亦聯之爲參議○谷雛李冬○香港華僑美術會開基之日○先生皆率行其個展○出品有國畫○西畫○書法○凡數百情○我國美人○自林主席以降○如于右任○孫科○居正○王世杰○邵景○朱家驊○黄慕松○黄紹竑○張發奎○葵廷鍇○余○吾知將來示範於後學青年者○必無量數矣○

（延中某主管機關審定○現凡三種○一日西洋畫法全科教本○一日國畫法指南○一日書法進奉○萬國函校美專用之培就及萬學員○

經製油畫到前綫去○可知先生藝術感人○無遠兩弗屆○八月前我首卻二次全國美展○先生作品○經家受入選○尤爲港粵藝提生色○抑先生不使以書畫鳴○若中西音樂○與夫國技○以辭術○攝影○游泳○均有所長○蓋其個性好建設○喜研究也○先生現方盛年○著作刊行○現凡三樓○一日西洋畫法全科教本○邱資甚富○

漢謀○區芳浦○劉石心○張遠峯簽各長官○紛錫題詞奬贊○各國畫家雲埠參觀之衆○亦爲尚所未有○香港國際美術會主席西洋名女畫家容臣夫人○對之尤無不欽崇○除向國畫思潮○陳諸會中○曰研究國畫○私人又似其國畫及蜀奈一情飛躍○以鉛筆量外○曰時中西報章○均紀其事○而介紹其佳景卯○富時油畫到前綫去○均紀其事○而介紹其佳作者○或刊油畫到前綫去○或刊國畫悲賢之或史有爲之出個展者○如大光報是也○先生大雅扶物○不忘國敵○偶展覽日

麥界聞人黄賓虹○張谷雛李鳳公等作品○今年仲春○應萬國校美專廣州青年會之請○又赴穗市個展○男女學員○及廣州區界人士○凡來其個展者○日達數十人○此間藝人李仝金爭盛譽○毆坤藝賞者○日界盛譽○以書畫描寫婀娜○妙筆通寫○對先生能以書法描摹髮○熱心國事○傷婀娜○熱心國事○均頌揚不置○徐如社省南寧氏國日報亦刊其富國防性之

曹思晃牧師

師牧晃思曹

香港銀鈀聖保羅堂主任牧師思晃先生○誕於港江○前澳門議例局員曹善案之第四文師○本港前任華人代表曹善允之胞侄任也○性況默○喜讀書○幼攻園學○家聘粵席名傳○精長○習葡文於澳門政府公學○西一九一〇年○益學英文於培義會督骨封先生為牧師於教廣州主堂○斯特陰服務楊羌會外○兼任大艮○石岐，江門，三區繞迴○一九二三年○應澳洲維多利省美利濱埠李會督長之名○充華人教會主任牧師○坪得五載○旅澳之日○曹參加全澳洲教會大會議○復好從各科學專家遊○於一九二八年○回港○是年二月十一○由其壽增會督主理○與吳光中學教員何女士王瑛結婚於試校禮堂○三月八日○奉杜結義會督委為本港聖保羅堂主任牧師○先生乃偈議展任牧師址○並於其側附建張堂址○牧師莊一問○費共四萬金○尤援華人禮科堂○臣學○先生向來不作無益之消遣○最戲興趣者○為宣道學○與分祈心理學○尤善於傳祥○故世界著名演講家艾迪博士○歇士德博士等○來港佈道○恆相先生作舌人○現繫廣州協和神科大學宣道學講師○西對杜會議務○尤熱於接受與負責○如國聯會奇港分會蓋事○聖保羅男書院蓋事○女書院董事○奇港吳光分校董事○香港基督教聯會中英文秘書○反對蓄婢會值理○南華聖書○中華園內佈道會總會值理○港粵教區常備委員會委員○現年四十有一○子三人

奇港聖保羅書院○修業期間○感基督教理之美陶○心馬嚮往○於一九一三年四月十三日在聖保羅堂受洗禮○五月十四日受堅信禮○學成後從事教育○先在母校工作兩年餘○嗣求深造於廣州和神科大學○至一九一九年畢其業○旋就聯會粵文秘書○反對蓄婢會值理○中華園英國聖公會南華會幹事長○是年厭月○偷會皆乃冊立先生為華差會幹事宜○是年厭月○偷會皆乃冊立先生為華差會幹事宜○助理英國聖公會南區常備委員會委員○次安道○幼安民○長安邦○

Rev. P.•S. F. TS'O,
THE VICAR OF ST. PAUL'S CHURCH.

The Rev. P. S. F. Ts'o who is the fourth son of the late Commendador S. I. Ts'o of the Portuguese Government, a member of the Legislative Council of Macao, and who is also a nephew of the Hon. Dr. S. W. Ts'o, was born in 1895 in Macao, to which his ancestors migrated from Chung Shan District, Kwangtung.

Coming to Hongkong in 1910, he studied in St. Paul's College, till he graduated. After his graduation, he joined the teaching staff of his mother school for two years.

Then he left Hongkong for the study of theology at the Union Theological College Canton. After he graduated from the Union Theological College in 1919, he became a secretary to Archdeacon E. J. Barnett, who was then the Secretary of the Church Missionary Society, South China.

In 1923, a call came from Australia. He responded to the call and accepted the invitation from the Mission of the Epiphany, Melbourne. He went there as Chaplain to the Chinese Mission and worked under the late Archbishop H. C. Lees. When he was there, he was able to attend the Australia Church Congress in 1925.

He stayed in Australia till the year 1927 and landed in Hongkong in January, 1928. On the 11th of February, in the same year, he was married at the True Light Hall by Bishop Mok Shau Tsang, to Miss Amy Hoh, a teacher in the True Light Middle School. He was inducted as vicar of St. Paul's Church by Bishop Duppuy a month after his marriage.

Mr. Ts'o is known as an able interpreter. During the visits of Dr. Sherwood Eddy and Dr. Stanley Jones to the colony, he was asked to be their interpreter. His Hobby is reading. He takes great interest in the Art of Preaching and Psycho-analysis.

Mr. Ts'o is a tutor of the Union Theological College Canton on the art of Preaching, a councillor of the League of Nations' Society Hongkong, a member of the Council of St. Paul's College, of St. Paul's Girls' College and of the True Light School, Hongkong, an English Secretary of the United Council of the Hongkong Chinese Christian Churches, a member of the Standing Committee of the Kwang Yuet Diocese of Chung Hua Sheng Kung Hui, a director of the Anti-Muitsai Society and of the Bible Society of South China, and a member of the Assistant Committee of the Chinese Home Missionary Society.

何玉瑛女士

士女瑛玉何

曹忠晃夫人，何玉瑛女士，原籍粵之連平人。於耶穌降生後一千八百九十八年，生於廣州市。爲雲山珠海蒙氣所鍾，呱呱墜地。已牟娑秀媚。英氣逼人。惟亦遺不屈。父早見背。遺雖六人。賴母鞠育。女士居長。岕友性成。念母氏之劬勞。顧他年之生計。故每日除助家務及

教席兩年。乃呂所得束脩作爲大學準備。一九二二年改進嶺南大學。專攻文科。一九二五年又學成。卽於史學文科學業修證。兼將教育科年修證書。卽於是年應眞光中學之聘。充敎育校務主任。女士篤信耶敎。以基督『非爲役人乃役於人』之訓。故樂於服務。當其在中學及大學肄業時。喜與同學組織社會服務團。聯袂結隊。往附近村落。舉行衛生演講。組織村婦人敎育會。及兄弟識字運動。故當時白鶴洞一帶。該女士其人。而樂與之親近。一九二六年曾代表華南基督敎育會。赴京出席全國基督敎敎育大會。代表廣東省。一九二八年與羅文錦律師結婚。聖保羅書院敎席兼其才名。任職凡三年之久。一九三〇年代表香港女青年會赴大會。一九三五年廣州眞光中學。在香港開設分校。

於攝弟妹之外。並從敎求學。日無服務。苦辛。作學覽之代價。始益于所請苦其心志。勞其筋骨者歟。稍攻進南中國最著名之眞光女校。每校攻硏纯。卽將來得下女英才而敎育之爲己任。在校時。每於保育嬰兒。每將研究耶穌聖道。西歷一九一六年畢所肄。校中富局以女士品學優異。聘充眞光校敎硏。二年之後。以女校進其職。翼其己任。一九二〇年畢呂最優等畢業。且留校當深造。

故分校校長。女士生平樂與兄愛爲樂。理頭愛心理學。兒童故事。兒童各方面表示。其智識恩聘。港中各界咸度該校將人。一九三四年起枕舉爲香港女青年會會長。香港反對畜婢會副會長。及港皇保羅堂婦女服務團秘書。均連任數屆。呂迄於今教區婦女服務團秘書。均連任至今席。一九三六年史枕抿爲坚保堂婦女服務團主席。女士富於求學。樂於才力。勞於服務社會。實港中婦女界之偉大人物也。

長於小學敎育。特聘充基督敎育。對於兄愛爲樂。對於兄弟各方面表示。小學敎育。一九三五年廣州眞光中學。在香港開設分校。呂女士富師資。故聘充中學及分校。羅女書院敎席兼其才名。任職凡三。年之久。一九三〇年代表香港女青年會赴大會。

Mrs. P. S. F. TS'O, B.A.
President of the Young Women's Christian Association, Hongkong.

Mrs. P. S. F. Ts'o, whose maiden name is Amy Hoh is a native of Lingping, Kwangtung, born at Canton, in 1898. When she was 13 years of age, her father died, leaving six children behind with but little means. Being the eldest child in the family, she needed to find money not only for her own education but also for her brother and sisters. She managed however to study at True Light School, Canton, which is the oldest educational institute for girls in South China, having been established 60 years ago. After graduation from the school with unusual honour of being the first in every class, she took up the normal course and finished the course in 1916. Saving some money from her salary as a teacher at her school for two years, she again joined True Light Middle School, Pak Hok Tung, and was again engaged as a teacher of the school for two years after her graduation there in 1920. She entered Lingnam University, Canton, in 1922 and graduated with the Bachelor degree of Arts and with the educational Diploma in 1925. At the request of True Light Middle School, she joined the teaching staff and remained in the post until she married Rev P. S. F. Ts'o, vicar of St. Paul's Church, Hongkong, in 1923.

She is an earnest Christian, and her life motto is, "Not to be ministered unto but to minister". That is why in her school days, she organized a Service League for the villages. She went very regularly with a number of girls into the villages near Pak Hok Tung and Lingnam, teaching and preaching. She taught the villagers, particularly the women and children, about hygine, about book and, above all, about God. Consequently, she was a well known figure among the village people.

In 1926, she was sent to Shanghai for the National Christian Education Conference as a delegate, representing Kwangtung Province.

Since her marriage, she has lived in Hongkong. She was engaged as a teacher in St. Paul's Girls' College for three years.

In 1930 she was invited to attend the National Young Women's Christian Association Conference at Shanghai.

When the Council of True Light Middle School Canton decided to open a branch school in the Colony in 1935, she was repeatedly asked to be the Principal of the new school. It is said that as she is known as a born teacher and is richly equipped with knowledge of Child Psychology, Story-telling, methods of teaching, School Administration, and with ten years' experience of teaching, it is a great pity that she does not take up education as her life work. Finally, she accepted the post.

As to her social activities, she is the President of the Young Women's Christian Association, Hongkong, Vice-president of Anti-Muitsai Society, and the Secretary of the Diocesen Women's Auxiliary, these three posts she has held ever since 1934. She is also the President of the Women's Auxiliary, St. Paul's Church.

柯應李先生

生先李應柯

柯應李先生○號宏楊○粵之潮陽縣洋內鄉人也○現屆中壽之年○為本島汕頭花邊公司創辦人○歷業總司理○性況誠○志不凡○少曾肄業於香港青年會○敏而好學○成約為同儕冠○精於民十一，曾受縣大元帥委充梅善後委員會委員○同年八月，汕頭抽紗同業公會○圖交涉免稅事○請其代表赴平稅務處請開○卒得成功○同業受益不淺○民十七，參加非律濱華商總會先洨其赴申選舉出席○燿舉其代表出席○兼陳敦主任○欲為墓怦教信

計氏生為○先生為發展其業務○送分設支號於汕頭北平等處○徐採結其故鄉萬錦婦女所成之抽紗製品外○復搜羅蘇湘粵以及北平各地之刺繡紗工○前為大觀○用備具邦來遊者所探擇○故一歲之中○周遊國內○及征僕僕○不以為苦也○先生燥忙於商務○對於社會○亦肯服勞○

○念人貴自立○乃輟讀從商○本港為遠東第二市場○商界奇才○咸集於此○先生果何所恃○而龍駝駢數十年○以躋今日之地位耶○是亦有故○蓋彼有遠大眼光○復擬深長效應○營謀方法○以提倡工藝為主○將吞華巧妙之美術錢繡

徒○向來注重養體育與教育人才○氏七，於香港僑鮮中華海沿會○氏九，於原籍創設造德學校○且年助經費百金○近今不替○又為本港華人游泳會贊助員○旅港潮州中華基督教分會發起人○其對本港各教會，及海而侍遇會○捐助亦不貲○是誠有心世道之士○未可以其一介

盡力介紹於世界人士之前○發揚國光○從而代各地女同胞取價款優厚工值○實大有禅於圜商人兩沒視之也○

Mr. KWA ENG LEE.

Mr. Kwa Eng Lee is a native of Chaoyang District, Kwangtung Province, born in 1886.

He obtained his education at the Y. M. C. A., Day School, Hongkong, and after he was graduated, he began to practise business in the Colony. He established the Swatow Lace Company in Hongkong with the main destination to promote the Chinese drawn work and embroideries, which are highly recommended in the Western Countries. His able management enables him to further his business to such an extend that to-day there are branches of his company in Swatow and Pieping.

Besides his commercial activities, Mr. Kwa has been devoting a lot of his time and interest in dealing public weal. He has been appointed by His Late Excellency Dr. Sun Yat Sen as a committee in the management of the affairs of the Chaochow and Mei-hsien Districts. In 1928, he was appointed representative for the Chinese Chamber of Commerce Manila P. I. in the Carnival Exhibition of the Philippine Islands. He is one of the founders of the Chinese Bathing Club and a patron of the Chinese Swimming Club, Hongkong. In 1920, he established the Chin Tack School in his native village and contributes to it a yearly fund.

He is a faithful Christian and is one of the original members of the Chaochow Chinese Christian Association, Hongkong Branch.

Married in 1905, Mr. Kwa has two sons and four daughters. All of them have received a thorough education.

○燕清先生○名熊超○字俊英○別署言情○行三
○粵高要金利鄉人○現年四十有六○為本港開
埠富人黃瑞生公之文孫○錦綸公之哲嗣○生而
秀慧○幼神童稱○讀於官立英漢文學堂○（今
易英皇中學）○博聞強行○在校大考十次○卒業升
○嘗精降○且得全校績分最高之特別獎○名未

MR. WONG YAN CHING.

學皇仁○壯年廣東高等師範○學成囘港○就金
壓洋行辦理機務○時報清李○革命思潮澎湃○
先生固熱血之士○年十六○已加入同盟會香港
支部○後寧摧批保證金萬五圓○而辭金星致
從事革命○聯絡各方○造攻粵督署之役失敗○
李公經堂卒○為喚醒國魂○組新少年報於港○
先生與胡漢民等○為喚醒國魂○與趙三○主其事○時此間有某○
保皇黨俄開報詆譭文○題為「中國應否革命」○惹含

色商報○先生任總編輯○
假招華工為名○運赴戰地工作是實○其慈理某公司
御命來此○以巨資向各方疏通○先生囘拒於報
章○學東辭某代設公司私許先生二千金○先生
妮却○反感助之○某慈理知報而退○四名人不
致枉死與威者○皆辦王某○勤辦工作○不滿
五色背料處惕統○皆辦王某○勤辦工作○不滿
於人○先生著為清鄉事忠告王背料一篇○王不
故極為港僑所尊欽也○先生現育子女凡九人○

江門人士之口○題結
俊英三字○遂奔侍於
革者根據執行○而黃
港貴物眼災者之具窘
成績○華集各界簽備
○先生具熱眼書○扶
中小學校○同時借途
張落○遂創江門女子
中小學○同時借途
病遊江門○先生赴外
○省塵於是地教育之
○遠其岳父羅澤森，

始○庠兼大光，華僑，南中，南方，等報編輯又興
黃李二君合料中華中學○四年後○等報編輯又興
小學，及光中女中小學○學務發達○一日千里
○去年秋○史符宣國民進熱心教育部立案○計先
校董會○在祖園偽委會○發教育部立案○計先
生至身教學兩旁○迨二十年○除上遊外○就其
工商，南綫，東方，趙燕，中和，南方，香江
，朝報○與廣州之公報，新國華，現象，珠江
，廣東，民報等○不特著作等身○尤擬毕創各校
○最得社會歡迎者○仍有香江之倚張，華字
○去年秋○史符宣國民進熱心教育部立案○計先
俊外史，新西遊記讓平行本○在編纂中○則有
大小俊合傳○新脂虎，民報等○老愛奴上下集，大俠笑史，大
○廣東，民報等○計有藍綠劫○言志深港○待人接物○莫不出於至誠
言○志志深港○待人接物○莫不出於至誠
也○先生詢各社團請○出任中華教育部常委
，華商總會與孔聖會等料之委
辭，眼續，及義學貢花，等欵○雷勢力以赴

請詞○於是中國，世界公益，新少年等報○率
起側之○先生誅伐尤力○某報遂遣責於國人○
及民國成立○從事革命者○多作官去○尤以報
界為泉○惟先生徵留○未幾革命元老朱爷中軍紐
政先民國新報編輯○旋甹任總編輯○後亦囘某
讀聞辭版○乃先後創香海女校○先生興
辭君奔石等創討賊軍○功成某退○任香港展報
事○朝年，復創香江吮報○自期
黃李二君合料中華中學○四年後○等報編輯又興

現象派○及同志料中華女學○咸歆先生任其事○

香港華人名人史略（一九三七）

Mr. WONG YAN CHING.

Mr. Wong Yan Ching was born in Ko Iu District of Kwangtung province in 1892. He was first educated in the King's College Hongkong and then in the Queen's College. Later he was transferred to study in the Kwangtung Provincial Higher Normal College, Canton. After graduation he was for some time the compradore of a foreign firm Hongkong.

As he was a faithful follower of the late Dr. Sun Yat Sen, he made great efford in forming the Republic of China. He was either chief editor or associated editor at different times of the various Newspapers in Canton or in the Colony.

Besides being a well known journalist Mr. Wong is also an enthusiastic educator. He has been a teaching staff of many famous schools in this Island. About a decade ago he founded a girls' school in Kaingmoon and later he founded the Kwong Wah Middle school, the Kwang Wah elemantary school and the Kwang Wah Girls' school. He is now the principal of these schools.

He is noted for his activities in social and charitable affairs. He is member of the Committee of the Kowloon Chinese Educational Association and of the Chung Sing Benevolent Association. He has written many Novels which are so interest and are welcome by most of the young people, so he is also called as a Novelist.

The readers of his humourous novels may easily think that Mr. Wong must be a very funny man; but, on the contrary, he is a man of dignified appearance. He talks very little yet works very much. His sincerity and honesty endear him to all the people with whom he associates.

During the beginning of the establishment of the Republic of China most of the journalists of the Kuomintang, the national party, were appointed as officials in the Government; but Mr. Wong declined all the posts offerred to him. He does not mind very much about wealth and fame, but he likes literary works and teaching best.

郭振成先生

郭振成先生

郭振成先生，百粤之中山縣人也。年剛而立。為香港振成商科專門學院之創辦人，兼監督。壯聘贄。志不凡。幼壯業於港濱。每試輒冠其

九二八，漫遊華南北。從事致祭教育及實業。放其遠大銳利之眼光。深悉商業人材之重要。於一九二九年春，在港舉辦振成打字專門學院。於澳卑利街。斯時規模甚小。就學者僅六人。先生抱不屈不撓之精神。弗以曲高寡和而小餒其志。卒也期年而生徒大增。一九三一年，港

中各大西報均為文紀述其打字技街之新奇與敏捷。復以學員畢業後。各商行機關。時皆聘用。成績顧著。從游日眾。乃造就成泉。故為普及起見。乃遂實成街。積極擴充。無

曾。極得師次之愛戴。其商學造詣。對於海記等科。閒具心得。開目，離機，龍子，打字法。尤有神出鬼沒之妙。故能致授英倫商學會佼等文憑。達先德上各中西商行委辦。年任及冠。教授懇期迄成。儀器亦順完備。先生因。印任茉大洋行司理。行內職員逾二百。米命。雖謹。英散粗稅。足見其多藝多才矣。公元一於社會工作。素感興趣。

生先成振郭

Mr. KWOK CHUN SHING.

A.A., A.R.I.P.H., F.COM.SC.A., F.C.I.

Mr. Kwok is a native of Chungshan District, Kwangtung Province, who is the Founder & Director of the Chun-Shing Institute of Commerce, Hongkong. Having obtained a fair knowledge at his town, he proceeded to Shanghai and continued his studies in the Ling Nam College, where he stayed until was graduated.

He began his commercial career in a famous business concern in Shanghai. Late in 1928, he had a tour throughout North and South China to investigate education and industry. Realising the depression of trade would soon be spread to the Orient, Mr. Kwok, since that time, had a firm decision to establish an institute of commercial subjects, where pupils may be trained with a technical profession before they start to face the depression.

In 1929, he established the Chun-Shing Institute of Commerce in Hongkong. At the beginning, he was little sympathized by the public and he had but six students. This weak start would have disappointed most people. But Mr. Kwok had the optimistic foresight that he could not fail if he tried hard. So he did, notwithstanding bad circumstances and the handful number of students. In the following year, the number of students increased rapidly and at present the institute is considered to be one of the up-to-date Commercial Institutes in the Colony, and its testimonials are well recognised amongst local banking and business concerns.

Mr. Kwok Chun Shing is also deeply interested in the social affairs and is now holding various positions in different Associations of the Colony.

譚紹海先生

夫功名富貴○固宜於枣一時○而忠孝廉
節○尤應流芳百世○譚紹海先生○事親
孝○與士信○臨財廉○取予義○此其大

譚 紹 海 先 生

生亦善書○世以小歐稱○且楷行篆隸
學案大字○蠅頭小楷○無所不能○有索
書者○咸恂然計之○好未經謀面○曾不
辭情○是先生秉性惜淡○海棠利○而復
能利物濟人○有任俠風○凡以惡泉者○
必百計應之○故人皆願識荆○先生少西

遊八桂
陽朝平
樂○山
水流連
採索嘉
十年○
光緒末
來歸○
肩荷地
方公益
慈善事
業○歷

茗之所以枝徵而列於是書也○先生乃順
德梁山人○其尊甫瀋川考廉○為宋九江
先生弟子○業有理學名○先生學具淵源
○杜尤孝友○生平非先王之言不敢言○
非先王之行不敢行○方弱冠己以『道學』
見稱於鄉塞○又其尊甫書工八法○而先

八人○

不竭力以赴○至今桑梓樂道之○先生又
曹寀嶺南學校教席○桃李遍於門下○近
氣倘寫香江○所交者皆名流雅士○其跆
蘭蕙之投契歟○淑配盧氏○有銀行○溫
恭有禮○勤儉持家○幷幷不紊○生于女

Mr. TAM SHIU HOI.

Mr. Tam is a native of Lung-shan District, Kwangtung Province. He is prominent not for his position but for his high learning in Chinese and great virtue in old Chinese Style.

His father was a learned man and had obtained the scholastic degree of How Lian. Mr. Tam inherits the gift of talents from his father. He showed his conscientiousness in his studies when he was quite young. He had obtained a good knowledge of Chinese literature before he started his business career.

He was a teaching staff in the Ling Nam University, and at present he is a staff of Messrs. Ts'o & Hogson, a famous firm of solicitors in the Colony.

Mr. Tam is a man of broad sympathy. He is ready to give assistance whenever he is asked to. Besides, he has partaken many social and charitably affairs in his native town and in Hongkong.

Mr. Tam has eight chidren and all of them acquire a thorough education.

關心馬醫師

關景良醫師。字心馬。粵之番禺西關村人。夲近古林。本港西醫之老前輩也。乃祖尤著公。自闢港僻來此間營鍼業。至萬亦昌公。為港粵牙科醫師先進。乃父元昌公。至一八八七年。身攻習學於拔萃書室。先生初討於拔萃書室。至一八九七年。學業成。一九零七年。張制軍之洞聘其為醫學院教席者。為西人白德力孟臣。唐士剛德利。威士剛德利。陳公少白。夫人蔡氏。語英文。在雅麗氏醫院當通事。侍人和謁。有大衆故事之稱。習聞張總理革命言論。復見時事多不平。如朱少鈞王孟琴何君閭楊鶴齡楊通安楊贊人。均以排滿為己任。惟事而深火熱之中。約束生人於痛不顧。且救民於水深火熱之中。約束生人於痛苦呻吟之下。里巷服務於那打素醫院。先生於一九零三年學成。張制軍之洞甚其醫學湛深者。

先生性孝。慈命毅違。（太夫人蔡氏。在雅麗氏醫院當通事。侍人和謁。有大衆故事之稱。）不聞其參預。曰。先生性孝。慈命毅違。

生先馬心關

江君與華。劉君泗楊等三十餘人。先生與孫總理同一宿舍。共晨夕者垂五年。極相友善。繼理舉所業。卸出而致力革命。盂拳書稱用其。以財帛者。或曰。先生為恩想極新之人物。觀其與陳君子采。發起前髮不易服會。早在民國紀元前兩年。（卸滿清宣統二年冬月初三。似庭華商會所舉行。是日聯袂以蘭西樂隊百廿人奏樂行禮。敦請六老人為公証。到會者五六百人。並遊行本港大馬路。故會成立紀念影片在後幅。）何以照次革命

力。曾連仕華商會所主席。發奇港油蔴地小輪公司主席等職。現份任華商會所值理。奇港油蔴地小輪公司董事。先生行七。昆季均有聲於社會。淑航江氏恩梅。甚有慈德。子榮厯。任吉陸安。克我國首都紅十字會醫官。榮賢。習醫于奇港大學。榮庭。足歷坡業商。榮貴。昆李咸有聲於社版。人以榮嘉之。先生對於民國成立以來。未嘗名發三樓樓樓四人。在雅麗氏醫院鶴齡樣。同振一影。時逾清光緒十三有七月初六日也。影片在後幅。卸公元一八八八年十月十日也。

坡業商。榮貴。足歷于英華書院。榮庭。卦業于培正分校。榮元。以榮心志恋於本業。亦骨致於本社園兩畫。於本社園兩畫。

仕民生中學教員。慈莊。請於米利濱書院。就讀于小學。女榮馨。遍林慈珍。遍鄉芳譽。

Dr. K. L. KWAN SUN-IN.

Dr. K. L. Kwan Sun-in has the distinction of being the Chinese Medical practitioner of longest standing in the Colony. He received his English education at the Diocesan school and was the second graduate of the Hongkong college of Medicine. In 1893 he was appointed house Surgeon to the Nethersole Hospital and in 1907 he entered the service of the Chinese Government at Nanking as an Army Surgeon for three years. Dr. Kwan returned to Hongkong and commenced private practice in 1911. He was chairman of the Chinese Club Hongkong in 1921-1922 and 1935-1936 and Chairman of the Yaumati Ferry Company 1933-1935.

Here the author must mention that Dr. Kwan was a schoolmate and a roommate of the late Dr. Sun Yat Sen, the founder of the Republic of China. Dr. Kwan lived with this late great revolutionist at the same room in the dormatory of the Medical College for a period of five years. In the next page we can find a picture of five persons who are the late Dr. Sun Yat Sen, the late Mr. Yau Lit, the late Mr. Chan Shiu Park, the Late Mr. Young Hock Ling and Dr. Kwan. This photograph was taken on the front of the second floor of the Alice Memorial Hospital Hongkong.

Being a roommate of the late great revolutionist Dr. Kwan had an intense hatred of the cue which was a special token of the Manchurians who reigned over the Chinese empire at that time. He originated "the League of Cue cutting but dress remaining unchanged" in November 1909 in the Chinese Club. The Late Mr. Kwan Yuan Chong, father of Dr. Kwan, was the first man to cut his own cue on that day and more than five hundred men followed. On the next page there is a picture of the important members of the league at that time.

香港華人名人史略（一九三七）

THIS PICTURE WAS TAKEN IN OCTOBER 1888 ON THE FRONT OF THE SECOND FLOOR OF THE ALICE MEMORIAL HOSPITAL HONGKONG.

前排自右至左為尤少紈，陳少白，孫總理中山，楊公鶴齡，後排為關先生心焉，

斯照底片，為心焉先生所珍藏，編者以此中人物，所為革命元勛，關係民國史實，統有價值，特商借刊之，

DR. KWAN SUN-IN.

THE LATE MESSRS. YOUNG HOCK LING, SUN YAT SEN, CHAN SHIU PARK, AND YAU LIT.

剪髮不易服會成立紀念

此會港准當地政府設立。於遜清宣統二年冬月初於日。假庄本港大道中六四號二樓華商會所開幕。發起人為關心焉，陳寳東，陳于棠三君。

贊成人為王元琛，關元昌，吳秋湘，胡禮垣，溫清溪，區鳳墀六老。實我族復興之光榮。吾國中興之前奏也。

吾圖中興之前奏也。

之翼郭	君某	彭李曾	裘子陳	波江黃	馬心關	東寶陳	君某
墀鳳區		溪清溫	湘秋吳	璨元王	昌元關		垣禮胡
(父之生醫港斯)	(父之生先忠東)	(父之生哥保天)	(祖之士博忠寵)		(父之生哥心馬)		(父之郎律銘位)

THIS IS A PICTURE OF "THE LEAGUE OF CUE CUTTING BUT DRESS REMAINING UNCHANGED" WHICH WAS ORGANIZED IN NOVEMBER 1909 BY DR. KWAN SUN-IN.

後攝
前攝

(88)

羨潛德之幽光

盧伯禎 題

香港已故華人

名人史畧

何啓爵士

何啓爵士○蓋原百粵樟西○於公元一八五九年○生於香港○乃此間設有學問及歐令人定戴之○已故聞人也○幼英俊不凡○曾肄業本港官立中

爵士字其新婚夫人返港○再育一女○一八八一年○

央書院○精長○為翩壯志○貧氣英倫○先退巴黎○常詡為富不仁○為仁不富○遇兄弟世庄○而與拉者○必先貴以大義○張民代為和解○故閣素數十年○仍兩祖濟底其也○爵士生平熱心社會○勇於股務○無政府機關○華僑團體○殆不以教劇之任料推○故名卷之践見后○盥束之源○任外交部次長○亦任合開監督○○厚不以教劇之任料推○故名卷之践見后○盥

八八二年始○政救大律師案○彼持船公正原潔○常詡為富不仁○為仁不富○遇兄弟世庄○而與拉者○必先貴以大義○張民代為和解○故閣素數十年○仍兩祖濟底其也○爵士生平熱心社會○勇於股務○無政府機關○華僑團體○殆不以教劇之任料推○

○大學與科學士○及外科碩士兩學位○宗詩有兵西學○其此才記○女名金○張○刻○鍛○銳○鎔○水苑○讀于港大特○水元○水宇○水利○水皂○水惠○水鑄○

心社會○勇於股務○無政府機關○華僑團體○殆不以教劇之任料推○故名卷之践見后○盥

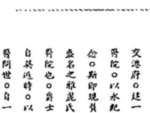

THE LATE SIR HO KAI

盧麻學校政診○組入阿故旬大學習醫○雙臥陛漂○注復功誼○數年苦詩○追後城○○盡爵遠底送○交港蔚○廷一醫院○以水妃○爵士遠其遺發○採八年制者不同○人以其成功迭○多樂就之○○一八九二年○英廷是為妃爵士勤結○投以C.M.G.○一九一○年○復錫以爵士榮街○爵士德廷名立矣○公祭復從事著述○計刊行者○有『中國之計論』○『鹬舆蚌』『中國基礎與政革』○『讚廣州稅務司帝博士之中國地稅及從海軍計』劉書壽代○『原有為建政見之質貧人論』○政長中國之貧貧人論』○○亦悉以拍之○其謙通篁方鵙臏○廠閣華人者○○○士資格○彼閣以身相屬○即退英國林肯法科院○勢力精研○卒殺放院高級法律學士資格○彼閣以身相屬○即退英國

生於香港○乃此間設有學問及歐令人定戴之○已故聞人也○幼英俊不凡○曾肄業本港官立中

色人種○而有所苓蒂○屢向之表示感謝○且以爵士天才活潑○不宜以醫自囿○勖其政習申轉之學○彼閣以身相屬○即退英國○爵士可其請○即退英國○功縣體○又爵士於任華人代表時○曾與曹善先等劃科聖士提反底書院○以保存祖國之禮教文化○爵士遠虔其遺發○不久亦棄世○○夫人偈之○為華人唯一獨立教育機關○不受當地教育司檢查○其學級採六年制○與全港學校均採八年制者不同○人以其成功迭○多樂就之○念○斯即現貨不久亦棄世○

先保民○國防○太平○三局紳士○定例○議政兩局議員○東華醫院弱閻安事子○在港盎三十年○不特喬烱唯其馬育更敬○即港府遇有事

THE LATE SIR HO KAI.—C.M.G., J.P., M.B., C.M., KT.

Among the Chinese there are many who have profited by a thoroughly sound and high-class European education, but there are few who have had a more education, but there are few who have had a more distinguished academical career, or who have used their advantages to better purpose than the late Sir Ho Kai.

Born at Hongkong in 1859, he was the fourth son of the late Rev. Ho Tsun Shin, of the London Missionary Society. He was educated at the Government Central School in Hongkong and subsequently in England at Palmer House School, Margate; at Aberdeen University, at St. Thomas' Medical and Surgical College, and at Lincoln's Inn. He took the degrees of M.B., C.M., Aberdeen. Then he became a member of the Royal College of Surgeons, England, and was Senior Equity Scholar, Lincoln's Inn, in 1881. Upon returning to the Colony he started to practise medicine but found that the Chinese were not yet prepared to avail themselves of Western treatment unless it was offered free. Sir Ho Kai therefore presented the Colony with the Alice Memorial Hospital, named after his late wife, Alice, eldest daughter of the late Mr. John Walkden, of Blackheath. Sir Ho Kai then commenced practice as a barrister-at-law, and he was so engaged since 1882. He served as a member of the Sanitary Board for over ten years and on the Public Works Committee for five years. He was a Senior Non-official member of the Legislative Council, and was for many years a member of the following public institutions:—The Standing Law Committee; the Examination Board; the Medical Board; the Po Leung Kuk Committee; District Watchmen's Committee; the Governing Body of the Free Hospitals; the Tung Wah Hospital Advisory Committee; the Governing Body of Queen's College; the qualified Architect's Advisory Board; the Interpretation Committee and the Advisory Committee of the Hongkong Technical Institute; and Rector's Assessor of the Hongkong College of Medicine of which he was one of the founders. In short it may be said that he had the distinction of serving on the Committee of almost every public board appointed during his last twenty-five years; and that his time was always given ungrudgingly in the public service no matter at what sacrifice to his own interests as a professional man. For upward of twenty-six years he was continuously resident in the Colony; for twenty-six years he was a Justice of the Peace for Hongkong and for three terms (eighteen years) represented the Chinese community on the Legislative Council. Hence it was not a matter for surprise that he was looked to by his fellow countrymen for advice in their dealings with the Government, and was also often consulted by the Government in their transactions with the Chinese community. On the occasion of both visits of the Duke and Duchess of Connaught and of Prince Authur to the Colony, he received and welcomed their Royal Highnesses on behalf of the Chinese and in recognition of his many public works and services he was created as C. M. G. in 1892. He was conferred with the honour of Sir in 1910. Among his publications are:—"A Critical Essay on China"; "The Sleep and Awakening"; a letter addressed to Lord Charles Beresford on "The Open Door"; "An Open letter to John Bull on the Boxer Rising"; articles on Sir Robert Harts' Memorandum on the Land Tax of China and his army and navy scheme, 1904; the "Foundation of Reformation in China"; criticisms of the views of Kang Yau Wei, 1898; criticisms of the views of Viceroy Chang Chi Tung, especially on his recent work, "Encouragement to Learning", 1899; Persons responsible for Reformation in China; and Two Critical Essays on the Progress of Reformation in China.

Died in 1914 at the age of Fifty nine. At his funeral thousands of persons followed his remained to the cemetery and many social organizations held a memorial service in honour of him, showing how many lives he touched.

韋寶珊爵士

THE LATE SIR WEI YUK, BOSHEN.

韋玉爵士，字寶珊。稱號之中山縣。於公元一八四九年。生於香港。父韋光。歷任本港有利銀行華總理。爵士出自富裕家庭。總角受書。名傾早席。甫富十歲。漢學功深。繼進本港官立中央書院專習英文。融會新舊文化。學議愈形堂富。年十八。破浪乘風。赴英肄業於利時打學校。越年。轉進蘇格蘭大東書院。修業四載。成績優異。師友佩敬。劂後進來人士投考故書院者。皆家育稱。寶爵士曾給故院一好印象故也。爵士為我國留學歐西之第一人。於一八七二年。學成返棹。卽進有利銀行供職。以學問及才幹兼優。至為富事人所倚重。其父棄世。一八七九年。行將之史歐。遂使繼父職。行。

相聚請克名譽或重要職位。茲畧舉其顯著者述之。一八八一年。為東華醫院首總理。一八八三年。為太平局紳。一八九三年。為國防局紳（此局乃由爵士倡辦者）一八九六年。為定例局議員。一九〇八年九月。醫校英國O.M.G.勳章。一九一一年。英廷以其勤績殊錄以爵士榮銜。又爵士早已有從九龍築鐵路至廣州之獻議。惜清廷官吏不之計。洎廣九鐵路興築。爵與其原定計劃一部份相同。今中英政府有廣九粵漢兩路接抵之磋商。將屆實現。此後遂抵北平。當非數事。畫非爵士龍洞堝先慷之明証耶。爵士於一八七二年。柴荊本港。定例局議員誠之長女為室。（黃誠字平甫，本港定例局華人議員之第二人，）爵士有第二女。田安。回培。均蓮於法學。為當時港中著名律師。計其父子連續與該行發生關係者。歷逾六十年。可謂數矣。爵士長於才。而為於服務。除銀行本職外。凡港中社會公益善舉。靡不贊助。故政府信任。僑胞愛戴。各機關團體。乎

THE LATE SIR WEI YUK, BOSHEN C.M.G., J. P., Kt.

As a conscientious worker on behalf of the Chinese community of Hongkong, and as a man who did a great deal to produce the good relations existing between the Government and the Chinese, the late Sir Wei Yuk's name deserved to be specially remembered by all section of society in the Colony. On many occasions he was of invaluable assistance to the officials and his counsel was largely instrumental, notably at times of riots and strikes during the past half of a century. In settling matters amicably before they assumed the serious proportions which they threatened to do in several instances. Sir Wei Yuk was a Cantonese (Chungshan District), born in Hongkong in 1849, and came of excellent family. His father, the late Mr. Wei Kwong, was a well-known banker, and formerly compradore to the Chartered Mercantile Bank of India, London, and China, in Hongkong.

After ten years' study of Chinese, under private tutors, Sir Wei Yuk commenced his English education at the Government Central School, under the late Dr. Frederick Stewart, LL.D., and in 1867, at the age of eighteen years, he proceeded to England and attended the Leicester Stoneygate School for twelve months. In 1868 he went to Scotland and studied for four years at the Dollar Institution. He soon became a favourite with both masters and fellow pupils, and the impression regarding his nationality that he made and left behind him became a tradition in the school, ensuring to others from the Far East a most friendly reception at that institution. The late Sir Wei Yuk was one of the first Chinese to go abroad for Western education. On his return to the East in 1872, after a European tour, he entered the service of the Chartered Mercantile Bank of India, London, and China (now the Mercantile Bank of India, Limited) in Hongkong, and on the death of his father, in 1879, he (after a temporary retirement, according to Chinese custom) took up the vacant position of compradore. Sir Wei Yuk and his father served the bank for fifty-three years in Hong Kong—that is to say, since it was first opened.

In 1883, the late Sir Wei Yuk was appointed a Justice of the Peace, and, in 1896, became an unofficial member (representing the Chinese community) of the Hongkong Legislative Council. He worked in the greatest harmony with his colleague, the late Sir Ho Kai, C.M.G., M.B., Kt. and while not noted for long speeches, was regarded as an invaluable adviser in connection with all legislation in any way touching the interests of his fellow countrymen. In many other capacities also he had striven for the public good. He held numerous appointments, and served on may committees, for when his help was required for the furtherance of the public weal it was never withheld. It is impossible to give a complete list of his appointments in a brief biographical sketch such as is here essayed, but a few of his appointments may be mentioned. He was chairman of the Tung Wah Hospital (Hongkong's leading Chinese charitable insitution), 1881-83 and 1888-90; a permanent member of the committee of the Po Leung Kuk for the protection of destitute women and children (of which he was one of the founders) since 1893; a permanent member of the Hongkong District Watchmen's Committee (which was formed on his suggestion); and a member of the Standing Law Committee since 1896.

Moreover, he served on all the commissions appointed by the Government to inquire into matters affecting the Chinese since the commencement of his public career. The Chinese Government was indebted to him in no small degree for the assistance he rendered in bringing to justice Chinese criminals who had fled from Chinese territory to Hongkong and elsewhere. For the services which he rendered during the plague epidemic of 1894, the general public of Hong Kong presented him with a gold medal and a letter of thanks, while the Chinese community also addressed to him a letter of thanks.

Sir Wei Yuk may be regarded as the father of the Sanitary Board. For many years, previous to the formation of the present body, he took greatest interest in sanitary matters, and he was the friend and adviser of Professor Chadwick when that well-known authority visited the Colony to report on the sanitary condition of the city of Victoria.

He suggested the construction of a railway from Kowloon to Canton, and thence to Peking. He spent large sum in furtherance of the scheme which failed however, owing to the obstacles placed in its way by Chinese officials, who at that time strenuously opposed the introduction of anything from the West. During the past decade, however, several lines of railway were constructed, between the places named, and they follow closely Sir Wei Yuk's original plans.

The Honour of Knighthood was conferred upon him by the British Empire in 1910.

劉公鑄伯

THE LATE HON. MR. LAU CHU PAR.

鑄伯劉公○寶安縣人○姓賴頻○甫七歲○卽棄學○以家貧○肄業於西營盤馮義學○苦讀不輟○試輒列前矛○堅辭揀西嘉之○十二歲喪父○賴母勤事女紅○以供修膳○未幾○兼習旁行文○益自刻苦○獲獎免費生○拔攷進皇仁書院

○學益大進○試輒獲獎金○學費衣履○皆有以自給○十七歲畢業○啟迪社會○初浮沈于士商者十年○而學行言論○已懍然具本泉○中西人士○咸倚重之○每遇疑難○性引公為助○前後歷住地方委職○以數十計○廉不殉公為心力○為傷胞造福○富其被選為華醫院總理也○同時祇任為香港清淨局員○會役甚○港史防侍雜○聽夕紛紜詳察○遇病者○卽昇入醫院○庶興智

精研政治法律○故於立法行政○多所啟發○壓任凡九年○傷胞以公一言而殘安居樂業者○亦史儻數數○局外人因不盡知之也○公弁生長香江○學成復國來審一日忘祖國也○遇清戊子○鹰台港巡撫招致中丞之聘○越二年○泊克繼教員○乙巳○鹰北洋移委員○越清政府之招○任浼案繼科○兼洋務會科洋大臣楊制府之招○任浼案繼科○兼洋務會科○而衛生局○巡警局○皆資助理○徒以當時國○廣付定區○存活槁枲○閒者嘉之○歐洲戰起○

遠○入者多死○欲速內地○又爲法令所禁○且惠救之家○例須黃泥○報遠及十餘戶○家具推殘○不可以日○居民長援○丘有景廩不顧○伺陳逃去者○全港蕭條○公與清淨局力爭○公慨然不顧○其以規往監視○不應洗者○禁勿洗○富洗當時○公必規往監視○不應洗者○禁勿洗○富洗當時○莱勿援○鏟走汗喔○易無係容○史後受約束○居辭獲保全○且力請富道除禁速之例○氏心始定○漸復舊觀○公在任凡十二年○局員有不協者○必攄理於至○如得教化之不變○則當暴抵几○未審少屈○則蓋暴抵几○○益自策勉○移科富分己○故華僑除受其福者○頭不勝舉○此則公共著者也○富其被任爲定例局員也○所以爲傷僑謀者○一如其往清淨局時○所阿附○鼎然以成骨自見○公論數十年○於此閒利病得失○復骨

是未定○敕然引退○其後農工商部菜紙公○復電促入都○將開以委職○及民國初立○粤史欲任以財政廳長○均辭不就○公語人曰○吾性不樂任進○倦出亦首○但欲於圖事有所補救○故旣不顧爲馮婷○非敢以是鳴高也○聞者建其言○而亢首史維史○益知其賢○後禮聘爲顧問○公辭無官守言責○然爲國努力○曹有方懷○如勤學也○然理齊鐘集資二十餘萬○故育才書社於港澳粤○以培育華人于弟○廣州之有公立學校○自公始也○其後港立大學等款達七十餘萬○亦公贊助之力爲多○如敏教也○（公偏設孔聖會於香港）附設義學三十餘所○以爲宏待孔教之地○就學者歲逾千人○海外之有孔聖會○亦自公始○公請於母省會○將原定路軌改近其故里先路爲奴婢○取息甚微○公餘陳省史○小試於其鄉○農人稱頌不置○創市塲○創農實苦○時以子女賢妓○困於重息○于女多次於其地設車站局○香西莆無市政○儲貨出賢○既定其國○尤愛其鄉○富廣九煩方建鐵時○公捐鉅貲○時以子女賢妓○困於重息○于女多次○立工塲○建醫院○附以農林實業○規模粗具○成一模範村矣○其拖於鄉有如此者○其閒在港善故○則有華人永遠墳塲○招孤寡家○收貧寒○則有公立醫局○華商總會○東菜兩會○廣華醫院等○其餘若中外凶災○莫不竭力捐募○以賞贎恤○氏二○漢陽淨飛兵禍○公以義富系縣○敏然捐儲脈款十五萬○存活槁枲○閒者嘉之○歐洲戰起○

吾國參馬。公扶國民外交之義。協大有銀號贈聯軍以飛機一架。乙則贈以紅十字摩托車一輛。而中英邦交。益加親睦。論者咸以為識大體云。公歷任治安局員。國防局員。公立醫局副局長。保良局副局長。東華醫院長年顧問。保良局總理。撫查種審值理。衞生局則例審查員。糧食價值稽核員。徵收輸出戰務用品值理。戰務仙款值理。募幹事員。教員研究值理。考查工程師局員。法例審察員。公項稽核局員。孫家仙款幹事值理。英國欽設工藝製造研究會會員。北般島工藝製造會永遠會員。華人永遠墳場幹事值理等。責重事繁。心勞力瘁。其病殆平伏於此矣。公性恬淡。徒以榮親故。納粟得同知。復以劉中丞奏保加知府銜。賞戴藍翎。乙卯順直賑捐出力。將制府奏保。以道員儘選加鹽運司銜。賞換花翎。鼎革後。以有功民國。獎給四等嘉禾章。復晉給二等大綬嘉禾章。二等寶光嘉禾章。以襄籌國內公債。得今嘉獎。賞給樂善好施，蒙公好義，等匾額。以襄辦港事。宣著勞績。英廷特諭嘉獎。并獎給二等寶星。公致力舉事。猶念食貨者。國之大命。遂以貨殖為本業。先後創設銀行凡十有二。皆歸公主持。治事之暇。亦問事著述。刊行於世界者。有自治須知。西禮須知。社會主義平議。各一卷。壬戌年春。海員罷工事起。相持久不下。商民交困。舉推公出任調停。公為華僑大局計。不憚唇焦舌敝。復向司所力爭。局外亦多有不及知者。衆情不諒。致謗交集。迨事獲解。而公之心力益瘁以至不起矣。公於壬戌四月七日仙遊港寓。享壽五十有六。哲嗣四。長子德譜。現在本港享有盛名。

THE LATE HON. Mr. LAU CHU PAR. J.P., C.M.G.

As the successful career of the Late Hon. Mr. Lau Chu Par may be an encouragement and an insperation to every poor youth, the author has endeavoured to collect the materials and write this biography.

The late Hon. Lau Chu Par was a native of the Bo On district in Kwangtung Province. He was born in Hongkong in 1856 and was gifted with a high talent for learning. As his parents were so poor, they were compelled to send their child to study in a free school in West Point. His father died, when he was only twelve years old. He had a very good mother who realized that a higher education was necessary to her child and tried her best to send him to the Queen's College.

As the late Hon. Mr. Lau was a good and obedient son, he understood that the school fee he paid was obtained by his mother's hand works, he made his hardest efford in studying. Consquently, he was always stood first in his class and was much praised by his teachers and school mates. The bounties and prizes he received every year from the college were sufficient to cover his school fee, and thus he lightened the burden of grief of his mother.

After he had been graduated from Queen's College at the age of seventeen, he began, at once, to give his efficient and trustworthy services to his community. He held many appointments and served on many committees. It is hard to give a complete list of them here. However, a few of important ones must be mentioned. He was chairman of the Tung Wah Hospital; Member of committee of Po Leung Kuk; Member of committee of the Hongkong District Watchmen; member of the Sanitary Board (Now Urban Council) and member of the legislative council of the Hongkong Government. He was also made as an official in the Ching Danasty.

He died in 1922 at the age of fifty six.

李公煜堂

THE LATE MR. LEE YOK TONG

李公煜堂。原籍粵東台山東坑。復遷居同邑西關堡冠舟里。幼研經史帖括之學。抱家風破浪之志。基伯叔昆季先後以貿遷美洲。心焉嚮往。年十八報謝。附帆船偕行。日心考察商務。旁及遠西富綠之術。在香江。小為拭展。敬立金利源永利源等藥材行。善於擇人任事。歲獲贏利。值清季甲午之役後。公深慨列強暴。華夏板蕩。益知興復之不容緩。遂斥資經營工商業。如廣州電力公司。及機器麵粉公司。泰山源出入口貨庄等。事屬草創。跟於開辦。成致鉅未彰。而公志曾不之拂綏。時嘗母財外輸。有裨民生。園人心之拂綏。時嘗母財外輸。温庇實難。乃首創香港聯益保險公司為率。而往六月。以積勞引退。嗣後多致力於商務。倡

康年。聯泰。上海聯保。羊城各公司。踵其後。今仍與外商競退。抵抗其經濟侵畧。他如寧陽鐵路公司。香港廣東銀行。四邑輪船公司。開粵航輪船公司。安樂園食品公司。上海新新百貨公司。漢口德豐棧打包公司。杭州西冷飯店等。或任總理創辦。或被推為董事或主席。信乎其規劃經心。衡物老幼。整宏董大。閎堂燗然。公躬身處閣閣。而目營八表。規

設香港廣東銀行。二十年來。苦心為策。資本日增。分行廣及中外。振務推。屢集議規模。未知所定。公鼓窗肝膽。行務中推。屢集議規模。開陳利害。各信推人成為之感勸。至於不起。老成潤耆。國人成具展恩。公生平素性懷怫恭謀。言行不二。其語人也。以孝悌忠信為本。且清而不介。儉而好施。旁以餘力。用之於公益教育善慈事業。青年會。胡起侯。各學校。及廣惠肇醫院。上海廣肇醫所。兩廣迎賓館。哈爾濱公醫院。南京台山男女青年會。印信加資助提挈。其於生鉻橋。正為社會人士所共聞共見者也。北平台山會館等。其一園內機關團體充任要職。除粵省財政司長外。曾為大元帥府參謀。總統府參謀。廣東省長。董事。中央財政委員會委員。國救會議員。公於歐戰後。為視察列強從事發展工商事業。而謀復興之努力。周遊歐美各園。嘗著『九園遊記』一書。用資園人借鑑。蓋欲望園黨琛之心。老而益壯。公生於民國紀元前六十年。壽八十有五。卒於民國二五年一月一日。孝子七月廿七日。終於民國二五年一月一日。男女子基達。計七人。公生於民國紀元前六十年。男子炳辛，炳垣，炳推，炳根，炳起，炳炤，炳煥，女公子基達。自平少平，珍平，寶平，究平，虎平。分赴日本美國或香港廣東內地各學校肄業。園民政府造齊前歡。於民國二五年八月十四日頒給褒揚令。照錄於后。廣東省台山縣。李煜堂。振興實業。贊助革命。輸財濟餉。為策匪淺。特趙給褒揚令。以昭激勸。

THE LATE Mr. LEE YOK TONG.

The late Mr. Lee Yok Tong was a native of Toishan District, Kwangtung Province, born in 1851.

He obtained his education at a school in his native village and when he was eighteen years of age, he followed his kinsmen to America, where he started his commercial practice. When he had acquired sufficient experience, he came to Hongkong and established the Kum Lee Yuen and Wing Lee Yuen, dealing in Chinese drugs.

After the Chinese Fleet was absolutely annihilated by the Japanese in 1894 the late Mr. Lee realized that it was difficult to restore the prosperity of our country besides the promotion of her industry and commerce. For this sake, he went to Canton and organized the Electrical Power Company; the Mechanical Flour Mill, and the Tai Sang Yuen Imports and Exports agent.

Later, he organized the Luen Yik Insurance Co., Ltd., in Hongkong. This is the first Chinese insurance enterprise in the Colony, and years later there are the Hong Lin Life Assurance Co., Ltd., the Luen Tai Insurance Co., Ltd., the Shanghai Fire and Marine Insurance Co., Ltd.; the Luen Po Insurance Co., Ltd.; and the Yeung Shing Insurance Co., Ltd., all of which are established with Chinese capital and are at present severe competitors of European insurance firms in Hongkong.

Besides the above mentioned, Mr. Lee is either a founder or a promoter of the following business firms:— The Ningyang Railway Co., Ltd; the bank of Canton; the Sze Yap Steamship Co., Ltd.; the Yuet Hong Steamship Co., Ltd.; the Sun Sun Universal Providers, Shanghai; The Shui Fung Cotton Packing Co., Hankow; and the Sze Lang Hotel, Hangchow.

Mr. Lee is a zealous nationalist. He joined in the national party long ago and rendered great assistance to the revolution of China.

In 1905, when the government of the United States of America announced the restriction of Chinese imigration into that country, a meeting was held in Hongkong by those prominent merchants who had close connection with the American trade to respond to this matter. Mr. Lee was appointed one of the committees of that assemblance. Consequently, the Americans were afraid of this resistance to justice, so the restriction was far less rigorous.

Before the establishment of the Chinese Republic, Chinese were divided into two parties. The nationalists who achieved the revolution on one side and those who plotted restoration of a monarchical government on the other. It happened that the China Post, which belonged to the nationalists, was endangered by the latter, and the situation was very hazardous. Mr. Lee undertook the enterprise and preserved the dormant force of the former.

At that time, the Ch'ing Dynasty Government had put a rigorous search on the nationalists, but Mr. Lee, who was one of the members, made his own shop, the Kum Lee Yuen Drug Store, a concentrating centre for his comrades so as to avoid the views of the Ching detectives.

When the Republic of China was just established, Mr. Lee was appointed as Treasurer of the Kwangtung Province. Mr. Lee, raised $800,000 in the shortest span of time for the purpose of supplying munition for the army. Six months later, he resigned from the post and came to Hongkong, where once more he set himself in the business sphere.

Mr. Lee was a man of broad sympathy, and every cause of good will finds him a willing supporter. He was in close connection with the following institutions:— The Lingnam University, Canton; the Chih Sin College, Canton; The Chinese Y.M.C.A., Canton; The Hong Kong Kong Kee Son School; the Public Hospital, Canton; the Kwong Shui Hospital, Canton; the Liang Kwang Association, Nanking; the Cantonese Guild, Harbin; The Y.M.C.A. and Y.W.C.A., Toishan; and the Toishan Chamber of Commerce, Peiping.

Mr. Lee was a counsellor of the Commander-in-chief, China; counsellor of the President, China; Director of the Industry Guild, Canton; Committee of the Board of Finance, Nanking; and member of the Chinese National Calamity Convention.

Mr. Lee had a tour around the Western countries and had written a book entitled "A travel over nine nations."

Mr. Lee died on January 1st. 1936, with a ripe old age of eighty-five. He had eighteen children and all of them are well educated. Mr. Lee Chi Chung, his eldest son, is the General Manager of the Shanghai Fire and Marine Insurance Co., Hongkong.

竊謂太上不朽。立德。立功。立言。天下達尊一，德一，爵一。仕宦而至將相。祿位而至公卿。寬乎尚已。而貧賤敗殺。味嘗甘苦。段則已焉。以陶朱之致富。惟簡公耀初。予頗數致書。國人膏日費。交遊稱其信。德則集中而貨殖。宜其所託可謂仁。其此

門不容車。既鮮鶴原。爲家墜東備之奉。軋軋紡車之聲。蜜蜜線之痕。落葉添薪。古桅是仰。機杼聲影。圖畫依然。遭遇如此。亦足悲已。越二載。江華以行侷供身。年十七。籍摩頂貢人簿。聖賢嘉謀。廣東簡氏族自治社。叛自題清瓷統二年。原舉先生爲社長。來身似受。勵行如創。則排敎解紛。兄弟周睦。則攝使海。二十餘年之鐘舉。搭於楊澔。爲橋爲揀。街狸持籌。竹瓷書。七十二縣之宗盟。高山仰止。此其三也。四○日人坐。才不足以服眾。則位高者貼危。德不足以說服。則重者場題。簡總會理值。民國十二年。壓任香港樸木行商會主席。先生於民國廿三年。公推香港來第三屆總理。開善則服。見義務爲。駁六馬朽索無馬。得一覽而大舉足足。此其四也。五日建祖祠。駐族之敵。以敘族之誼而無間。老成人於馬是式。處李世而無間。吾粵簡氏聞宏祠其舉。照南昆仲建倡。先生完成斯在腳。族其成人於馬。則漢素不振什在腳。無論紛紛。何者者。則廣祚不能。此其。無少姜之其。財用紛答。則漢素不成。

雄才。微爲蔽行。宜必都三公位。享萬鐘祿。勒諸舞鼎。著之風磬。昭茲來許戢。然則將其生平。撫成得忍。顧惟德之表指善著者宜也。自古英雄崛起。多由賃賤。自郡謂萬之魚覽。傅說樹立。半出突微。能度安集於秋淵。派愍咨於雨而起家寬素。坐擁厚封。無遇乎。文正義田。賙諸族人而逮給。守錢虜。往往難之。先生之少也。家徒四壁。

臣浸。乙卯水災。遂成澤國。南海鼎安圍隄鞅決。先生癃懷悠庶。批撥其財用原論其多容。爲而至。逆乃高率遠距。而尢外聯。史在香港敗木行九家。及賢倉四五座。一帆風順。而先生之年已高矣。蓋水勢遠流。湯湯其托。夫狂瀾。卻浩浩相傷夫先生之才既展。而善行息浪於江中。萬餘脆輕。故木愁雲驚於天表。黃鶴樓雲於江中。長跪

巨浸。乙卯水災。遂成澤國。南海鼎安圍決。其占魚夢。迎兒鴻敝。先生癃懷悠庶。工程移著其墜牢。爲財用原論其多容。一鄉譙桑田之萃圍。以獨力障桿里之安危。用能度安集於秋淵。派愍咨於雨而。此其一也。二曰衛鄉圍。荏苒之故害。甚於天災。由於人事。自官失其取。馬疢者牧。氏陷其情。桑杵之安穴。先生築磚模。以杜奸究之前。姣案

以助守望之力。設圍牆。以助守望之力。設圍牆。以杜奸究之前。姣案

二曰衛鄉圍。荏苒之故害。甚於天災。由於人事。自官失其取。馬疢者牧。氏陷其情。桑杵之安穴。先生築磚模。以杜奸究之前。姣案

THE LATE MR. KAN YEW CHO

故案儻之捐款興伐。而熱心之辦像先。此其九年之開科南海第六區氏學校。先生任校童氏園廿四年。在本鄉地建學校。先生捐出貲。力有餘而必彈其力。財有餘而必散五日。六日興學校。氏智有餘而善用其財。與子孫言慈。詢詢然。惴惴然。簡子吉滂。與兄言慈。一沆涼涛之風。克勵精勤之業。此其六也。簡公耀初。粵南海良沙海人也。在簡港經商。兩年茌茸泰山遊。享受六十年九日善。修港志。將來辨文行界。所栽叢評。盍非之以仰景仰前微之意云爾。

THE LATE Mr. KAN YEW CHO.

The late Mr. Kan was a native of Nam-hoi District, Kwangtung Proivnce, where he was born in 1867. He was bred up in a poor family which could scarcely afford him a thorough education. His father died when he was yet an infant and it was his mother who went through hard and soft to rear him up. It would be surprised to learn that the late Mr. Kan received no other higher eduation than his homely tuition when he was young, yet he could become a rich merchant later. When he was seventeen years of age he was sent by his relations to go to school. It spite of the short span of two years in school, he obtained a fair knowledge in writing and counting. Before he was known to his community he had been an apprentice in Canton, and through his frugality he could accumulate a little savings.

In 1891, in partnership with a kinsman, Mr. Kan established a lumber firm in Canton under the name of Wing Cheong. Through his able management and foresight, this shop soon prospered to such an extend as enabled him to initiate a firm of his own in Hongkong. This ambitious and industrious man worked on energetically and before his death in 1936, he owned nine lumber shops and five go-downs, and was considered to be one of the most influential lumber magnates in Hongkong.

In his life there were many good deportments and charitable deeds and the following descriptions are the most popular ones. First of all is that he was generous in contributing a large amount of money to build a dike in his native village, which is located on the bank of a river and is often threatened by floods. Secondly, about half of a century ago, his village was threatened by bandits who used to rob and made disorder every now and then. The late Mr. Kan gave his own money to build many ramparts and earthworks to resist the robbers. Therefore, though all the neighbouring villages were deeply afflicted by the outlaws, Mr. Kan's village was always in the safest situation.

Lastly, the late Mr. Kan paid much attention to education. He spent considerable time and money for the purpose. In 1910 he was a director of the Kok Man School, and in 1935, just a year before his death, he founded a school in his native village with his own means.

Commercially, Mr. Kan was a committee of the Chinese Chamber of Commerce, Hongkong; Chairman of the Lumber Merchants' Association; President of the Tung Wah, Kwong Wah and Tung Wah East Hospitals; and committee of the Nam-hoi Chamber of Commerce, Hongkong.

馮公平山

THE LATE MR. FUNG PING SHAN

馮平山先生○諱朝安○廣東新會縣人○以商業起家○生平樂善好施○尤熱心捐財興學○近世言慈善者必稱之○少讀書於家○年十六○棄儒業商○從其尊父之遠遊○既壯有室○其地有貧人棄子某○見先生就俊偉○計為大器○欲以其女為人某○迺挾其庭姬萬治產具○先生娩詞謝之○

者甚眾○後居香港○每年先與辦慈善事業○遂被選為東華醫院首總理○及永遠顧問○保良局首總理○團防局紳董○太平紳士○香港大學永遠校董○院費因盆充裕○皆先生之力○值癸丑軍與○為院廣開財源○院費因盆充裕○值癸丑軍與○尚不與焉○民國十三年甲子○於銀號即領提取○一提存款即致萬金○的○家其彩繁○醫院有積存之資中致萬金○先生謂宜相讓起計殷富○紛紛起而相讓○級業○乃以其產業文據為質○保不提金以○銀市卒稍可安○

大學經費○平山圖書館建築及開辦料費○兄童工藝院建築費○皆出鉅資○諸凡相助○而景堂圖書館○為起念其先人者○經營尤大○景堂其先德字也○計先德用於教育之資○凡百餘萬金○其慷慨若此○尚不與馬○民國十三年甲子○先生遊於歐美○考察商務○既歸所得○益不遺餘力○至其言行○尤積詳款式○少於其幼時○於先世遺產○視為父母祇生○未嘗過問○嘗曰○人能於分占物時○則必為富者○於有事出資○則必無學於己○又謂處世為人○第一不可為人欺人○又以古人格言○見蘭先生語○必請回傲先生○學經驗之語○必增退道德○見金蘭先生所輕格言爾覺乙○先生就其成之○而位記頌其語和○故其退事堅定○與人諸和○事也○則必無學於己○又謂七十生辰時○索集捐於慈善事業○人皆諧作○不欲其開道詳會商所○民國念五年六月十九日○卒年七十有二○中外人士○聞之甚悼其悲○嘆遺命不用詳依○惟速葬於江門○先生能以自奉者○恨港府特派人員○親友行列○以行弔之別○悼港府特派○

地人士所推為富者○人之力○每舉科其眾○人累年謀其就之○其本山公園之建築○蔣新會書院○之成立○其他○象白沙公園○旅港新會商會○先生亦勇於任事○往往以一人之力○成象○

生歌與成之○自是益為富○先生所輯格言爾覺乙○書以增退道德○

蔣先生之力勒○會之成立○

孔堅會中學○香港華商總會圖書館○不視其事者○於廣東高等師範附屬小學校建築費○香港大學堂基本金○圖書樓購書費○漢文云○

先生誠篤○先與米○不卽索值○俄民科以存沽○歲大歉○愛育善堂○及各善院紳童○及剝○全不至○來糶值○不取其事者○於廣東高等師範附屬小學校建築費○

先生至廣州○任方便醫院○○○○有勒有篤○時翁街多以運糶用致富○之道○以此備有嬴○以入巴蜀○為化房懲遠○來足發展所長○乃北湖大江○過武漢○逾三峽○以遠漲商業○光緒士辰○○乙己○先生○清光緒癸未○丁外憂卒○服関○

於奇港則男女義學凡三校○平山小學○復約同志組織○賴先生之組織○其指財而兩○積善之家○為世所重○○戚其私子幼承庭訓○兄弟九人○○曾卜素素業於香港大文科○生子慶龍○長卒者七○素芬亦華○尋素業於香港大學文科○生子慶龍○卒其子汝村○亦早大○偏室李氏○生子汝桃○初○祖其子汝村○德配李氏○生子汝桃○於五旬後而素華○素芬○始生○李氏○亦早卒○偏室李氏○初○生惣家庭多故○不欲蓋萎○至是親友以其剝繼○不悅勤之○乃立庶室郭氏○生女四人○長卒者三○生女八人○長存者七○

廣州中大附小開會以表哀思○先○生平不育○五旬後而素華○素芬始○不悅勤之○生怨家庭多故○○○孔堅會中學○香港華商總會圖書館○生平不育○求學中○曾卜素業於香港大文科○銘德○為世所重○積善之家○成卜其必昌大○云○

贊○香港大學堂基本金○圖書樓購書費○漢文云○

THE LATE Mr. FUNG PING SHAN, J.P.

The Late Mr. Fung Ping Shan was one of the most prominent Chinese merchants in Hongkong. He was born in 1860 in the District of Sun-Wui, Kwangtung Province. In his early youth Mr. Fung was deprived of the opportunity of completing his education on account of poverty, and consequently, when he was only fifteen, he followed his uncle to Siam where he started his business career.

It was some years after that he returned to China to be married, and after his marriage he returned to Siam to continue his business. While in Siam he came in close contact with a certain rich merchant who took a ready fancy to him, deciding to betroth his daughter to him, with the promise of the rich dowry. This generous offer, however, Mr. Fung declined without hesitation.

In 1882 Mr. Fung's father died, and he returned at once to China to attend the funeral. Shortly afterwards, he went to the Szechuen Province, where he started a business of his own, dealing principally in Chinese drugs.

After making a fortune, he returned to Canton in 1891, and was at once elected Director of the well-known Fong Pin Hospital, and many other charitable institutions. In 1904 there occured a severe famine in Canton, whereupon Mr. Fung, amongst a number of other philanthropists, was asked to deputise for the Hospital and proceed to Hong Kong to purchase rice, which would be distributed among the sufferers. The rice was purchased, but the necessary fund was not fully subscribed in time. Yet the rice merchants trusted Mr. Fung and delivered the rice to Canton without delay, thus saving many lives from the disaster.

A few years later, when he settled down in Hongkong, Mr. Fung served on several occasions as Chairman, Director and Adviser of the Tung Wah Hospital and Po Leung Kuk. He was an unofficial Justice of the Peace, a member of the District Watch Committee, Life Member of the Court of the University of Hongkong, permanent adviser of the Po Leung Kuk, and a life member of the Chinese Chamber of Commerce.

Himself a self-made man, Mr. Fung's great desire was that those who came after him should enjoy the opportunities that he had missed. He initiated Free Schools and Vocational Institutions both in his own town and in Hongkong. He gave generously to the building fund for the Higher Primary School of the Normal College in Canton; and in his native district he established the King Tong Library to the memory of his late father. He was mainly instrumental in the establishment of the Aberdeen Industrial School in Hongkong, towards which he donated $100,000.

To him it would seem monstrous that Chinese boys and girls should grow up in ingorance of their cultural heritage. He was one of the founders and staunch supporter of the now defunct School of Chinese Studies of the University of Hongkong; and the Fung Ping Shan Chinese Library is an abiding testimony to his devotion to Chinese learning.

In commerce, the late Mr. Fung was one of the founders and a permanent Director of the Bank of East Asia, Ltd., and many other public and private Companies. Besides his many commercial activities in Hong Kong, he had numerous connexions in the principal trading ports in North and South China, as well as in Siam, French Indo-China and India.

Owing to his genial disposition, Mr. Fung, both in his private life as well as in business, was much liked by all classes and nationalities with whom he came in contact.

He died on the 2nd August, 1931, at the ripe old age of 72, and is survived by three sons and six daughters.

陳公子丹

THE LATE MR. CHAN TZE TUAN

同人胼修香江人物志。特賢之嘉言懿行。已廣
事徵飾。古哲之潛德幽光。尤樂於傳述。得增
城賴太史陳熙先生，為詰封光祿大夫子丹陳公
撰行狀。亟錄於后。

公諱步蟾。字于丹。一字幼侔。其先自閩遷粵
之統平縣居美鄉。越十一世。至曾先公。乃箕

○狀業於東莞陳捷學伯陶，香為許孝廉之捷門
下。與澄海陳荇農汝南，潮陽蕭郁卿師瑾珊。訂
文字交。連邐講習。學益大進。然會于邁。安
統初元。必水冠堂開門祝。復集令多人。虛會備方物。遂
已瘁止。與海內名宿。公乃捐業怡之學。而致力於詰古文
辭。與海內名宿。耽騁於詞理文圃間。乃名大
噪。時父兄所營商業。日益興盛。步蟾公前卒。其
于退讓。公則侍煥堂公相繼主持於香港。奇港
為五洲出入門戶。形勢壯濶。鑿氣宏遠。公廣
交游。尚風義。聲氣宏達。公廣

宅前溪。卽今所居也。曾祖有秋。祖慶瑞。父
煥榮。皆以世德清望聞於鄉國。累晉封貤純表
來大夫。而煥榮公史以樂善好施奉旌坊純表
三十六柱。亦名結詩樓叢書。其志趣可觀矣。
李也。煥榮公有三子。長步瀛公。次步育公。公其
季也。步瀛公隨父經商成倖業。而習雅重文行
所詩華。陸烟任邸。為公善行。而陳祖敬宗族尤
相詳。公必備。身躋旅外。歲必一歸。展墓拜祠。皆
親視其事。整理塋廛。修舉饗祀。訓示禮法。
必詳必備。陸棲山居家正本制用篇。王茲其宗
約。王士青宗規。奉為圭臬。數十年如一日。

結其詩陳列會所。借資優厚。公卽以詩酒名其
樓。史輯集師友文字。兄箚牘時答。悶不備列。繁為
以至教子課本。治家訓言。其志趣可觀矣。
閒。時有女子綵嫦哀情。公卽以勤人哀寫
作感慈苦。弁卉呼就
島人會集盡之。閑其編敎勸。開寫史
瘞遠近有義卒。必捐貲建
其役。廣東水災。
飢。必捐貲
四方名流至者。尚風義。
必所動款洽。而
於驗人恭客。講
閭力協助。戊甲
官遗民。尤加禮
重。

同二妃兩案閒歎。偶或遺三數日而
詞閒若孫志。遠就同鄉。為邦人師。必
行文學兄弟重來。自臺斲夕遊從。則
遣訂交。嗚濁漓俗風。敍爾於結詩樓之
見其言論丰采。岸然深慨。公於絅人中。文
藝學兄。皆有起送流俗氣概。王
諸方。李原卒以王戌年終。而其
生母到太夫人以壬戌年終。乃
別營灤伍西阡定。以水愛居海
偏。得生事死物。亦篤於孝而連于
禮矣。公處事忧倔。有多疏解閒目。不拘苔禮。
至此奉奉忠志之邦。余年發居海嶠。公於酬人
公乃龍之馬。余年發居海嶠。公於酬人
至深歎談。王
知其言隋。而
見其言論半采。

行彥方。邁居海外。清商業。能以德
欲。余猶自其所居。往來於時。爲邦人師。日
遵訂交。自臺斲夕遊從。
令揚的余狐行。而相與談笑。則例初如往。
劑增損。亦必以諫議
配李氏。纒配則爲原卒。原女名也。公諱封夫人
于五。曰興邦。亦公卒也。
人生。黔光公卒。
遜邦。倜宴虞氏生。由齡。虚齋。由勤
女二。長適王。次適計。其子若孫之
女二。記昔年公與約。諸乎真志。吾二人交至寓。知歌其真
列舉世次行實。予曰。是香風志
也。記昔年公與約。請乎真志。吾二人交至寓。
就爲後死。必光爲先死者作傳狀。斯庶得情
信。挽其餘緒。振錄其生平本末。

增城賴熙撰狀

郎九切磋砥錯。成就不能遠大。乃貧氣遊遠方
自居上。益勉往來精進。知學問之道。非朴
報卉其會。桷博士弟子員。食廩餼。舉俊行
也。公善健父兄志。蓄庶成學業。出就有司試。
李也。步瀛公隨父

THE LATE Mr. CHAN TZE TUAN.

The late Mr. Chan Tze Tuan, grandfather of Mr. Chan Yeung Chai, shipping manager of the Kin Tye Lung 27 Bonham street west, is considered to be a learned merchant in the past.

The late Mr. Chan Tze Tuan, born with a literary gift, was under tutor of the Chinese old classics at an early age. He was arrayed with a formidable scholastic degree as "gung Seng" in the Ching Dynasty when he was still within his "teens."

Later, he came to Hongkong with his father, and settled in the Colony as a merchant. Though he was in the business field, yet he continued to do his literary works.

He was a man of broad sympathy. His humanity and generosity might be seen from the fact that during the disastrous flood in Kwongtung Province in 1908, he raised a large amount of money by means of selling his literary works and contributed all the money for relief.

In the family, he was an obedient son and a strict father. He taught his children in such a way, that all of them are good, obedient and diligent.

As to his ancestors they were originally natives of Fukien Province. They removed to live in Yau Ping District Kwongtung Province about two hundred years ago. So the late Mr. Chan Tze Tuan may be called a Cantonese or a Fukienese.

He was died in 1934 at a ripe old age of sixty five.

郭公少流

郭公守怡○字少流○廣東三水人○生於香港○幼習中英文於本港○新舊學均精通○年十七較讀○近廣州營赴小呂宋等地經商○公元一八九四年○法國東方滙理銀行開設分行於香島○公即

妾為該局永遠總理○其他如港大校董○基督教聯校校董○雅利氏醫院值理○聖約翰救傷會董事○及財委○華人後備警察財委○華商總會顧問○旅港三水商會永遠會長○保護兒童會值理等職○無不樂就○而於提倡教育○尤力與財俱○曾慨捐鉅款○以興築聖士提反女校郭少流大堂○及創立香港大學生理學緖等○此均為港中人士所共見共聞者也○至於造福鄉土者○尤為足稱○如籌建三水博愛留醫院○與縣蓋旅

逍放行任華經理○直至一九零六年○以持勞告退○旅行圍留不絕○乃惑其萬寶接替○仍任保家○一九二九年○由其子郭贊君接任華經理○計與旅行前後有四十餘年之歷史○公退隱後○惟致力於公益慈善事業○光緒兩申年○曾任東華醫院總理○戊戌○任保良公局總理○庚申○復兩任該局首總理

港三水工商會會址○均龍悉力以赴○色人甚德之○港府敬公甚公○特委為太平紳士○復給以榮譽奬章○法屬越南政府亦錫以龍寶星○公平生雅喜遠行○當周遊世界○凡名勝之地○靡不有其足跡○始能善養其浩然之氣○故辭於本港古稀社之列也○一九三六年六月○在港寓,谷亥○復兩任該局首總理○俊港府史仙遊○享壽七十有八○

郭公少流（流少公郭）

THE LATE Mr. KWOK SIU LAU.

The late Mr. Kwok Siu Lau, a native of Samshui, Kwangtung, was born in Hongkong in 1859 and received his early education here.

At the early age of 17, the late Mr. Kwok started his business career. He held positions in Canton and Manila. In 1894, when the Banque de l'Indochine opened its branch here, he was elected the first compradore, and remained with the Bank as such until 1906. He continued to stand surety, but retired from active work. In 1929, his son, Kwok Chan succeeded as compradore. His connection with the bank lasted forty odd years.

After his retirement, he devoted much time for philanthropic work and public activities. He also travelled intensively, and had made visits to all parts of the world.

He was a member of the Committee of the Tung Wah Hospital thirty odd years ago, and the committee of the Po Leung Kuk. He held the position of Chairman of the committee of the Po Leung Kuk on two occasions, and was nominated Justice of the Peace and also permanent director of the Institution.

In the cause of education, the late Mr. Kwok donated large sums for the erection of the Kwok Siu Lau Hall in the St. Stephen's Girls' College, and the founding of the Chair of Biology in the University of Hongkong.

He also devoted much attention to matters in Samshui, and helped largely to the Hospitals there. He also purchased the present site of the Samshui Chamber of Commerce in Hongkong and gave it to the Chamber.

He was a member of the Court of the Hongkong University; a member of the Committee of the Church Missionary Society Associated Schools; member of the Committee of the Alice Memorial and Affiliated Hospitals; Finance Committee of the St. John's Ambulance Brigade and Association; Finance committee of the Hongkong Police Reserve (Chinese Company); Adviser to the Chinese General Chamber of Commerce, Hongkong; Permanent President of the Samshui Chamber of Commerce and Committee member of the Society for the Protection of Children.

He was awarded the Certificate of Honour by the Government of Hong Kong, and the "Officer du Dragon D'Annam" by the Indochina Government. He was a member of the Septuagenarians, and died in June 1936 at the age of 78.

陳公任國○廣東省台山縣水南鄉人○七歲至十七歲○在村里從師習經史之學○年十八○素儉不入商○就同邑沖美遠音濟堂藥肆之聘○孳孳不倦○服務三年○旋改應新昌埠岐生堂藥肆之微聘○亦約三載○美國三藩市致中和藥肆聞其說○

○公不好名○自民國肇建○從不以革命先進自稱○一志經商○不求官職○來港創料理海通有限公司○務拓實業○以利民生○當組織時○親歷美洲各埠○所到之處○華僑皆表歡迎○以親旅館○陸海通藥行○陸海通保險有限公司○陸海通輪船旅館○陸海通飯店等○先後辦立○六國飯店○編致酒店等○先後辦立○嗣以年事日高○而暫卸符祥君○料事幹練○克耀大志○

退使總理公司事務○若遇要公○仍須商承之也○公陰任陸海通有限公司董事○並克任上海縣保水火險有限公司董事○兼會主席外○又克任廣州府醫學院○台山水圖則正學校○曾慨捐鉅巨款○又公深得慶壽時○於廣州公育○當公七秩開一青○足為後學林式也○公年登之冠○樂善好施○關心教基督教義諸○兄事具有愛心○故鄉人美其名曰阿姿○以其和平○與人無忤○

特建之往○公為好逃父兄向外發展之志○欣然就道○受任後○整理有方○營業大進○任事六年○為謀捐立展計○乃奶辭告退○在三藩市自設保滋堂藥肆○業務日盛○時富滿清末葉○當地巖柴華僑入境○公以己國衰的異族主政○美奔之何○遂傾向革新自後事業○具族主政○美奔之何○遂傾向革新自後事業○

同盟會為會員○歷次起義公債捐款○均樂輸將○革命首領孫總理引為同志○來往甚密○加入南學堂○次男元喜○年四十一○畢業於德國柏林大學○聲醫學博士○湖公生於遜清同治元年正月念三日○卒於民國念五年九月初三日○享壽七十五歲○

婴邬氏為室○生二子一女○長男符祥○年五十五○曾讀於上海南洋公學○及廣州公學○享壽七十五歲○

國任公陳

THE LATE Mr. CHAN YAM KWOK.

The late Mr. Chan Yam Kwok was a native of Toishan District, Kwangtung Province, born in 1861.

He acquired his education at his native village and when he was eighteen years of age he worked in a Chinese drug store in his neighboring town. Three years later, he transferred to another shop and again he remained for three years.

Then he crossed the oceans and proceeded to America, where he worked in the Chee Chung Wo Chinese Drug Store, San Francisco, California. He stayed in the post for six years and when he had accumulated sufficient means to be independent, he established the Po Chi Tong, which was also dealing in Chinese drugs. His experience and business acumen enabled him to become prosperous in the shortest span of years.

Mr. Chan was a faithful nationalist. He had helped a great deal in building of the Chinese Republic. He was an intimate friend of the late Dr. Sun Yat Sen and had for several times assisted the latter in revolutions. After the Republic of China was firmly established, Mr. Chan did not boast for his merits but ran on his business as usual.

Then he came to Hongkong and devoted himself to the commercial field. He initiated the Luk Hoi Tung & Co., Ltd.; the Luk Hoi Tung Life Assurance Co., Ltd., the Luk Hoi Tung Hotel and Restaurant; the Luk Hoi Tong Dispensary; the Luk Kwok Hotel; and the Nathan Hotel.

Besides the above mentioned, he was also director of the Shanghai Fire and Marine Insurance Co., Ltd. He contributed a large sum of money to the Public Hospital in Canton and the Chik Ching School in his native town.

Married at twenty, Mr. Chan had a couple of son and a daughter. He died in 1936, with a ripe old age of seventy - five and to the mournfulness of most people of the Chinese community.

THE PROMINENT CHINESE IN HONGKONG

BY

Prof. WOO SING LIM

PRICE; $ 3.00
$ 5.00 (Cloth)

THE FIVE CONTINENTS BOOK CO.

63, HENNESSY ROAD, WANCHAI,

HONG KONG

All Rights Reserved

中華民國二十六年六月初版

◉ 中英合璧 香港華人名人史畧一册

每册 硬面定價伍元
軟面 叁元

編著者　中山吳醒濂

發行者　五洲書局
香港軒鯉詩道六十三號

承印者　聚珍印務書樓有限公司
營業部：香港威靈頓街五十號
工廠：灣仔洛克道卅二至四十號

香港・澳門雙城成長經典

書名：香港華人名人史略（一九三七）（中英合璧）
　　　The Prominent Chinese in Hong Kong（1937）
系列：心一堂 香港‧澳門雙城成長系列
原著：吳醒濂 編著
主編‧責任編輯：陳劍聰

出版：心一堂有限公司
通訊地址：香港九龍旺角彌敦道六一〇號荷李活商業中心十八樓〇五一〇六室
深港讀者服務中心：中國深圳市羅湖區立新路六號羅湖商業大廈負一層〇〇八室
電話號碼：(852) 67150840
網址：publish.sunyata.cc
淘宝店地址：https://shop210782774.taobao.com
微店地址：　https://weidian.com/s/1212826297
臉書：　　　https://www.facebook.com/sunyatabook
讀者論壇：　http://bbs.sunyata.cc

香港發行：香港聯合書刊物流有限公司
地址：香港新界大埔汀麗路36號中華商務印刷大廈3樓
電話號碼：(852) 2150-2100
傳真號碼：(852) 2407-3062
電郵：info@suplogistics.com.hk

台灣發行：秀威資訊科技股份有限公司
地址：台灣台北市內湖區瑞光路七十六巷六十五號一樓
電話號碼：+886-2-2796-3638
傳真號碼：+886-2-2796-1377
網絡書店：www.bodbooks.com.tw
心一堂台灣秀威書店讀者服務中心：
地址：台灣台北市中山區松江路二〇九號1樓
電話號碼：+886-2-2518-0207
傳真號碼：+886-2-2518-0778
網址：http://www.govbooks.com.tw

中國大陸發行　零售：深圳心一堂文化傳播有限公司
深圳地址：深圳市羅湖區立新路六號羅湖商業大廈負一層008室
電話號碼：(86)0755-82224934

版次：二零一九年四月初版，平裝

心一堂微店二維碼　　　　心一堂淘寶店二維碼

定價：　港幣　　　　九十八元正
　　　　新台幣　　　四百四十八元正

國際書號 ISBN 978-988-8582-65-5